Amanda Coe is the acclaimed screenwriter and novelist who in 2013 won a BAFTA for the BBC Four adaptation of John Braine's *Room at the Top*, starring Maxine Peake. Her other credits include *Life in Squares*, *Margot*, *As If* and the recent BBC One adaptation of *Apple Tree Yard*. Her novels *What They Do in the Dark* and *Getting Colder* are published by Virago.

EVERYTHING YOU DO IS WRONG

Amanda Coe

FLEET
2018

FLEET

First published in Great Britain in 2017 by Fleet
This paperback edition published in 2018 by Fleet

1 3 5 7 9 10 8 6 4 2

A CIP catalogue record for this book
is available from the British Library.

ISBN 978-0-349-00507-2

Typeset in Caslon by M Rules
Printed and bound in Great Britain by
Clays Ltd, St Ives plc

Papers used by Fleet are from well-managed forests
and other responsible sources.

Fleet
An imprint of
Little, Brown Book Group
Carmelite House
50 Victoria Embankment
London EC4Y 0DZ

An Hachette UK Company
www.hachette.co.uk

www.littlebrown.co.uk

Black on grey. Birds like black filings swooped across the sky by a magnet. Party bag toy. Magnet pulling them along, shape swelling, dense with birds. Up, long now, ragged, away. Grey sky. Cold. Wet. Freezing cold and soaking wet. The sea. That's a fact. Dragging me back, then giving up. I want you, forget it. I love you, fuck off.

Soaking cold and freezing wet. If no one comes, I'll die. I'm going to die.

I'll die, then.

PART I

Since Harmony Ansholm knew, and mourned, that in all her fifteen years nothing had ever happened in Evensand, the first big storm of the winter was like a trailer for a blockbuster that would never make it to a screen near you. But it still stirred her that morning as she looked up from her trudge through graphs, to see the weightless peach and lemon shells of takeaway cartons chase each other up the pavement below the library and past the evergreens planted in a line outside, their needles beginning to ripple, showing silvery undersides. By eleven o'clock, the tiny agitation of the Edwardian window frames had amplified into an assault on concentration, and the street light outside, with which her eyeline was oddly level, the Quiet Room being on the library's first floor, started a stately, weighted nod on its pole. Seen so close, the wedge-shaped head of the light was an improbably massive thing. You didn't think of that, from the ground. If it fell, it would do as much damage as a falling tree. Harmony, imagining metal smashing through the glass, slid her files up the table and repositioned herself in the next chair along, closer to the door. Nothing would happen, but you may as well be on the safe side, or what was the point of an imagination?

The Quiet Room took up half the library's upper floor, and today Harmony was one of three occupants, apart from the invigilating librarian reading the *Daily Mail* at the desk by the door. He sat straight, head cocked critically to the print, running his thumb down the edge of each page before he turned it, as though he was conducting research, not reading. He was, though: Harmony had seen him at the sudoku. As usual, her own brain had fogged shortly after she took out the maths sheet. It was impossible. Declan said not, but it was. She tried to focus on the questions, for his sake, but the sight of how many lay ahead, becoming denser and more difficult the closer you got to the bottom of the page, like a forest you were bound to get lost in, made even the basic numbers of the first problem fall away from meaning like leaves shaken from a branch.

The windows shuddered acoustically. Did Declan like music, she wondered? Probably. Not that she'd even have heard of the kinds of bands he would be into. Reaching under the table, Harmony inched out the two-finger KitKat she'd stowed in her bag for lunch. She was starving. A hundred and six calories. She could still have the apple she'd brought at actual lunchtime for a mere fifty-two calories. The trick was writing it all down. Besides, if she was hungry her concentration would be even worse.

The weather's percussion usefully disguised her cautious tearing of the wrapper. Mum had never bought KitKats, because Nestlé and baby formula for African women; also sugar. Now Harmony had a multipack stashed in her bedroom. A guilty pleasure, which was a phrase Mum had hated about as much as she hated Nestlé. Feigning attention to her maths, Harmony broke off furtive morsels under the table and passed them to her mouth. Tiny shavings of chocolate and wafer sprinkled the white paper of the worksheet, smudging into brown blots as she brushed them away. The numbers were impossible.

The skitter of ball bearings hitting glass made everyone look up, as a gust of wind flung a slack handful of hail across the window. The storm was starting in earnest. Harmony felt a lift of excitement. It was a Declan day, after all.

'No food in the library.' The librarian was staring straight at her.

Framed against the pane, Harmony absorbed the judgement of the other, older library dwellers. In a rich blush of humiliation, and willing herself not to chew, she released the last of the second finger – the best bit, with the thick little rim of chocolate at the end – back into her bag. The librarian returned to his *Daily Mail*. Wanker.

'I'm diabetic,' she announced in a demitone, unsure if she wanted anyone to listen. 'Blood sugar?'

By the time she left the Quiet Room, after forcing herself to sit for five minutes so that her exit would look unforced and incidental, the rain was pelting in fat, squalling drops. As soon as you stepped outside you could hear the sea, although the library was at the back of the 1960s precinct, streets away from Evensand's so-called promenade. Harmony battled the freezing wind channelling through the torso of her parka to zip herself up, spitting away the fronds of hair that whipped into her face. The roar of the sea felt like a roar in your blood.

She could be diabetic, for all anyone knew. She'd never had an actual test for diabetes. Maybe that was why she got so bloody hungry. Once out of view of the library, where she would never be able to work again, she scrabbled in her bag and shoved the linty end of the KitKat in her mouth.

When she reached the end of Court Street, the boiling sea was blackboard grey, dashing dirty foam across the small stretch of shops that ended in the Co-op. The first proper storm of the year, no doubt about it. Shoppers were running urgently to their cars, and, as Harmony watched, the transparent cover a mother was trying to fix to her toddler's pushchair flapped free and took off like a kite above the trolley park. The little boy raised his arms and spread his stubby fingers into stars, in unflustered exultation at its flight. It felt as though anything might happen, even though Harmony knew it wouldn't.

At home, the radio in the kitchen declaimed a severe weather warning. If the weather was very severe by four, Declan might cancel. Harmony didn't know what she would do if that happened; if *he* didn't happen. Their lesson was the peg on which she hung the meaning of her week. The rain and wind were bad, but the radio was saying it wouldn't get properly worse, properly severe, until the night. And if Declan didn't come, she reassured herself, he wouldn't get his twenty pounds, and surely he needed the money.

Harmony suspected some sort of arrangement with Mel about Declan's fee. It was quite likely on the down low, since Stu had a general policy of refusing help from his sister. He called it charity – like Perks in *The Railway Children*, as Mum had once pointed out, forcing him to accept a bag of Mel and Ian's unwanted clothes that would have otherwise gone to Oxfam. Harmony, along with Mum, wasn't so proud. Unlike her cousins, she never got any extras. Not until Declan.

Whatever the arrangement, and Stu's possible ignorance of it, twenty quid was twenty quid. More than once Mum had resorted to raiding the treasure-chest money box Harmony had been given when she was a little kid to make up Declan's cash to the full twenty. But today, as for many months, Stu had left it all on the kitchen table: two fives and a lot of shrapnel. Harmony sorted this into more respectful piles of related coins. Although there weren't any coppers, which would be an insult, there were still a few marginally embarrassing five pences. She scavenged tens from the depleted treasure chest and exchanged them. During this, Harmony ate the apple she'd intended for her lunch, which was woolly and disappointing, followed by a slice of peanut butter on toast. Protein was good. At her age, you needed it for growth, if in fact she was still growing. She spooned more peanut butter from the jar, then, after she'd put the spoon in the sink to stop herself eating more, continued to scoop gouts of it out with her finger. From the nutritional information on the label she calculated that she'd eaten about five hundred calories' worth, not including the toast. There was no point after that, so she put two more slices of bread in the toaster. During her final instalment of toast, Harmony tried to watch a YouTuber she liked, another guilty pleasure unsanctioned in Mum's day. But the internet was down, probably because of the storm.

It had been Mel's idea, to get her a tutor. Declan was coaching Mel's youngest, Eddy, through the entrance exam for St Benedict's, the private school his brother Aidan attended and which his eldest brother Joe had left the previous summer. When Mum agreed that Harmony could think of going 'somewhere' for sixth form – the 'somewhere' meaning nowhere they had to pay – Mel had pointed out, deflatingly, that she wouldn't get in anywhere at all without GCSEs. Then, more helpfully, she had suggested Declan to tutor Harmony through her maths. Nebbing, as usual, according to Stu. Stu didn't have much time for school. The one time Mum had dragged him to parents' evening at Severn Oak he became clammy and silent, like someone trapped in a lift. But since he wasn't her actual parent, he didn't have any real say over her education, and Mum had been surprisingly keen on the tutor idea, despite her own customary dislike of Mel's interference. Harmony had been keen herself, even before she met Declan in the flesh. The flesh.

Upstairs for a wee, she got caught by the bathroom mirror. Her fringe had become far too long, apparently overnight. Holding the puff of hair back out of the way, Harmony gave herself over to such prolonged scrutiny that her reflection gradually became as bizarre as an over-repeated word: face, face, face, face, face, face, face, face ... Why had she never realised that her forehead was so grotesque, both abnormally high and oddly bulging? Plus, spots. As she was combing the fringe back down a violent bang came from downstairs, at the back of the house. Her first thought was that someone was trying to break in, because it was far too early to be Stu forgetting his keys, and then with a bigger gut lurch she thought she might have got the time wrong, or Declan was early, but when she inched through the dining area, where they never dined, to get a view of the back garden, all Harmony could see was an upended plastic garden chair on the empty flower bed that stretched beneath the window, white against the black earth. The chair wasn't theirs: if they ever wanted to sit in the garden they just took normal chairs outside. The noise must have come from the wind seizing the chair from next door's garden and hurling it at the window.

Harmony marvelled at the weather's malevolence. It wouldn't take much, she saw, for the panels of their sagging, ancient fence to give way. It had happened before, as evinced by the contrast of the new panel in the middle, orange and unweathered. Of course, it had had some help.

Best not to think about that. The point was, the sea couldn't reach them, even in a storm this bad, even if the fence broke. Although the house stood in the last row before the beach, with the road intervening it was too far for the sea to reach, however furious. Only the wind could do them damage. And she hadn't missed Declan, thank God.

Despite the storm, he was exactly on time. He always was. Harmony wondered if he waited outside, checking his phone until the two zeros of *4:00* appeared. Numbers were his thing, after all. She was already on the other side of the door, watching the numbers on her own phone. She answered the bell so promptly that he jumped, his finger lifted to the button. In turn, she got the usual slight shock from seeing him really as opposed to the Declan she made up for herself in the rest of the week. In her mind he was a bit ginger, but now, chivvied by the wind into their narrow hall, he wasn't. His hair was matt brown; not even chestnut highlights. Still gorgeous. He brought his smell, too, gels and sprays sharpened by the astringent, salty cold.

'Weather!' Declan said, dealing with his coat. It was a grey North Face, nothing special.

'There was a warning, on the radio.'

His smell made Harmony think of him in the shower, which made her blush. Also usual. For the whole hour of their lesson, she was aware of the skin on her face flaming.

Mum had always made him a cup of tea, but Harmony found the idea of offering and making Declan a drink herself both too weird, in that it underlined Aurora's absence, and too embarrassing, in that it drew attention to herself, so she'd been telling him for months the kettle was broken. As he got the workbooks out of his backpack and slapped them on the table, Harmony switched on the lamp. The wind was wuthering against the window like a crap trick-or-treater.

'So, how did you get on? Any problems?'

They sat. Declan, his pencil poised by the first question, glanced over at her worksheet. He swivelled the page to get a better look, although even with it upside down, he must have been able to see the multiple rubbings out. By some miracle, she'd got it right.

'Excellent stuff.' His pencil jumped to the next question. He swiped his mouth and chin, concentrating on her graph. She wondered how often he had to shave.

'So, talk me through this – why have you plotted x as five here?'

Harmony tried to focus on the pencilled blob she had speculated on earlier. As ever, the monolithic need to concentrate blocked her concentration. Declan sighed. The storm made its noises. She grabbed at the smudged number on the line below the graph, just above his adorably bitten fingernails.

'Because of the cube of fifteen? Sorry.'

'Nothing to apologise for. It's right.'

He smiled at her. White teeth, one at the bottom set a tiny bit crooked, the two incisors slightly proud of the rest. She could have identified him from his dental records. Oh God, she loved him so much.

'Cube root,' he said.

'Cube root.'

But the right answer was a fluke. As always he was very patient with her, though she could see the effort it cost him from the way he jammed his hand up into his hair and tugged harder at it each time she failed to understand his explanation.

'Slow down,' he said. 'Don't panic. It's all there in the numbers – you're panicking.'

It wasn't just panic, though, was it? It was him, the real smell of him, the freckles on his cheekbones, the peaty brown of his eyes. How old was he, anyway? When he started, Mum had said twenty-four, tops.

'Harmony.'

Harmony tried again, dutifully transcribing numbers as Declan spoke. Suddenly the edge of understanding appeared and she grabbed at it, paddling frantically, before the current of him could pull it away. It was just numbers, beautiful and simple. Two lines. Equals.

'X fourteen, y twelve.'

'Perfect.'

Declan sat back, smoothing his tormented hair back into place. His forehead, unlike her own, was normally sized and unblemished. Harmony twiddled her fringe down past her eyebrows as he checked the time on his phone. She knew he had Eddy as his next lesson, and that it would be more than his life was worth to be late for Mel. Beyond the hoop of lamplight that encircled them, the dark had thickened. During the blank week, when she gorged on the possibility of their lessons, this was the moment when she declared her love.

But instead he made her do a timed worksheet on what they'd just covered.

'You know the drill.'

Ten minutes. Declan set the timer on his phone and leaned back, his gaze set above her head at the black, uncurtained view to the back fence and the sea beyond, twiddling his pencil as an analogue to the digital milliseconds she could see flickering past out of the corner of her eye. The storm screamed to be let in.

'So noisy . . .'

'Concentrate.'

He wasn't even looking at her. Probably, with the lamp on, he could only see himself bounced back from the streaming window. There would be five minutes of him left after the worksheet. As Harmony sneaked another look, she saw Declan's expression change. Before she could turn to share his view there was human tapping at the glass, a thinner, animal skittering of paws.

'Harmony!'

It was Mel, cowled by the hood of her anorak, Toothpaste leaping up so that his muzzle slobbered a streak on the pane before she tugged him down by his lead. They must have come from the beach. She didn't wait for Harmony to open the back door but crunched round to the front and was trying the handle there before Harmony reached it herself.

'Just a sec—'

The wind wrenched the door away the moment she released the latch, smashing it against the radiator. Mel would have charged past with similar force, but Toothpaste's delight at seeing Harmony brought her up short. She shrieked at the dog to sit.

In her whole life Harmony had never seen Mel in such a state. She was in her dance-teaching kit, Lycra over greyhound legs and the usual puffa'ed and zipped accoutrements, but it was as though a stranger had taken possession of her face, its angles flayed red by the storm and snaked with wet hair. Her eyes were huge and sightless with shock. She didn't even seem to see Declan there, at the entrance to the living room, as she shook her iPhone at Harmony.

'Bloody thing! I can't get reception! Toothpaste!'

Mel yanked the lead. Aidan, or Eddy? Fighting the suck of panic, Harmony turned to the landline balanced on the radiator, but the dock was empty. She or Stu had left it somewhere, and wherever it was it would probably be out of charge. Harmony pushed Toothpaste's wet, freezing muzzle away from her crotch but Declan was too engrossed by Mel to notice. Before she could go to look for the phone, Declan had stepped forward, offering his mobile.

'Hi, Mrs Bale.'

Mel stopped short, squinting down at his handset.

'Is it still 999 for mobiles?'

Please don't let it be Eddy or Aidan. Let it be Uncle Ian.

'I'm not sure,' said Declan, but Mel was already dialling. The phone connected. Mel swiped the dewdrop from her nose, already more herself at the contact with authority. She was trembling, though, in strange, convulsive jerks, as though she was having some sort of fit rather than suffering from cold.

'Ambulance – hang on, yes, ambulance. Shit. Police, maybe? Listen—'

The unlatched front door crashed back against the wall, reasserting disaster. Reaching to secure it properly, Harmony saw a splintered wedge gouged out of the laminate by the edge of the radiator. Mel hadn't reacted to the noise. She lowered her voice, as though what she had to say wasn't fit for Harmony to hear. Her chattering teeth made her words come out in oddly clustered spasms, like ice cubes fused into clumps.

'Yes, it's. A body. A girl. A dead. Body on Evensand. Beach.'

It was the first time Declan had ever looked at Harmony properly, and her at him, as though they were two humans. Hours later, in bed, as the weather continued to assault the house, Harmony savoured the reciprocity of that moment of shock. His eyes, yellow-green-brown, those eyelashes, had looked properly into hers. That had to be the start of something, surely.

'Dead, yes. By Brazen Point, the golf. Club end, she's. Naked.'

For once, the storm had made good on its promise.

Mason was on lates. His shift had barely started when they got the call, just after five. He and Soccolo were parked up on the road to Brazen Point, waiting for their takeaway brews to reach a drinkable temperature as they argued about the transfer window, so they were at the scene in minutes. They were flagged down near the entrance to the golf club by the woman who'd rung 999. A Mrs Melanie Bale, local dog walker, though she'd ditched the dog by the time they got there, he had no idea where. They left the patrol car at the gate and floundered with her down to the beach, screaming to be heard over the waves and wind. The ambulance had been dispatched at the same time as them but had further to come, from Whitby. Mason's hand shook with adrenalin as he tracked the slender, staggering figure ahead of him with his torch. The woman wheeled a few metres from the sea's spewing edge, trying to get her bearings. From behind her, Dan's wavering beam illuminated sectioned patches of empty beach and roiling sea, hazed by the icy rain that was driving itself into his eyes and mouth.

'Maybe – washed – sea!'

He followed as the woman slithered up the bank of gravel, closer to the bottom of the cliff. Soccolo laboured behind them, cursing the world, while Mason aimed the torch low at the woman's scrabbling legs, trying to help her find her way. He reared, bucking the light up at the cliff face, then braced the torch back to where it had shone. The edge of the projection had caught part of what they were looking for: a foot, he saw. No shoe, or sock. When he swept the torch further it revealed the whole of a body. A girl. She was fetal, bare and lifeless. What skin became.

'Chuffing—'

Soccolo caught up with them. He was already removing his coat to throw it over the body. Mason thought about his partner disturbing the scene at the same time as wishing he'd done it himself.

The ambulance drove as far as it could on to the beach, no messing. Its headlights created a pool of light for them to work from, bringing colour to the monochrome as the paramedics brought their bustling routine to urge the body back to life. Mason recognised the drill from the few RTAs he'd attended: a checklist of vital signs and chest-pressing and oxygen before they got the girl into the ambulance. At his first RTA – two idiot little twoccers who had run a stolen Audi into a tree – he had thought all this was hope of life, until Soccolo had disabused him: it was stats, not having too many deaths on their data sheet. The paramedics would never call it. Let the doctors do it, back in A & E. Their allotment of death was more generous than that allowed the ambulance crew.

It still looked like hope, though, the way everyone teamed up against the adversity of the weather. The square young woman doing chest compressions had to kneel on the edges of the silver insulation blanket they'd covered the girl with to stop it flying away in the gale. Every screamed word was swallowed by the storm. Soccolo, reunited with his coat, cannily escorted the woman who had made the 999 call back to the golf club and the warmth of their car. He would offer Mrs Bale a lift home, leaving Mason to be taken in the ambulance. Got to love Soccolo, he played all the angles.

Left alone to watch the paramedics work, Mason havered. The question of when a medical matter became a police matter, if there was crossover like this, was tricky. Once the girl was called as life extinct, the howling beach would be a crime scene. How was he meant to secure it on his own? The paramedics stretchered her into the ambulance, strapped up to the oxygen tank. Mason climbed in after them. He watched the gelid mask all the way from Evensand to Whitby, unclouded by any breath. The atmosphere in the back, though solemn and exhausted, was matter-of-fact. They'd given up. Over to him, then.

But in A & E – overstretched, due to the storm but when wasn't A & E overstretched – the harassed triage nurse optimistically dispatched them up to the acute assessment ward. Mason saw once they reached it that it wasn't just the empty beds that had triggered her decision. The other occupants of the ward were all elderly; variously demented, dehydrated and dying. One more body would inconvenience no one. Mason loitered in the corridor. A curtain had been pulled around the bed, preventing him seeing anything beyond backstage distortions of the flimsy material that implied some concerted, continuing degree of effort. The paramedics were long gone. This was the hospital team, with their own boxes to tick.

Just as Mason had decided to call the station, Soccolo arrived, coffee on his breath. He was unimpressed to hear how little progress had been made, but then the day Soccolo was impressed by anything, pigs would be seen flying in formation over Brazen Point.

'Got spannered, decided to go for a chuffing paddle, end of story.' Soccolo dropped heavily into a chair that faced the nurses' station, not displeased that this was the indoor turn their shift had taken. Soccolo hated being out in the car nearly as much as he hated having to get out of it to do some policing.

It was bound to be different for him. He was an old hand, in tasting distance of his pension. Dan, not yet a year out of training, was trying to tamp down his excitement. A murder investigation. So far, none of his working life had corresponded to the hopes he'd had for it. Mason had known before he started his training that some people didn't love the police, but since his IPLDP it came as a daily shock to him just how automatically hated he was, by such an uncriminal range of ages and conditions. It got him down. And the fact that he hadn't realised this before applying got him down even more. 'Classic Dan' was the verdict of his mates, if he bothered to confide after a couple of drinks. They didn't like cops either. No one liked them, apart from three old ladies in Easingwold who mistakenly thought they could catch the lads who'd been nicking their garden furniture.

'Have they called life extinct?'

Dan detained the stacked little nurse who had gestured him to the row of chairs. She was heading back into the ward carrying a small, tubular piece of medical equipment.

'Soon.'

She gave him a look over her shoulder before she disappeared behind the curtain. Mason smiled back. The only compensation for the cop hate was women. They didn't like him either, but they all wanted to shag him. Dan's easy-going nature and bland handsomeness had always seen him right, but with the uniform on there was no comparison. He should have been pleased, but after yet another lass who was vocally excited by his handcuffs then got his name wrong as they fucked, he felt ready for something real. What was wrong with a cuddle? Sitting in the corridor with Soccolo, he was almost tempted to confide. But Soccolo was old school. For him, over the side was what it was all about, the more the better. Even at his age, long married, he didn't do badly for what he referred to at his least offensive as *skirt*. Listening to the older man's extended recovery from the stairs – his partner's phobia of lifts was the only thing that forced him into anything close to exercise – Mason teetered on the edge of a complicated reflection: since he'd become a copper, lasses had treated him the way they complained men treated them – as an object. It verged on … not racism, obviously, but it was surely more than sexist. There must be a word.

Soccolo ostentatiously checked the time on the hospital clock against his watch, as though this would bring the end of the shift sooner. It was only twenty to ten.

'Do you think we should call in?' Mason suggested, bracing himself. 'See if she matches any mispers?'

He still felt slightly self-conscious about using professional shorthand. During training, one of the other cadets had successfully wound him up that 'sexoff' was short for 'sex offenders'. Soccolo didn't flinch, though, at 'mispers'. His own speech was often incomprehensible to civilians.

'Suit yourself.'

Mason thought of the woman who'd made the 999 call. Mrs Bale. In the heat of the moment, he hadn't asked her if she'd pulled the girl out of the water, or whether the body was already on the beach when she found her. The girl couldn't have been in the water long without being washed out to sea, could she? Good point. The woman might even have picked up the girl's clothes, moved them. People did all sorts of things you wouldn't want or expect. She may have seen a car driving off, or someone else on the beach. Dan knew Soccolo would have checked on all this when he'd driven Mrs Bale home. He may be as idle as fuck, but some points of procedure were as routine as brushing your teeth.

The pale blue curtain continued to billow, feet shuffling beneath. How much longer? Driven away by some large, unendurable emotion, Mason paced down the corridor, escaping the view into the ward. He called in and got nice Claire in the office, who would have given him a cuddle if he'd asked. She was about fifty, with vast underwired tits that still made you look. Though come to think of it, wasn't she one of Soccolo's conquests?

He gave her the details, estimating the girl's age within a generous range of 15 to 25. Caucasian. Medium build and height. Hard to tell hair colour because it was drenched, but she wasn't noticeably very blond or very ginger. No distinguishing features, from what he'd been able to tell before the paramedics had rushed in and started working on her. No clothes. No jewellery, not even ear studs, no visible piercings. No obvious tattoos either, which made it unlikely she was from round here. Or absconded from care, which was the most frequent local provenance of missing teenage girls, if she was a teenager.

Claire had a 16-year-old on the system. She'd absconded

from care near Selby two days before, but part of her description, surprise surprise, was a massive 1Direction tramp stamp at the base of her spine.

'You haven't got a name . . . ' He could hear Claire tapping details into her keyboard.

'They're still working on her,' said Dan. 'It's touch and go.'

More go than touch. He felt a bit sick. It was the adrenalin. 'Anything else distinctive?'

There was something, but Mason couldn't bring himself to mention it. He'd noticed, before the paramedics threw the space blanket over the girl on the beach, that she had pubes. Not many lasses did, not the ones who came his way, anyway. And of those who did, it was a waxed landing strip, nothing like the dark V visible on that stark, gritted body.

The call finished, Dan got out his pen and notebook. He stood by the lift, mindful that if it came to court he'd have to read out his notes. There was nothing weird in him noticing. It was decent policing, and possibly useful. Carefully, the notion of court forcing his neatest handwriting, he wrote 'odd features'. Then, deciding this was too obscure to jog his memory, he added 'pubic hair'. As far as he knew, no one actually looked at your notebook.

For a moment he couldn't remember which of the identical corridors he'd come down. He'd got himself turned round. Then he saw the sign back to acute assessment and retraced his steps. From the entrance to the ward the bed at the far end was exposed, no screen around it, stripped and empty. Over, finally. Dan was aware of his adrenalised boner; the same as when he'd first spotted the body on the beach. Everything had happened in the bare couple of minutes he'd been on the phone.

Murder was surely asking too much, though. Soccolo was

probably right: the girl had done it herself. Gone out in the weather and come a cropper. But suicide or accidental death would both still warrant an investigation, a statement to the coroner in Northallerton. Dan hadn't been to an inquest yet. Even that would have its own excitement. And if it turned out the girl had run away from care after all, there would be a shitstorm of publicity.

Then he realised; he'd overshot. There were no doors to any of the wards, just openings into this corridor that traced a square around the nurses' station at the centre. He'd been thrown by Soccolo's disappearance from the line of chairs where he'd left him. Now, retreating by a ward and looking in the opposite direction, he saw the jaundiced bulk of his partner among the beds, talking to a doctor. Female, mid-thirties, Asian. Eyes like a Disney character. Up by the window, the curtain had been pulled back to expose the bed with the girl in it.

Mason huddled into this centre of activity. The youngest nurse there, the one who'd given him the smile, smiled at him again. The scowl of her Scouse brows imposed a fierceness at odds with what appeared to be her natural friendliness. Or it wasn't friendliness, just his uniform.

'We've got her back.'

'You what?'

Soccolo came up close beside him and nodded at the bed. The girl was still masked, but her mouth made shapes beneath the frosting plastic, the patch of mist shrinking each time her chest lifted for the next breath in, expanding again on the exhalation. She was either gulping down the air forced into her or struggling to speak.

'She's alive.'

Shit. Not murder, then. Dan couldn't help the disappointment. Alive. What were they supposed to do about that?

Only two days had passed since Mel had found the body on the beach, and everything for Joe's birthday dinner had been in the fridge since. Assessing her abandoned preparations, Mel skimmed the top off the trifle, where the hundreds and thousands had haemorrhaged technicolour dye into the cream, which had also begun to crack. No one would be the wiser, once she'd whipped another carton to cover the custard. When she sniffed the fish, though, she had doubts. It smelled fine, but it did smell of fish. Better not poison the new girlfriend. Before Mel left for classes on Saturday morning, she asked Ian to pick up more salmon. There was no point troubling him with a search for lime leaves, as the recipe requested; they could do without.

Sunday lunch would have suited Mel better for the rescheduled celebration, since Saturday was her busiest teaching day, but Joseph said it was either Saturday night or him and the girlfriend postponing to the following week, and she was damned if all the rest of that food was going to waste.

It was odd, she thought, that the police still hadn't rung. They would, Ian reassured her. She had moved the body, for one thing. Schoolboy error, he teased.

'Never move the body, Mel.'

She felt very far away from him when he said this, even as she enjoyed the warmth of her husband's big hands at her waist; his moist, familiar kiss. The body had been on its back. Even thinking of the first contact with the freezing, rubbery flesh made Mel retch, the way she'd retched at the time. No blood – but wouldn't the sea have washed it away? She was the only person in the world who knew what it had been like, out there beneath Brazen Point.

She'd been walking the dog. Despite the forecast, the snugness of their double glazing had misled her about the storm's ferocity. It was howling out there, the rain brutally horizontal. Mel had braced herself and headed for the golf course.

She wasn't planning to be out for long, just through the top of the course to the sea and back. She hadn't had time to take Toothpaste out at lunchtime because she'd been busy with all the cooking for Joe's birthday, and Aidan had been so drenched when he got in from school she didn't have the heart to ask him to go straight out again. Once they were clear of the road, she let the dog off the lead. He looped ecstatically across the dark, deserted links, ears blasted back by the gale.

By the pale swatch of a bunker on the fourth hole, Mel saw Toothpaste stop and squat. It took her a few minutes to reach the bunker herself, battling the wind, and to locate the trio of tobacco-coloured shits at the slope's edge. With the tide at its highest, the sea flung its spray close enough to scour Mel's cheek and tang her lips with salt as she crouched. It was as she bagged the turdlets, sugared with wet golf club sand, that she caught a blaze of white against the black water. Fitfully illuminated by the bobbing beams of Toothpaste's light-up collar, indispensable now that they were far from any street lighting, the white patch had looked to Mel like the gleam bounced back from a reflective strip. It wasn't until she followed Toothpaste out of the golf course, nosing his way against the wind towards the sea below Brazen Point, that the whiteness moved in the water and became uncanny. Mel's gut dropped as she saw what she was really looking at, this close: an arm, bent at the elbow. And then she was running, overtaking the dog, who was wary of the smashing waves.

The girl was flung at the sea's edge, half in, half out. Like something from TV, but real. Bare skin, eyes shut, longish hair filthy with sand. White. Dead. Mel had given all her details to the burly policeman who'd accompanied her home that night. Two days now, and not so much as a text.

On Saturdays, Mel kicked off with Pre-primary Ballet at ten and carried on straight through to Grade 4 Modern just before teatime. No lunch break, though Gaynor, the mum of Jodie-who-helped, always brought her in a cappuccino. Thank God for Jodie and her 17-year-old knees. The way Mel's knees were going she'd end up like her own dancing teacher, Mrs Beagles, who towards the end had taught mainly by bestriding a chair with arthritic elan and demonstrating footwork with her hands.

Back from class, Mel scrambled to shower and get ready and shout at Ian and the boys to restore the house to the order she'd requested that morning. Mud on the stairs, clothes on the bathroom floor, the kitchen surfaces ravaged.

Eight o'clock came and went. As all the food was prepared but uncooked, there was no issue of dinner being spoiled, but holding back past the usual time for their first glass of wine was beginning to make both Mel and Ian ratty. There were a couple of bottles of Prosecco chilling in honour of Joe's birthday, or the two of them would have cracked by twenty past. They had an obligation to the ceremony of the cork; marking the celebration, even if it was a couple of days late.

'Sod it.'

By twenty-five to nine, Ian had opened a beer and turned to his default pastime of surfing new cars on his laptop. The remorseless light from the corner lamp exposed at the crown the bald spot that lurked beneath the apparent luxuriance of his ungreyed hair. Aidan appeared, to plunder the bowls of crisps she'd put out and be batted away. Finally, at nearly nine, when Mel had given up and started on the crisps herself, Joseph let himself in and shouted a hello. He had keys, since he was notionally still living at home. He made no mention of the delay, but his new girlfriend apologised effusively for both of them, in a fluting voice with an unexpected Home Counties accent.

'A southerner!' said Ian, taking her coat, already charmed. The entire family crowded in the hall. It was the first time any of them had met her, though they all knew she was Lottie. She apologised again, offering up a dripping foldable umbrella with several broken spindles.

'I don't know why I even bothered.' There was a mournful comedy in her tone. She turned and offered her hand to Mel. Toothpaste rapturously nosed the girl's crotch before Ian intervened to remove him.

'Lovely to meet you, Mrs Bale.'

'At last!' Mel ignored the stab of Joe's warning look at this and waved Lottie into the living room. 'Mel, please.'

A Nice Girl. Mel felt a rush of relief. She'd feared the worst about Lottie having a flat, assuming it meant council, and possible single motherhood, but had been too wary of Joe's outrage to prod him about it. She was a pretty girl as well; tall and slim, with shiny hair and large, even teeth. She looked nothing like Lauren, Joseph's previous and as far as Mel knew only girlfriend, who had been small and busty and had always reminded Mel of one of the hamsters Joseph had been so devoted to as a small boy. Apparently boneless, but capable of giving you a nip. Lottie already seemed to be displaying an eager friendliness (*'Oh, lovely house!'*, an exclamation precisely no one had made before, although Mel often expected them to) that verged instead on the canine. In their household, any resemblance to a dog was the highest form of praise.

Joe had yet to speak, beyond his desultory hellos. Dropping beside Lottie on the couch, he took her hand, marking a gauche pride of ownership that shocked and touched his mother. The soft little bugger. She saw the reason for their late arrival: the blood ran high in both their faces. They'd been shagging. No wonder Joe had yet to meet her eye.

Despite the inhibiting presence of Aidan and Edward, who lolled mutely along the other sofa scrutinising Lottie and demolishing more crisps, Mel discovered more about the girl in five minutes than Joe had disclosed throughout their relationship, which had begun a surprising two months ago. Lottie, she informed them, was a psychiatric social worker.

'Interesting!'

Mel wasn't entirely sure what this meant, in terms of

qualifications and prospects. Possibly the medical aspect made it a cut above being just a social worker. As Mel nudged Eddy to offer Lottie the depleted crisp bowl, she realised that despite the girl's soft look of extreme youth she must be at least three years older than their Joseph. This explained her having a flat. No wonder he was so keen to spend every waking hour there. An older woman. Never had Mel felt so much the mother of boys.

'Mum found a dead body on the beach.'

Eddy delivered this up with the crisps. Lottie smiled in friendly concern. Mel thought she could see some training coming into play.

'Yeah, I heard there'd been a ... that someone had been found. I didn't know it was you who found her, Mrs Bale.'

'Mel, please.'

Mel quelled her irritation that Eddy hadn't let her introduce her story.

'It was a girl with no clothes on,' Edward told Joe.

'Drama queen.'

'Aidan. Enough.'

'Well, he is!'

Ian intervened.

'But she did, didn't she? He's not exaggerating. Your mum did find a body, unfortunately.'

Joseph was agog for the details, his interest finally torn away from Lottie. But there was so little to tell, even if Mel tried to embellish the account she had given Ian on the night it had happened. So much of it was feelings, the untellable panic and futility. An obscenity in that marred nakedness, the girl's softness exposed to the world. She left them to their speculation, trusting Ian to filter out anything unsuitable for Edward, to go and rescue her filo parcels from the oven.

They had caught a little, the pastry browned at the edges like a pirate map. She broke off the worst shards and primped the rest as appealingly as possible. By the time Mel carried the serving dish to the table and called everyone in, the conversation had moved away from the body on the beach and back to Lottie. Joseph was still gazing at her with calf-eyed devotion as she spoke, with Ian, Aidan and Edward scarcely less enraptured. Mel quelled a pang and asked Ian to hand her the sweet chilli sauce. Lottie was talking about her dad, who she loved to bits but who apparently could be slightly controlling.

'Ian?'

He gallantly offered the dish of sauce to Lottie first, who declined.

Clearing the starters, Mel paused as she saw that Lottie, still talking, had about a third of her food left. But the girl handed the plate over without hesitation. Mel was unused to leftovers. If anyone in their house didn't finish something, which was rare, plenty pounced to polish it off. She paid attention to how the girl tackled the next course. While Lottie chatted about her schooldays – somewhere outside Guildford, though not private – Mel watched her settle a mouthful of salmon on to her fork, then, delayed by total engagement in the conversation, wave it animatedly near her mouth before returning fork to plate and, using her knife, shredding the fish sufficiently to disperse it about the plate's surface to give the illusion that something had been eaten. A token sip of wine – the level in the glass had hardly sunk, and she had already held her hand over the rim when Ian had hoisted the bottle for a refill – and she resumed her pantomime of eating.

Their eyes met. Lottie gave Mel a ready, even-toothed

smile, her hazel eyes crinkling at the corners with genuine warmth. Anyone, any parent, would describe her as a lovely girl. Perhaps Joe had been wrong about her eating fish? Mel had asked, she was sure. Or it was some stupid weight thing? They all waited politely for Lottie to finish her food, until in frustration even Joe interrupted her to ask directly.

'Aren't you going to eat that?'

Lottie puffed her cheeks. 'It was delicious, Mrs Bale. Sorry, I'm really full.'

Joseph leaned across and skewered the unmolested chunk of salmon that remained on Lottie's plate, encompassing it in a mouthful. All three boys were large, like their dad. It had been Mel's life's work to keep them fed. As Mel collected the plates, Ian halted her to dispatch the piece of fish she herself had been unable to stomach. Beneath her careful flavourings, the faint sea taste had awakened the sickness that had been curdling her appetite since Thursday. Her body seemed to reject some kinship with the freezing flesh she'd dragged from the water. A fish on the slab. A mermaid. A corpse.

Pudding, then. Joseph followed her with the plates.

'Lottie seems lovely,' said Mel.

'Mum.'

He said it as though she wasn't allowed an opinion, but she saw how pleased he was.

Oh God, he really loves her. She de-clinged the film from the trifle bowl and, before he could lift it, made him wait as she skewered candles into the cream, placing them round the edges of the bowl like numbers on a clock, with the odd one in the middle. Nineteen candles. If Joe was nineteen, she was going to be fifty, whether she liked it or not.

'Is this really necessary?'

The parody of Ian's dryness Joe had started when he was about twelve had come to fit him, like a child growing into a school blazer bought far too big. Now, he sounded just like his dad. But at the corner of Mel's eye, he made the same shape as Stu: lean and narrow, like all the Ansholms, where the Bales were stocky.

'It might not be necessary, but it's traditional.'

Mel knew how much Joe would have hated it, if she'd forgotten the candles. She wished her profiteroles didn't look so clumsy. They had come out of the oven unaccountably bloated, despite the million times she'd made them. She collected the jug. Thank God for chocolate sauce.

'How did you and Lottie meet, anyway?'

But the impetus to answer was lost as the desserts entered, to traditional delight and a round of 'Happy Birthday'.

'I've never seen a birthday trifle before.'

'What do you have on your birthday?' Edward asked.

Lottie pulled a face of hangdog apology.

'Cake.'

'We always have trifle. Cake's a bit boring.'

'I know, right? This is amazing.'

Serving spoon at the ready, Mel asked her what she would like.

'Hang on!'

Ian, whose disappearance into the kitchen Mel had assumed was related to replenishing drinks, reappeared with a supermarket tarte au citron and put it on the table with the closest he came to a flourish. He'd bought it, he explained, when he was replacing the salmon.

'What for?' Mel asked him, removing the extinguished candles from the cream.

'Thought it looked nice!'

This was a matter of opinion. The pale yellow circle certainly looked very neat in its foil case, next to her slightly dog-eared job on the top of the trifle and the mutant profiteroles.

'Lemon tart is my absolute favourite!' Lottie exclaimed. Ian waved a lofty arm, gracious.

Mel asked Lottie again what she could get her. The correct family answer was 'a bit of everything', but the girl rejected the offer of either trifle or profiteroles in favour of Ian's sodding lemon tart.

'You know it's not home-made,' Mel told her. Lottie said she didn't mind.

Mel watched as, in contrast to her behaviour with the salmon, Lottie enthusiastically trowelled sections from the yellow triangle straight into her mouth. When she accepted the offer of seconds, Mel took pleasure in cutting her a comically obtuse slice, almost a third of the whole. This, too, swiftly disappeared.

'That's what I like to see,' Ian said. And actually winked. At Mel, at least, not at Lottie. Joseph looked as though he would have liked to be the spoon going into Lottie's mouth. From across the table, Aidan was staring frankly down her top.

'So I don't know if the police have arrested anyone yet,' said Mel. She'd found a dead body on the beach, for Christ's sake. That was what had happened to her lately.

'You know, for murder.'

Lottie guarded her mouth as she spoke, to protect them from her crumbs.

'Actually, Mrs Bale, she isn't dead. Sorry, I was going to say when you went to serve up.'

'The girl I found?'

Lottie put down her spoon. 'It's a bit weird, actually.'

'Weird?' Edward was enraptured. He had hitched his chair closer to hers and was gazing at her hair.

'There's been nothing on the news,' said Mel. 'Or from the police. You'd think they'd have been in touch, considering I was the one who ... '

Lottie grimaced. 'I think they've been waiting to see if she'll say anything. About an attack, or ... '

Mel saw her doubtful look at Edward. The girl rattled her fork on to the bare plate. 'So yummy.'

But it was too late. Edward wanted to know what kind of attack – was she stabbed, he wondered eagerly?

'Or raped?' asked Aidan, trampling straight past Mel's silent signals about his little brother.

Neither, Lottie said. But the girl hadn't spoken yet and she had no ID, so no one knew who she was or what had happened to her.

'And how do you know about this, Lottie?'

This, from Ian, was not couched at all in the way Mel had been about to put the very same question. Far from scepticism, his tone suggested that Lottie must be quite remarkable to have access to such privileged information. A smear of whipped cream adorned the fold of his right cheek, just where it was at the cusp of becoming a jowl.

Lottie dabbed at her own cheek with her napkin. 'Oh, you know. Just ... working at the hospital.'

Suddenly she seemed embarrassed by the attention. Mel intervened with the offer of the last sliver of lemon tart, which she declined. Aidan finished it instead, as Mel reached over and thumbed the cream from Ian's face.

'Lovely girl,' he said as they shared the en suite basin for teeth, well after midnight.

'I could see you thought so.'

They swapped a look. Mel bent to spit.

'Well, she is, isn't she?' He prepared to swill a capful of mouthwash. 'Very chatty. Bubbly.'

Of course you wanted your son to meet a lovely girl, of course you did.

'Bloody hell, Ian.'

She'd warned him about 'bubbly' before. It was on the list with 'feisty'. Probably 'lovely' should be on there too. For a moment, Mel realised how very much she missed Aurora.

'I'm dreaming!'

The wail pierced the wall. Ian, spurting lurid green, pulled a face.

'Here we go ... '

Mel's feet found her slippers. 'I don't mind going.'

Ian sluiced the basin with the tap, feelingly.

'He should be well past this sort of thing by now.'

'He's got an active imagination.'

This had been a family article of faith about Edward since he had first been able to speak. Mel went out to the landing. Edward stood sobbing at his bedroom door, afraid to go further in case Ian lost it with him. Funny old boy, he was. So solid-looking, but so sensitive. She had known it was a mistake to discuss the girl on the beach with him there.

'Oh dear, was it a bad one?'

Mel followed him into his room, where he continued to drip unselfconscious tears on to his outgrown dinosaur rug. He had never much liked dinosaurs, but had inherited the rug from Aidan, who had once been passionate about them.

'I dreamed Declan was killed, like the woman. He couldn't swim.'

Declan? The tutor. God, she had paid him, hadn't she,

amid Thursday's chaos? Surely he would let her know next week if she hadn't. Mel sat on the bed, smoothing the sheet to entice Edward back in.

'I bet Declan's a really good swimmer, don't you? Everyone can swim.'

'Not Grandad.'

True. Ian's dad famously strode around within his depth, bogusly sculling his arms.

'Everyone nowadays learns to swim.'

This was her best tone, her mother-of-boys tone.

'Besides, she wasn't killed, Lottie said.' Mel fussed the duvet round him. 'And don't say woman, say lady.'

She promised to stay until he fell back to sleep. After she'd turned off the lamp Eddy held her hand, his boneless boy paw almost as big as hers. Why did 10-year-old boys always smell of biscuits?

'What do you think happened to her?'

He was whispering, in honour of the dark.

'I don't know, love. Maybe it was an accident.'

'What kind of accident?'

Mel hoisted both legs up on to the bed. It had been a long day, and the submission to comfort was a kind of bliss. She had almost forgotten the strange pleasure of watching her children fall asleep, the slow, trustful slackening into absence, like watching someone die. Long breaths, the heat of each exhalation briefly warming their joined hands, clasped between their facing heads. The non-bridge of Edward's nose, like his brothers' and Ian's, a straight drop between his wide-set eyes, now closing.

'She's very pretty, isn't she?'

He meant Lottie, of course. Mel agreed that she was. She also, when Edward suddenly spoke a couple of minutes later, in defiance of even deeper sleep, murmured agreement that Lottie had lovely hair.

'Do you think ... she puts something on it?' he asked, from far away.

Rays stretched from the shininess of Lottie's hair, word and image tangled together into a child's crayon drawing, the smell of wax bringing Mel comfort. Warm, like the sunshine. *You mustn't eat the crayons; have some proper food, you're fifty.* Yellow. Yellow tasting like wax becoming pebbles on the dark shingle below Brazen Point, as Aurora laughed and laughed, spitting stones.

After that, there was only silence.

Five days in and Mystery Girl still hadn't spoken a word. Dan was pleasantly surprised to get the message to call the hospital. He'd assumed he'd be the one having to do all the chasing. When he rang back it wasn't the brisk, hot doctor herself, as he'd hoped, but some kind of secretary – you couldn't have everything. They thought the girl might be suffering some kind of memory loss. They'd got a psychiatrist coming over from York in the next few days to examine the patient and they wanted a member of the force to be present, preferably a WPC. Dan agreed, while deciding to say nothing about the WPC angle back at the station. If anyone was going to be in that room, it was him. His sergeant wouldn't turn a hair about him going, since Dan had been attending officer when the girl was found.

In the meantime, he thought he'd take a bit of initiative. Out in the car, it was a doddle to get Soccolo's consent to be left alone for a few hours. His partner was up to his elbows in a long-running neighbour dispute in Ruswarp. It was the only bit of policing Soccolo truly loved, wading in among the leylandii, being the sheriff. Dan dropped him off, relieved not to be involved. In the rear-view mirror he saw Soccolo reasoning with a belligerent, shaven-headed middle-aged man while the complainant laid about a ten-foot hedge with a trimmer and the complainant's wife filmed proceedings on her mobile from the censorious safety of their living room window.

Dan had decided to conduct a cheeky bit of house-to-house along the staggered row of neat bungalows that overlooked the far hook of Evensand beach. The bungalows had the best view of the crime scene, if in fact there had been a crime. As far as anyone could tell, according to the secretary who'd called from the hospital, it was hypothermia that had almost finished the girl off. Swabs had come back negative for semen, and there'd been nothing in her system when they'd taken the precaution of pumping her stomach just after she'd come round.

Mason weathered the further disappointment of the rape all-clear. If the girl hadn't been boozed or pilled up, and there was no sign she was a junkie, they were still talking about a blow to the head that had left her in that state; aggravated assault at least, he consoled himself – if not abduction, or worse? So, witnesses. He was being proactive, a quality much praised in training but unfathomably absent from what Mason had seen so far in practice. It was much better to be doing this solo. Nobody liked a smart-arse, as Soccolo would be quick to tell him.

Parking up on the curve of Whitecliff Road, Dan began at the beginning, with number one. There was no car in the drive and no response to his knock. He moved on, to number three. Again, no answer, although this time the car was at home: a red SEAT, he noted automatically, H reg, although he stopped short of clocking the whole number.

'Beechdale', said an oval sign by the tiny sun porch at number five. As Mason stepped through the porch, which was crammed with stunted geraniums growing in ancient yogurt pots and margarine tubs, a large man opened the front door.

'You're late,' said the man. He was plump, with a lot of butterscotch hair, squarely cut.

'Am I?'

The man wrung his hands, blinking expectantly. Some kind of mental health or learning issue, Dan saw. Although he looked around forty, he was wearing the clothes of an elderly person, a button-through shirt and zipped cardigan, both beige. On a different sort of man they would have appeared ironic, even fashionable.

'Did you call the police then?' Dan asked, bluffly. He had had the radio on all the way to Ruswarp and back and hadn't heard a call out to Evensand.

There was a delay, as if the man was translating to himself what Dan had said.

'You were supposed to be here at eleven.'

'Sorry about that.'

'Me dad's out.'

Dan asked if he could come in anyway. The man considered this for a second or two before saying he could. He stepped back from the door.

'Said they were sending another lady,' he managed. At least, that was what Dan thought he'd said. His host sieved the vowels from his speech by talking through clenched teeth, making him hard to understand. As they walked into the house, Dan asked who he was talking to.

'Malcolm.'

'Nice to meet you, Malcolm.'

Malcolm opened a door immediately off the hall and shambled into the room. Dan, following, flinched. The large space was sluiced in unexpected light – almost the entire back wall was a picture window facing the sea. Dan stepped up to get a look, already confident the panorama must include the spot on the beach where the girl had fetched up, but Malcolm, squinting and shaking his head at the glare, trotted to the window and twiddled at the rod of the floor-length louvre blinds, killing the view. A wave of dust exploded from the closing blades and made them both sneeze. Dan managed with a pinch of his fingers, but Malcolm brought a hanky from his trouser pocket and tended to his nose, carefully scanning the large square before fastidiously refolding it over whatever it contained.

The house smelled stale, as though no doors or windows were ever opened, and despite the imposed gloom Dan could see that Malcolm's old-fashioned clothes were hap-hazardly stained.

'Do you mind?'

The man looked at him, wringing his hands again. 'If I sit down?' asked Dan.

Malcolm shook his head. Mason perched at the edge of the sofa, its green velvet paled by exposure to sunlight. It was a nana's room, full of china knick-knacks, pastel and tidy, despite the dust. On the chill gas fire stood a pyram-idal plastic air freshener of a type familiar to him from his own nana's, its mummified gel core still producing a faint synthetic floral whiff.

The doorbell chimed, a reduced Big Ben preamble: ding-dong ding-*donnng*, which, after a stately pause, rebutted its own statement: *dong*-ding dong-dinnng.

'Who's that?' Malcolm wanted to know. Dan couldn't help him. Possibly it was the WPC he was expecting? Agitated, Malcolm went to see.

But it wasn't Lisa or Jade who came back with Malcolm from the front door; rather, a tall girl with swinging hair, an open trench coat and an air of harassed officialdom, signalled by the bulky paper file she clutched to her nicely showcased cleavage.

'Mum and Dad not here?' she was asking, as she followed Malcolm in. Mason stood. She was definitely no copper, Dan would have laid money on it, even if he hadn't known all the WPCs at their place. He introduced himself. In return, looking a bit fazed, she told him she was the Community Psychiatric Something or Other; he didn't catch the end. Her name was Lottie, not from round here by the sound. She produced a knockout smile, quickly wiped away with a lick of her front teeth he read as automatic rather than nervous.

Malcolm was still standing in the centre of the room.

'What's happened to Sally?' he asked effortfully.

Lottie sank on to the sofa, next to Dan, placing the well-stuffed file down between them with another more ingratiating smile aimed Malcolm's way.

'Didn't they tell you on the phone?' She sighed. 'I'm so sorry. Sally's had to go into hospital for a little operation. Nothing serious. I'm covering you until she's back. They should have told you.'

There was a small delay. 'They didn't tell me,' Malcolm said, fretful once more.

Deploying a tone of not entirely confident professional brightness, Lottie suggested he sit down. Malcolm checked her face and looked around for an anxious few seconds, keen to get it right, before choosing the matching armchair set at an angle to the settee. So how was this supposed to work? thought Dan. He was here first. All right, the girl – woman – and Malcolm had some sort of appointment, but he really didn't want to have to come back, probably dragging Soccolo. And he was running out of time before he was due back to pick up his partner. He turned on the charm.

'I was just asking Malcolm a few questions, if that's OK with you. It won't take long, to be honest.'

Lottie smiled again and said it was fine. Though as Dan launched into his set piece about the girl on the beach and what Malcolm had probably heard about it, she interrupted him to address Malcolm herself.

'Sorry – Sally left you a chart? Maybe I can be having a look while you two are chatting?'

Malcolm continued to stare, saying nothing.

'Behaviours,' prompted Lottie, and to Mason, 'Sorry.' She flipped open the cover of the file and Mason saw, on top of the pile of printouts and scribbled notes, a half-denuded sheet of brightly coloured smiley face stickers. How severe were Malcolm's learning difficulties, if he needed fucking stickers?

It appeared that Malcolm wasn't going to speak up about his chart. He wrung his hands, darting a beseeching look to Dan.

'Never mind,' Lottie said, and to Dan, 'Carry on. Sorry.'

Although Mason resumed his speech, he now had a feeling he was on a hiding to nothing. But before he had cranked himself on to the 'anything you saw, however small' part, Malcolm's face brightened and he spat something past his teeth.

'She's dead.'

'Well, she's not, actually,' said Dan.

'Yes she is.'

Beside Dan, Lottie had pulled a sheet out of the file and was pretending to examine it while listening in. He was beginning to find her quite irritating.

'What makes you think she's dead, Malcolm?' Dan asked, allowing himself a tiny pop of hope that the poor bastard had seen something in that spectacular view, something useful that had led him to believe the girl was dead. *Listen, don't lead*, that was the first guideline for questioning potential witnesses. He waited, looking as encouraging as possible, as Malcolm searched his face for the answer.

'She had a stroke,' insisted Malcolm, unhappily. He was pulling at his hands now, each hooked by the thumb of the other, an irresistible force meeting an immovable object. 'I found her at the bottom of the stairs.'

Next to Dan there was a slithering fall of paper as Lottie, knocking the file by her side, dislodged a large portion of its contents on to the floor. Malcolm exclaimed but made no move to help as Mason and Lottie scooped the sheets up between them. Dan's growing irritation wasn't entirely mitigated by the full view of her cleavage he got as she leaned forward past her almost equally fine knees. Proffering a retrieved fan of papers, Dan looked up to Lottie's face and saw that she was locked on to the contents of the page she'd just picked up.

'Oh, Malcolm, I'm so sorry.' She was no longer smiling.

Malcolm's mum had died in 2007. Of a stroke. Between the two of them, they sorted out the confusion. Malcolm had been talking not about the girl on the beach, but about the death of his mother, in delayed response to Lottie's query about his mum and dad both being out that day. Lottie was mortified, explaining on the way out of the tiny, stuffy porch a few minutes later, that she hadn't been briefed by her team and had only had time to glance over Malcolm's file in the car just before the visit. Asperger's, complex learning difficulties, elderly parents.

'It said parents on the top sheet!' she protested. 'Parents, plural. It hasn't been brought up to date!'

'I wouldn't worry about it,' Mason advised.

She seemed to him to be overreacting. Malcolm hadn't minded at all, from what Dan could see. If anything his mood had been unclouded by the three of them resolving the confusion. And anyway, didn't the nature of his condition make him immune to social embarrassment?

'I don't know much about Asperger's,' Lottie confessed. 'There was only one module, in my training. You had to do it as an option.'

The weak sun shone on her hair. They walked to their cars, parked one behind the other. Now they were outside, Mason's irritation had evaporated. Maybe he could convert this pointless interview with a bit of self-interest. But before he could move in, Lottie too brightened.

'That's what my boyfriend's mum thought, you know. That the girl was dead. She was the one who found the body on the beach. Melanie Bale?'

Melanie Bale. A pair of leanly muscled legs, lit by his torch, thrashing up the shingle. The woman who'd called in. 'Oh yeah.'

She smiled again, those full lips. Of course Lottie had a boyfriend. The only attractive woman, admittedly annoying, that he'd met since he'd graduated who seemed entirely indifferent to his uniform, and she wasn't single.

Dan's good mood remained undented. The day was already considerably more interesting than the usual run of petty burglaries and miserable accidents that occupied a shift. He still had the hospital appointment to look forward to, what that might throw up. And this to mull over: Malcolm's announcement, as he stood at the front door to let them out.

'She went in the sea.'

Surely he couldn't still mean his mother? Didn't you have to be in the navy or something to have a sea burial? Mason would have asked, but before he could, Malcolm was talking to Lottie, giving her the sheet of stickers that had slid across the carpet when her file had fallen to the floor.

'I don't want one of them,' he'd said forcefully. Annoyance opened his mouth properly, freeing the words. 'I'm not a bloody baby!'

The memory of Lottie's total, useless surprise entertained Dan all the way back to Ruswarp.

The girl Auntie Mel had found wasn't even dead. Stu passed that on, straight from the horse's mouth. Harmony knew it was Mel on the phone: apart from the fact that she was pretty much the only human being ever to call their landline, Stu had a uniquely abrupt, defensive voice for talking to his sister. He always stayed at the bottom of the stairs, where he'd picked up the call, as though Mel had him chained to the radiator with the power of her personality alone, and with his head bowed and his body slightly inclined away from the handset, he slid first one foot forward, then the other, in a muffled stamp that brought up crests of phlegm-coloured fluff from the dirty carpet. From upstairs you could hear the melody of Stu going 'yep', 'nope', 'summat like that' to Mel, countering the bass of him pawing the carpet, sherlunk, sherlunk, sherlunk.

Harmony was in the bathroom. She had been trying out laxatives, but it was awful. Not just what came out of your bum, but because of the way you had to charge off to the bog so randomly. Plus she hadn't lost even a definite pound.

And laxatives, the amount you had to take to try to develop an eating disorder, as opposed to oiling your wheels after too much cheese on toast, were quite expensive. Since the only cash Stu gave her was for food, she was in danger of having to decide between the cure for her problem and its cause: a multipack of KitKats or more Senokot. It was like 'The Gift of the Magi' that Mr Sanderson had made them read in Year 7 just before it all kicked off at school, where the wife had beautiful hair and the husband had a beautiful watch, and the man bought the woman a tortoiseshell comb for her hair by selling his watch and she cut off her hair and sold it so that she could buy him a watch chain, for the watch he'd sold to buy the ornament for the hair she no longer had ... a Möbius strip, Mum had said. Thinking about it did your head in in an awful, irresistible way.

Stu hammered on the bathroom door.

'Mo, I need a shave!'

Stu always shaved in the evening, which meant he had a beard shadow for the whole of the next day, unless he was going out after tea, when anyone he met would be treated to the three-hour window in which he was truly clean-shaven. Mum used to tease him about it, but Stu claimed it saved valuable time, since he had to get up at what he called the bumcrack of dawn. Sometimes, if he and his partner Craig were catering a festival, they set off before the bumcrack, in the middle of the night. Harmony had, in the past, suggested he grow a proper beard, but Mum always claimed she could never shag a man with a beard. Too pubey.

'Harmony!'

She flushed. They met at the door. This was when Stu told her about the girl not being dead. He didn't pass on anything else about the conversation with Mel. But Mel knew what he was like, which was why she rang the following day, ten minutes before Declan was due to arrive. Harmony was relieved to abandon the despair of experimenting with different tops up in her bedroom to pick up the landline.

'You know it's swapped round,' said Mel, already irritated, just to save the time. 'The lesson. I told Stu last night, did he not say?'

Harmony thought of her aunt in their hall, convulsed and sodden, brandishing her useless mobile, the dewdrop quivering off the end of her nose. Helpless, for a change.

'Harmony?'

Mel was talking about Declan. She'd rearranged the hour that Edward had missed because of last Thursday's events into a double lesson, but she had to take Aidan to some sports thing, which meant Edward would be home alone, so was it possible for Harmony to come to theirs to be with him and she could make up her own botched lesson with Declan there, after Edward's? Ian couldn't leave work in time.

Harmony, once she'd disentangled this, said that was fine. Mel didn't really ask her to babysit properly, for a whole evening or stretch of hours, but in the last months she'd started to ask her to cover these little patches. Harmony wondered if she could ever dare ask for laxative money. But Edward was her cousin and she liked seeing him, as well as Aidan and Joe. She enjoyed their big warm house with its interesting biscuit tin and Mel's home-made cakes and Toothpaste and, more than any of this, the sense of being at a busy junction of connected lives.

On the minus side, at their house she was a cousin, and a niece. Declan wouldn't be able to see her for herself, or, better, as mysterious. Like she was mysterious. Plus, with everyone around, there wasn't the chance for anything to happen, for them to have a moment. Like that was going to happen either. But it was nice, wasn't it, to have the sense of possibility? That after the definite, weird moment they'd shared last week as Mel gabbled to 999, their eyes might meet again. That his hand might slide across the worksheet to touch hers, and then. *Then*. That was definitely never going to happen at Mel's.

Harmony still said yes. It would take someone a lot braver than her to say no to Mel. Mel told her to get a move on.

Outside, although the weather had calmed since the maelstrom of a few days before, it was still freezing. Taking the turn away from the beach road up towards Mel's house, Harmony could see the mark of the storm in the uncleared motley of rubbish that cluttered the base of the bike stands by the Spar. She passed a bus shelter with one side blown out, which made sense of the panel she had seen a minute before in an unloved front garden, its poster of a giant jar of Dolmio askew in the cracked Perspex frame, exposed corners torn. And at the top of the road leading to Mel's, the little green with the mossed war memorial in its centre was filled by the gothic branches of an elderly tree, sheared off at the trunk with a white wound to its bark, not yet tended or cleared. Harmony wondered again about what Mel had actually seen, there on the beach. She'd been so certain about the girl being dead. And hadn't Mel said she was naked? Was that even true?

Skirting the green, which she usually cut through, Harmony was brought up short by a passing 'hi'. By the time she'd turned to see who it was, her own 'hi' back was pointless. The girl who'd spoken looked like a lot of other girls, with a doughnut bun high on her head and a cumbersome green parka. The flick of her pale eyes, though, as she'd passed, landed hard in Harmony's memory and ramped up her pulse, like something toxic hitting her bloodstream. Year 7, Mr Sanderson, one of the lot who'd formed the gauntlet she'd had to run every day before Mum stepped in and took her out of Severn Oak. *Jabba. Spunk Bucket. Great White Fail.* She could remember everything the girl had called her, but had forgotten her name. Chloe? Emily? Harmony turned back for another look, but Chloe/Emily had already disappeared past the war memorial. Good riddance, Mum would say.

'Oh. Hello.'

Up the road, Auntie Mel answered the door as though something was Harmony's fault. Impatiently flourishing a skewer, she explained she was in the middle of impaling a lemon drizzle, the better to douse it with syrup. Declan was already stuck in with Edward. Mel saw his grey North Face hanging on the hooks in the hall as Mel ushered her through to the kitchen. Toothpaste alone nosed her in welcome. Harmony cupped the warm, sueded dome of his head, murmuring endearments.

'Don't let me shoot off without leaving his money, will you?'

Mel meant Declan. Harmony looked up from the dog to her aunt, who was waving the skewer at the closed door of the dining room like a wand, and was startled by a sudden resemblance between Mel and her mum. It was gone almost in the moment she registered it. A turn of the wrist, a lift of the mouth or the voice – what was it, exactly? Mel and Mum weren't properly related; 'outlaws', they used to call themselves, since Stu and Aurora had never bothered to get married. Even if they had, the blood relationship was between Stu and Mel. The two women looked completely unalike, and yet for a breath, like a superimposed image marrying up with the lines of the one below, the way you could match a tracing perfectly to the outline you were copying, they melded. Of course, Mel and Mum had known each other for almost all their lives. They had been friends long before Stu happened. But it was weird. Bad enough having to manage her own thoughts about Mum without being ambushed.

'Oh, God, where does the time go?'

The outlines slipped, and Mel was back to being just Mel again. Harassed and angular, pulling on her fleece over her teaching Lycra. Harmony felt relief, the strangeness dissipating. Mel grimaced at the big clock above the table and thrust the skewer at Harmony.

'You'll have to finish it off for me. You don't mind, do you, love? Aidan! I'm leaving! Get your shoes on if you're coming!' she bayed towards the stairs.

She meant finish the cake. Harmony didn't mind. She took the skewer from Mel, who was scouting the worktops for her handbag. As Mel counted out the money for Declan from her purse, Harmony realised that it had worked out better than she had hoped. Eddy could be relied on to weld himself to a screen full of Minecraft the moment he was let out of his lesson, effectively leaving her alone with Declan. She poked a few more holes in the cake, with a vengeful thought for the girl who had greeted her out on the street, and reached for the bowl of syrup, its surface already pearled to a crust. Jabba. She would present Declan with a slice, but not have one herself.

Aidan, garish in sports kit, staggered in, his heels balanced on the backs of his gigantic untied trainers, only his toes shoved inside. Harmony couldn't have sworn the kit was football; she didn't do sport.

'Hey, Harm.' He picked up a banana from the bowl and tottered out, ignoring his mother's admonition to put his shoes on properly. Mel followed him, palming keys from the hook next to the door. Toothpaste trotted behind, eternally hopeful of a walk.

Dribbling syrup on to the thirsty, planetary surface of the cake, Harmony anticipated the last command to Toothpaste to stay and the solid finality of the closing front door. But instead there were voices, Mel's and a man's, reapproaching the kitchen. The man wasn't Aidan, although Aidan's voice had broken in the last year.

'Oh dear, you'd better come through for a minute. Toothpaste!'

Mel pointed the way with her keys to the voice that materialised, surprisingly, into a policeman. A young, hot policeman. He smiled apologetically at Harmony as he bent to rub Toothpaste's neck in greeting. She wasn't used to being noticed like that. A nice, young, hot policeman.

Mel explained that she didn't have time to talk to him, as she had to be in Glaisdale within the hour. But she wasn't using her briskest tone, so the niceness and possibly even hotness hadn't escaped her.

'Maybe my niece can give you some details,' she suggested, already backing out again, 'or you can leave yours with her. Sorry!'

'Can I at least—' He turned after her, but she'd gone. This time the front door shut.

His name was PC Mason, and he wanted to talk to Mel about the non-dead girl she'd found on the beach. It had taken them a few days to track Mrs Bale down, he explained to Harmony, because although she had given her name when she called in – Harmony remembered Mel spelling out her surname on the phone, very clearly, as her teeth chattered, B-A-L-E – using Declan's mobile had been a temporary source of confusion.

'Declan's here, actually,' Harmony offered. 'We were both there, the storm night.'

PC Mason brightened. 'Fantastic. Anything you can tell me would be brilliant. Anything at all.'

He took out a notebook from his trouser pocket and slapped it down on the breakfast bar. Harmony was interested to see it was exactly the kind of notebook, spiral-bound at the top, used by police on TV. Although wasn't it traditionally kept in the breast pocket? The PC frowned and delved back in his trousers, rucking the sleeve of his tunic so that Harmony could see the elaborate edge of a tattoo on his forearm. It was impossible to tell what it was; the last flourish of a Chinese motto, the curl of a dragon's tail, the toe of a posing glamour girl. Her curiosity drew PC Mason's own attention to the sleeve. He tugged it back in place and asked if he could borrow a pen.

'So, you were there on Thursday,' he prompted, furnished with one of Mel's sharpened pencils.

'Yes, with Declan. He tutors me as well as Edward. Eddy's my cousin.'

'So who was it who spotted her first?'

'Auntie Mel. Who called. Melanie Bale.'

It was only as the PC jotted some version of this on the small page that Harmony realised, her face beginning to burn, that he thought that she and Declan had both been on the beach with Mel. She was about to correct him when he asked if the girl had been in the water.

'Yes, I think so.'

It was true – isn't that what Mel had said, when she burst into the house? PC Mason had concerned brown eyes, and they were looking right at her. He was about the same age as Declan, she reckoned.

'Did you help drag her out?'

'No.' Well, this was also true, totally.

'And did you see anyone else on the beach?'

Harmony hesitated. She felt like a complete dick, but she was going to have to clear up the misunderstanding right now, before he put it all down in the notebook.

'I suppose it was pitch-black,' PC Mason said, encouragingly. 'And coming down stair rods.' Harmony remembered the garden chair flung at the window, which she had yet to return to next door. She agreed it had been.

'She was naked,' said Harmony.

Mason nodded. 'Poor lass. We didn't find any clothes out there,' he said, 'though they might have ended up in the water. You didn't pick any up at all, or your aunt?'

Harmony shook her head. Mel had burst into the house empty-handed, apart from her phone. She wasn't actually telling PC Mason anything that wasn't true.

'Has she said anything?' she asked. 'The girl. About what happened to her?'

The policeman told her that it was all a bit of a mystery. 'We can't get her to speak, as yet.'

'But hasn't anyone reported her missing?'

He smiled, without meaning it. 'You'd think.'

He concentrated again on the notebook, down on the table, as though it might contain answers to these questions. Between them, Toothpaste's tail began to drum the floor as he heard movement from the dining room. At any moment

Declan would appear, and PC Mason would ask him about the night of the storm and it would immediately become clear that Harmony had more or less lied about her involvement. As there were footsteps in the hall and Toothpaste rushed to the door, Harmony advanced to pre-empt Declan.

'Sorry, I'm supposed to be having a maths lesson now.'

'If I can just have your name.' The policeman's pencil hovered. She told him, holding on to the door. It wasn't a lie. She and Mum had used Stu's surname for years, despite the lack of officialdom. But she realised, watching him write the name in rounded capitals, that it came with the bonus that if PC Mason wanted to look into what she had said, 'Ansholm' might hold him up for just long enough to decide it wasn't worth the bother. Not that it would come to that. She could see how completely he believed her. To the cop, she was a witness. Harmony Ansholm: he trusted her, just like that.

As Dan had predicted, his sergeant didn't turn a hair when he said he was off to the hospital. An absent 'good lad' was Hildebrand's only comment as Mason squeaked the details on to the whiteboard and took off from the station. In the car, Dan niggled at the request he'd fudged. It was unthinking protocol, surely, asking for a WPC to be present at this interview with the psychiatrist. After all, he'd already seen the girl in the nip the day they rescued her, and there was no evidence of a sexual assault. Why would she need another woman in the room just to see a shrink? Dan hoped, though, that he wouldn't be challenged on the matter. The closest he'd ever come before to meeting a member of the psychiatric profession was at a lecture given by a forensic psychologist during his training. Even that – Mason had asked her a question about Hannibal Lecter, on a dare from the other lads – had made him feel excitingly on the brink of confiding something terrible about himself.

The psychiatrist, Lennox, was an immediate disappointment. For a start, he was a bloke. He looked like a lad you'd meet down at the rugby club: thirties, big-boned and upfront, his tie askew under his collar as though he'd borrowed it for the day. Yorkshire, but not local. They shook hands at the door to the side room they had been allotted for the exam. The shrink's hand was large and cool. PC Mason had no desire to confide.

In the room, a large piece of medical machinery had been wheeled to one side to create more space, but its armatures and screens still impinged uncomfortably on the backs of the chairs arranged for them round a small table. Lennox settled an A4 pad and pen in front of him before rolling up his shirtsleeves. The stacked little nurse with the eyebrows brought them plastic cups of water. Dan remembered her eyeing him up the night they were working on the girl.

'How is she?' he asked.

'You'll see,' she said. 'Poor lass.'

'You've called her Storm, I hear,' said Lennox. Mason didn't know about this.

'We've got to call her something,' the nurse said. 'Do you want me to fetch her?'

As they waited, Dan asked the shrink what he thought had happened to the girl. Why wasn't she talking? Lennox addressed the cover of his notepad, reluctantly.

'Dissociative amnesia includes something we call a psychogenic fugue state.'

Mason stared at Lennox, defying him to use smaller words.

'It's actually very rare, but it's the most familiar form of amnesia, you might say. It follows on from a traumatic event rather than having a physical cause.'

'A physical cause? You mean, like a blow to the head?'

Lennox grunted dismissively. He didn't want interruptions.

'Anterograde amnesia is caused by actual brain damage. Such as that caused, say' – he opened a concessionary palm to Mason, eyes still on his notebook – 'by a blow to the head. In that type of condition we would see an inability to create new memories. But as far as I've been told the patient's procedural memory is intact.'

'Procedural?'

'Her ability to remember routines, people she encounters. All that seems fine.'

'But if she's not talking—'

'Believe me, you'd be able to tell if it was anterograde. She'd be in quite a bit of distress. Anyway, hopefully we'll know more once I've seen her.' Lennox pushed himself back in his chair, trying to find some legroom.

'There's also transient epileptic amnesia – a form of temporal lobe epilepsy. We might expect that to show up on her scan, scarring from previous episodes . . . I'm still waiting on those results.'

'But if it's the fugue thing you said . . . traumatic in what way?'

Lennox shifted again. For a moment Dan hoped he might crown himself on a folded limb of the displaced machine behind them, but without looking the shrink reached up and fielded the hinged protuberance away from his head with a relaxed assurance that was unaccountably annoying.

'Psychogenic memory loss is like a form of PTSD. Post-traumatic stress disorder—'

Mason told him he knew what PTSD was, ta. 'So, bottom line, something bad happens to her and she forgets it all?'

Tattooing his pen against the cover of his notebook, Lennox grimaced. 'Possibly.'

As the nurse led the girl in, Lennox stood and offered his cool hand.

'Hi, I'm Andy.'

He hadn't given his first name to Dan. The girl hesitated, then took Lennox's hand to shake, not very hard. Smiled nervously. So that's what she looked like.

Dan realised the girl was looking at him now, her hand still uncertainly extended. He took it and shook, pretending confidence. There was no variation in her reaction, despite his uniform. Obviously she wouldn't have recognised him from the night of the rescue at Evensand. Obviously, she didn't.

'Dan,' he said, feeling like a fraud. Perhaps Andy would have been able to explain why. The doctor ushered the girl to the free chair, swinging his briefcase off the table and taking his own seat, his tree-trunk legs uncomfortably squeezed to one side, away from the medical paraphernalia. Scouse Brows left them to it. According to her badge, her name was Chandra.

'Right,' said Lennox, amplifying his normal-bloke tones to a professional resonance, 'I'm here to have a chat because we need to help you find out what happened, don't we? Before you were found on the beach the other day.'

The girl's face was turned to him. A maroon graze cross-hatched her right cheekbone, probably from where she'd been dragged along the shingle, probably by Mrs Bale getting her out of the way of the sea. Otherwise, hospital pallor apart, she looked healthy. Her expression remained neutral, as though Lennox was the radio while she was doing the ironing. Her hands were relaxed on her lap.

'Can I see if you understand me?'

She nodded, rubbed at her nose, an itch. No more smiling, tuning in a bit more.

'Good. Now, I understand the nurses have tried this with you, but just checking . . . '

Lennox pushed over the pad and pen.

'Would you like to write anything for us?'

As the girl picked up the pen, Mason felt himself sit forward in his chair. But after a second or two, to her own apparent frustration, she put the pen back down, her mouth tucked. Little shake of the head. He realised his heart was beating double time.

'Sure?'

Of course she was effing sure. Lennox neutrally dragged the pad back to his side of the table. Mason got the impression he was clocking something Mason hadn't noticed. That's what shrinks did, in their secret shrink way.

The girl didn't look like a Storm. She looked like a Lucy or a Jennifer. Mild and slightly sweet. Old-fashioned, even. Not like that other girl, Lottie, the psychiatric nurse or whatever she was. Although there had been something blunderingly naive about her, and one of the reasons she was annoying. This girl facing them, she was innocent, which was different. And her mouth didn't make you think of blow jobs.

As Dan watched, Lennox spent the next twenty minutes putting the girl through her paces, physically. Holding both hands out and turning them individually palm up and palm down, then alternating, an awkward Motown routine. After this, Lennox picked up his pen, held between finger and thumb, and tracked it up to and away from one eye, then the other. All the time he jotted notes that Mason saw slide off the lines of his notepad, because he never took his neutrally reasonable gaze off the girl. Next, the shrink stood. Following his lead, she stood on one leg, then the other. She wobbled. Who wouldn't? Her reaction to this was normal, a near giggle, a near exclamation before she righted herself. It pinned her as young, to Dan, really young. Or was it just because of her plainly brushed hair and lack of make-up? You never saw a girl like that round here. The clothes they'd come up with for her were normal enough: leggings, a dark blue t-shirt limp with washing and a deep pink hoody, unzipped, with curled silver script reading 'Club Tro' on the left, 'picana' on the side hanging right. But on her feet were hospital slippers made of greyed towelling. She was a patient, no doubt about it.

'Good,' said Lennox. The girl had stopped looking over at Mason. She'd learned by now that Lennox was in charge. He nodded his permission and she sat once more.

Mason had to make an effort not to yawn. The room was essentially a cupboard, without windows. Lennox took an iPad from his briefcase and flipped back the cover for the girl, tapped the screen to life. She started pleasantly and smiled up at them as Lennox's wallpaper – Mason could see from upside down a baby's gurning grin – appeared. But she didn't lift a hand. She didn't know what to do.

'OK . . . ' Was there a tang of Aussie in Lennox's accent, or had he just had too many holidays? 'Some photos for you to look at.'

The doctor swiped images up on to the home screen, explaining to the girl that she should stop if she recognised anything. She watched his fingers, learning. Dan hitched his chair closer, to share an angled view. The shots were of towns, places around Britain, some of them famous, some of them more ordinary. With increasing confidence the girl swiped past Big Ben, Edinburgh Castle, York Minster, Fountains Abbey . . . a bus stop, a street, a pub . . . on she went. To Mason, she seemed more interested in the process of making a new photo appear than the photos themselves. Then, after he'd decided for himself this was a pointless exercise, she stopped and considered for the first time. Both he and Lennox tensed, moving as one to take a better look at the inverted image. A Costa sign. The girl nodded dispassionately, meeting Lennox's eye. Lennox took a note. There was a Costa a few yards from the hospital, Dan knew. She could probably see it from the window of the ward. He'd piss on the shrink's chips about that later.

She next paused at a photo of a shopping mall. Then a McDonald's. Mason could feel Lennox's excitement begin to fade.

'Maybe that's enough to be getting on with,' he said. Then, unexpectedly, he leaned forward and asked her, 'Is there anything you'd like?'

The girl became very still, as though the surprise of the question contained a threat, or a trap.

'Show me.' Lennox pointed to the iPad, smiling. She shrugged, shook her head, rubbed her nose. There was no exaggeration in the movement. She wasn't particularly frustrated, Dan saw, by not being able to speak. She was simply confused. And hopeless. That's what Mason got – he didn't know if Lennox saw that. This girl wasn't going to try, because whatever she wanted, she knew they wouldn't be able to get it for her. Not in a despairing way, but because it was impossible. A McDonald's, now you're talking. Trip to see Big Ben, I'll have a word. Anything else, what difference was El Shrinko going to make?

Dan's heart actually felt heavy, if that really was his heart at the top of his stomach. Like it had been left in water and was swollen with the weight of feeling. Didn't she just want to know who she was and go back there? He thought of that moment as he'd stepped into the dead air of Malcolm's living room to be blinded with light. And Lottie, smiling to reveal her large, perfect teeth.

'We're on it. Don't worry. We'll find out who you are.'

Lennox's face told him he'd actually said this out loud. Well, fuck it. It was Dan's job. What was wrong with that?

Mel wouldn't have looked twice at the photo; it was the stark DO YOU KNOW THIS GIRL? that hooked her attention as she stood behind a man attempting to fathom the automated loan-and-return machine at the library. The flyer was freshly pinned on the community noticeboard, above the machine's unresponsive maw. Most of it was a head-and-shoulders shot, with the claustrophobic focus of a picture taken with a mobile. The white horizontal rod of a hospital bed frame drew a line behind the girl's head. As the conveyor spat back the man's Lee Child, Mel considered the young face, halfway to a smile.

She had saved the girl's life, but she wouldn't have recognised her in the street. A soft, tense face, features regular enough to be pretty, or not irregular enough not to be, but not pretty enough to stand out. A face you saw countless times every day, in all stages of life. Except, for a girl this age, the shot was unusual in containing none of the reflex curation of the selfie. This might have been because someone else had taken it – one of the nurses, perhaps. There was a shy surprise in the expression that suggested the girl hadn't been ready for or even aware of the pressing of the phone button. Her pupils were too dilated by the flash for the picture to reveal the surrounding eye colour, and the hair you could see, since it was pulled back, was a flat brown that could easily be dark blond. The pull of her mouth as she almost smiled suggested the teeth beneath might be prominent or crooked, though she might have just moved her tongue as the picture was taken. Otherwise, apart from the mark of a bruise on her cheek, there were no distinguishing features. Looking at the picture, though, Mel had a feeling. A feeling that translated directly into the thought: *she's not from around here.*

'Returns isn't working, love.'

The librarian intervened to rescue the man's books, which he followed to the desk. Mel stepped up with her own pile, offering them competently to the scanner. There was a knack. The two next Skulduggery Pleasants for Edward and a Tom Gates, as requested. What were they going to do about Edward? Declan had left a polite message asking her to call him to 'check in about Edward's progress', which couldn't be good news. It was so easy to let things slide. She shouldered her shopper, heavy with the books. A bag for life. That sounded about right. A bag, for life.

She'd fancied that young policeman, though. He was probably only a couple of years older than their Joseph, but the uniform changed everything. The solicitous way he had called her Melanie on the phone had been oddly arousing, as though he saw her in an intimate and unfamiliar light. No one called Mel Melanie now her mother was dead. Mrs Ansholm had chosen the name in tribute to her favourite film, *Gone With the Wind*. How disappointed Mel had been, on finally watching it, to discover Melanie Wilkes was a sap, and not even the main character. Oh yes, her mother had agreed, Melanie was wetter than water; it was the actress who played her, Olivia de Havilland, she'd loved. But obviously you couldn't go christening a girl Olivia in North Yorkshire in the 1960s. Mel would have been teased, so Melanie it was.

Such a pretty name, Mrs Ansholm had protested, when somewhere during the rupture of starting secondary school, Melanie had been shorn to Mel. Had it been Dawn who had renamed her? Secondary was when they had begun to be friends, and God knows, Dawn – later to be Aurora – was always keen on reinvention. Whoever was responsible, Mel had relished her new identity, trimmed of vulnerable consonants, suddenly contemporary. Soon after she had her ears pierced, and lobbied for a perm. And now she had been Mel Bale, mother of boys, teacher of girls, for so long that nothing of Melanie Ansholm remained, or so she'd thought until that young policeman had summoned her.

If I can just ask you, Melanie, if you saw anyone else out there on the beach?

Although he was just a voice on the phone, Mel had seen enough of him on the night when she was rushing out with Aidan to feel stirred by the singularity of his address. Puppy-faced, but manly. Dishy. Was that a word anyone used any more? It was barely a word she used. He gave her a number to ring, if she thought of anything else she'd seen, along with his name. PC Dan Mason. She already knew both, from the scribbled note Harmony had left next to the crumbs of the plundered lemon drizzle. She promised to call if she remembered anything else.

'Anything, Melanie,' he said. 'Any detail, however small, don't worry. I want to hear it.'

Young *man*.

He had rung when she was on her way to the Co-op, stopping her in the street to answer her phone. An hour later, Mel's tasks were almost at an end. Now that she'd done the Co-op and the library, there was only Skelton's, to pick up the elastic for ballet shoes. Both the library and Skelton's were living on borrowed time. Well, weren't they all? The elastic was bogglingly cheap: ninety pence for a metre, measured and cut at the counter. Mel had to buy it because half the girls she taught had mums with no idea how to sew the few stitches needed to secure the strips to the kids' shoes. She wasn't in the business of giving sewing lessons, so she'd started doing it herself. Ian wondered why they didn't just sell ballet shoes with the elastic already on. They did, on the internet, but the shoes were more expensive and anyway, Mel couldn't be bothered to explain to him that it wasn't the same.

DO YOU KNOW THIS GIRL? She saw on the way out that the flyers were even up on Skelton's window, obscuring the headless mannequins drooping under anaemically printed kaftans.

Jobs done, Mel traditionally popped into Scoffs, the café where Joseph worked, for a cappuccino on her way back to the car. She was aware Joe didn't enjoy her visits, but she'd have stopped somewhere, and Scoffs' location, at the foot of the steps up to the clifftop car park, was ideal. It seemed ridiculous to deprive the place of custom and herself of caffeine just to humour his whimsical embarrassment about her appearing in his workplace. He hadn't been back home since his birthday dinner over a week ago. He'd never stayed over at Lottie's that long before, if only for reasons of laundry. Mel assumed the girl had taught him how to use her washing machine.

Which reminded her: Harmony's clothes had looked in need of a wash when she'd come round the other night. Not for the first time, Mel put Harmony on her to-do list.

When she went into Scoffs Joseph had his back turned, taking an order. Mel sat at one of the few free seats, near the door, and waited. His white shirt looked clean, she was pleased to see. Scoffs was at the genteel end of the café trade – crab sandwiches and doilies, cups and saucers and tea in a pot. Old-fashioned, like the library and Skelton's, without the twee self-consciousness of heritage. But it did well, even out of season, full of pensioners bent over toasted teacakes, and school geography trips recovering with insurmountable wedges of Victoria sponge from the hike up the cliff path; walkers all year round; and even the occasional tourist gone rogue from Whitby. The manager, Elaine, who had been at school with Mel and Aurora, had inherited the business from her parents. She was too mean to hire more than one waiter, and Joseph had moaned about being overworked ever since he'd started the job. Mel and Ian both took that with a pinch of salt. Spoiled rotten. That was probably her fault. She'd never expected any of them to help. Maybe that was why she always popped in, Mel realised, as Joseph sighed and pencilled her order. Just for the pleasure of having him wait on her.

'How's everything?' she asked him.

'Fine.' There was a warning in it not to go any further. His eyes were ringed. Shagged out, she shouldn't wonder.

'Cos your dad's wondering if we should start renting out your room.'

'Yeah, if you like.'

Joe took the order slip back to Elaine, as if she didn't know what Mel had asked for. Watching him, she saw another of the flyers above the hissing coffee machine, Elaine's head bowed to the frother beneath it.

DO YOU KNOW THIS GIRL? Mel's fingers remembered the rubbery density of those bare shoulders she had scoured along the sand. PC Mason had asked about this, grunted in appreciation as she described the struggle to get that dead weight up out of the water before she ran back to call 999. He said this made sense of some bruising on the girl's upper body.

'Don't worry, Melanie, you did the right thing.'

She had done the right thing. Now Mel raised her voice above the crescendo of espresso manufacture.

'The police say I probably saved her life. That girl.'

Joe didn't respond, deafened by the machine.

'The police were just talking to me. You know, about all that.' She nodded to the flyer. A couple of OAPs craned round to look. 'They think she's lost her memory. Because of a knock on the head.'

PC Mason had confided this. Though hadn't it already been in the paper? The thought from the library returned.

'She's not spoken, you know. She could be foreign.'

One of the pensioners tutted and returned to his teacake. Joseph rolled his eyes at her.

'Really, Mum? Really?'

He meant she was being racist, like the old man. The kids liked to accuse her and Ian of racism, by which they seemed to mean noticing if anyone wasn't white, or British, or even local.

'Well, how would they be able to tell? She could.'

The cappuccino, when Joseph brought it, was too

69

lukewarm to relish. He'd slopped froth into the saucer as well, when he put it down. Reaching for a tissue to blot beneath the cup, since Joe had also neglected to bring her a napkin, Mel was reminded she'd got his post in her bag. Not checking up on him, then. Not intruding. An errand. She waved the envelopes at him.

'For you.'

Joe ignored her, on his dignity with a couple of early jacket potatoes. Putting the letters on the table, Mel extracted the one significant envelope from the junk mail and the probable dental reminder.

'Did you see?'

It was a large, official-looking airmail from South America. Gap year stuff. Off he'd go, into the wide blue yonder. What would his Lottie think about that?

'Don't you want to open it? It's probably that school, isn't it?'

'Clinic. I already emailed.' Mel waited. Joe took her empty cup. 'Change of plan.'

'Change . . . '

'Yeah, not really feeling it, South America. Think I might stick around here for a bit.'

Off he went, to attend to two oyster-eyed old ladies who'd taken a corner table and were keeping their coats on. Bloody hell. Mel got up and paid at the till.

'What kind of do is this then?' Elaine kinked her chin at the police notice.

'I know,' said Mel, tightly. She didn't trust herself to look at Joe. Elaine stared through her with amiable incuriosity. Relentless years of customer chit-chat had slackened both her ability and desire to have a genuine conversation, but she was primed to talk at all costs.

'They're sending experts, it said on the news.'

'Experts' provoked another Pavlovian tut from the pensioner in the corner. Elaine forged on. Tiny points of light shone through the piercings up her ear cartilage which she no longer bothered to adorn. She'd been a punk, at school.

'I suppose we'll be paying for it, mind.'

Elaine busked this final, edgeless observation as she raked Mel's change out of the till. Would it have killed Elaine to give her a free coffee? Mel popped the coins into the tip box, though God knows Joe didn't deserve it. A circular economy, wasn't that what it was called?

'Paying for what?' she asked, irked to have to get news from Elaine. She hadn't seen the news. Really, shouldn't PC Mason have told her what they were planning?

'All of it,' said Elaine blankly. 'I don't know. You know, experts and that. To find out where she's come from.'

Dawn had always been rude about Elaine when they were at school. But after she came back to Evensand with Harmony, she and Elaine had become friendly. Mel, inviting Aurora along to a grey family barbecue soon after their return, had been astonished when she turned up with Elaine in tow.

'Elaine Ashley?'

'Yeah, why not? We bumped into each other and decided to have a catch-up. She's nice. You don't mind, do you?'

Mel was still adjusting to Dawn's change of name, let alone all the other changes wrought by the intervening years. When Dawn had come back to Evensand with Harmony – the phrase 'with her tail between her legs' was irresistible, although Dawn wasn't seen to display any kind of shame, or indeed, a tail, despite her years living in Bristol – it turned out that she'd been Aurora for years. 'Latin for Dawn,' she'd

71

said, as though that made it any less poncey. Whatever she wanted to call herself, niceness had never been a quality Dawn/Aurora had been known to value. Of course she didn't mind, said Mel. Sunk low in the ranks of pregnancy (Eddy), toddlerdom (Aidan) and early childhood (Joseph), she was in every respect slow on the uptake. Dulled by hormones and cornered by Elaine, Mel had dimly apprehended the way Dawn/Aurora took up position under the golfing umbrella where Stu presided over the sausages with professional aplomb, and, despite the hovering presence of Stu's long-term girlfriend, Lisa, responded even to Stu's most token jokes with gales of long-throated, cleavage-displaying laughter. Later, drearily sponging the ketchup off Aidan's t-shirt that had been squirted there by Harmony, who was wired to hysteria by unfamiliar sugar, Mel clocked her old friend's progress to fleeting you-are-awful touches of her brother's arm and leg. But even after a gloomy joke by Ian about the difficulty of combining a sex life with raising and producing small children, when Aurora had provocatively announced to Stu she was 'so crap at sex', the penny had failed to drop. This only happened three weeks later, when Stu broke up with Lisa and Aurora and Harmony moved in with him. She wasn't sure how friendly Aurora and Elaine had continued to be after that, although Mel supposed the reignited contact was indirectly responsible for Joe's current tenure at Scoffs.

People, though. Mel climbed the steps to the car park at a pace that raised protest from her knees. People were bad enough, without your family making everything worse. What was Joseph playing at with this gap year business? It was Edward she should be worrying about. Really, she should be ringing Declan about him right now. She wove through the rows of cars with her shopping. Why couldn't Edward just be like his brothers? Well, like Aidan? St Benedict's was such a good school, and they gave a discount for siblings. Bloody kids. All the money, all the hours of work . . . The whole idea of Joe's year off had been to travel. The longer he stayed in Evensand, the harder it would be for him to leave. What if he ended up jacking in his place at Birmingham? What if he got Lottie pregnant? Mel pulled up as a sagging, chaotic crone reared out at her from the reflecting window of a people carrier. Jesus. It was her, she saw. The original bag for life.

Safely behind her own steering wheel, Mel conducted an examination in the rear-view mirror. It wasn't as bad as all that; largely a matter of the wind and her hair, combined with the way her lips tended to disappear when she was under any kind of strain. But here she was, more or less as she remembered herself. She thought again of that poor girl, lost to herself and the world. Experts indeed. What good was being alive if you didn't have a clue who you were?

It had just turned two o'clock. Mel was due to teach her first lesson at four: Grade 1 Modern, one of her biggest classes. If the journey was in her favour, Mel calculated she had enough time to get out to the infirmary and back to the church hall by then. Short of staking out Scoffs in the hope of catching Lottie meeting up with Joe there, Mel couldn't see what her options were. She needed to get the lie of the land.

Mel had been quite impressed to learn that Lottie was based at the infirmary. Had Joe known of the medical status his mother felt this conferred, she knew he would have done more than rolled his eyes. Inching through some post-lunch congestion at the out-of-town roundabout, Mel reflected on how much time she seemed to spend withstanding imaginary put-downs from her eldest son. Wasn't the effect of parenting supposed to be her presence as a voice in his head, rather than the other way round?

Of course, she could have rung Lottie instead of turning up at the hospital in person; presumably there was a contact number for her team on a website. But a call would give Lottie the opportunity to let Joe know Mel had been in touch, permitting the escalation of his Jiminy Cricket routine into a real-world intervention in his mother's behaviour. She could hear him asking her what the hell she thought she was doing, taking on his girlfriend. Mel could see it looked bad from the outside, but if being seen as a joke was going to stop her, she'd have given up leaving the house years ago. It was Joe's future. A future was such a fragile thing, like the moment after you dipped the wand in the mixture and blew a soap bubble. The tension as it distended from the wand, oily with all the colours of the rainbow, then detached, suddenly whole, and wobbled up into the air, clear and beautiful. Or popped.

The traffic delays were already galvanising Mel slightly as she asked in the hospital lobby for directions to Social Care. An elderly volunteer with a hairdo directed her to the fourth floor. Why were hospital lifts so slow, Mel wondered, as she ascended at a glacial pace in the company of a silent porter. Could it really have anything to do with health and safety, as she'd been told during maternity visits? They stopped at each floor, whether there was anyone waiting or not. The porter sighed each time Mel jabbed pointlessly at the button marked '4' while the doors cranked apart, hesitated, then cranked back. Either he, or the lift, smelled strongly of sweat.

Finally they were at the fourth floor. And here, providentially, was Lottie herself, about to get into the lift with another woman.

'Mrs Bale! Hi!'

Mel had to give the girl marks for immediate identification. She was aware she looked very different, haggardly ponytailed and zipped into teaching clothes, from the way she'd appeared, blow-dried and glad-ragged, at Joe's birthday dinner.

'I was just coming to see you!'

Anxiety tinged Lottie's wide social smile. 'Were you?'

The lift doors were inching shut behind her. Lottie yelped and pulled at her colleague, who staggered into the space with an exaggerated pantomime of squeezing in, although there was plenty of room.

'This is Val. Val, this is Joseph's mum.'

'Ooooh. Nice to meet you, Joseph's mum.'

Val was small and plump, her currant bun face alight with defensive irony. Lottie refreshed her smile as Mel told her that it must be nice, working at the hospital. They were only based here, Lottie explained. Most of their day was spent visiting clients.

'For our sins,' chirped Val.

Mel wondered if the two of them were on their way out now. They were, actually, said Lottie. As the lift continued up to Floor 5, releasing the despondent porter but not the smell, Val added that they could tell her where they were going but then they'd have to kill her. It was going to be a problem, Mel could see, getting Lottie on her own in order to have a private conversation.

The lift began its descent. Mel and Lottie continued to swap smiles, as Val hummed in a peculiarly artificial way. Mel suspected that Val prided herself on putting people at their ease.

'So were you just dropping by, or ...'

'Aye, aye,' said Val, jabbing her little elbow at Lottie. 'You're for it, lass.' She nodded at Mel. 'Future mother-in-law!'

Lottie obliged with a nervous giggle, while managing to lob Mel an unfiltered look of dismayed apology over Val's head. The doors inched open, back at Floor 4.

'Actually, Val, you go on, we'll ...'

And Lottie stepped out of the lift, encouraging Mel to follow. The last she heard of Val was a 'give her hell!' as the doors shut.

'Who was that for, you or me?'

'Oh dear ...' It was the same falling tone with which Lottie had handed her broken umbrella to Ian at their house, both wry and defeated. Beyond Mel's irritation at Val nailing more or less why she was there in the first place, Mel felt a further irritation. She was beginning to like the girl. What use was that?

Lottie led them down the corridor leading out of the right-hand side of the lift. She apologised for not having more time, but she thought she knew why Mel had come.

'Really?'

Had Joe rung after all, warning Lottie that Mel was likely to put her oar in concerning the two of them after her reaction in Scoffs? Was she that monstrously predictable?

'I don't want to interfere ...'

'I totally understand, Mrs Bale.'

'Mel.'

Lottie gestured. They were at the entrance to a ward. Three of the beds contained dozing elderly ladies, one flanked by visitors; the fourth bed was empty.

'She's probably in the TV room, if she's not in the loo,' said Lottie. 'It's fine to see her. Honestly. You saved her life.'

Mel, squared to block a penalty, fumbled after a balloon.

In dumb confusion she trailed after Lottie all the way to a small, oddly shaped corner room permeated by the ghostly tang of long-banned cigarette smoke. Now it contained a small wall-mounted TV playing a soundless quiz show to an armless three-seater sofa and two plastic chairs that had been dragged in from the ward. The girl stood at the junction of the right-angled windows, staring into the view with her back to the door. It must be her, though Mel wouldn't have recognised her from the night on the beach. She wore a lurid pink hoody that was much too big for her, her slight frame a surprise after Mel's remembered tussle to heave her out of the water. *A dead weight.* She'd never known just what that meant until she'd tried to crab-scuttle the two of them free of the sucking waves. For panicked seconds she'd been terrified both of them would be dragged under. How ready she'd been to let go.

'Storm? There's a visitor for you.'

Lottie's voice was gentle. Hearing her, the girl turned and smiled. It was a nervous smile, offered in lieu of speech. Lottie did all the talking, explaining who Mel was and that she'd just come in to see how she was doing. And then she backed into the corridor, apologising that she really had to go. She was already a bit late for her client meeting.

So that was that. Not so much the wrong end of the stick as a whole different tree.

Mel's unusual position of not knowing what to say stretched the silence into seconds. The girl made no noises or gestures to take the place of her missing language. She stood quite still, offering only the worn single coin of her smile. The white sky behind her, suddenly lit by occluded winter sun, pressed at the uncurtained hospital glass. Come on Mel.

'I'm glad you're OK ... we were all worried about you!'

The girl stepped forward and reached out to squeeze Mel's upper arm. It was a thank you. Her face was vivid with it.

'That's all right,' said Mel. 'I only did what anyone would have done, seeing you out there.'

The girl nodded. Her dark eyes searched Mel for meaning more deeply than Mel felt, suddenly, she could bear. She remembered the boys, as babies, staring up from her breast with that fiercely essential, locked-in gaze. She forgot what she had really come for. Mel Bale, mother of boys, teacher of girls. Being looked at like that was like being seen for the first time.

There were only five more Declan lessons before the exam. Harmony wasn't thinking beyond that point because she knew the exam itself was going to be a disaster, followed by the void of afterwards, without even the thought of seeing Declan to keep her going. It seemed incredible, since they were only at the beginning of March, but there was Easter, and another half-term when he was going to be away, and that would be that: exam time. Come the beginning of June, they would part. The only comforting possibility was that when she failed, he might tutor her for a retake, although she could already hear Stu saying he couldn't be much of a bloody teacher if she'd failed in the first place, could he?

Something definitely had to happen, then, before it all came to an end. Harmony knew it wouldn't. Why should anything happen to her, when even the heightening discovery of the girl on the beach seemed to have led nowhere? Already, over two weeks on, the little posters with her face on were getting pulled down or torn. The one by the Spar had a hairy-balled knob scribbled on it, angled to the girl's mouth, with a speech bubble saying 'I luv spunk'. There had been a piece on the local TV news, but who the girl was and why she'd ended up beneath Brazen Point remained a mystery as great as the value of x in the problem Declan had left Harmony with last week 'as a challenge'. She attempted it, out of love for him, but there was just too much wheeling in her head.

Hairy-balled knobs, for one. The defaced poster had brought home to Harmony the tragic fact that she was likely to turn sixteen without having seen an erect penis. Not properly, anyway. Part of the school thing back in Year 7 had been ambushing her with porn on phones, so she had an unhappy, fragmentary memory of angry purple willies at open holes or poking out from between massive, globular tits. Although at the time she'd burst into tears and run away, she still used the images as wank fodder. It wasn't good enough. As a family they were neither notably prudish nor notably open, and over the years Harmony had incidentally seen Stu's tackle, mercifully flaccid. There had also been a playmate called Jake, also homeschooled, who they had met when she and Mum had first moved back to Evensand. Mum had encouraged him to come to the house, and for a while he and Harmony had shared an interlude of cheerful mutual genital display behind her closed bedroom door when the mums thought they were building Lego. But stepdads and nine-year-olds didn't count. It was pathetic. How could she expect to do anything with Declan without at least some theoretical knowledge?

Harmony didn't have a laptop, and her phone, passed down from Mum, was basic and antique. Her only chance was the sclerotic home computer, when she was sure Stu would be out and the broadband wasn't on the blink. The opportunity had come, as a kind of luck would have it, on a Declan day. Feeling ridiculous, although she couldn't see an alternative, Harmony typed 'porn' into Google. It did the trick. Within ten minutes, including an almost immediate detour to put her hand down her leggings and bring herself off, she began to feel inured to the sickly, arousing shock of bodies doing unlikely things to other bodies. Why had she never thought of this before? There wasn't much hair, though, on the balls she encountered. This, she knew, was a porn thing: Mum had given her the lecture when she'd wanted to shave her legs.

Inspired, Harmony googled 'medical penis'. This turned out to be a mistake. Hastily clicking out of the page, Harmony amended the entry to 'medical condition penis', and, sifting squint-eyed through images that were realistically rather than pornographically nauseating, arrived at a shot that seemed exactly what she'd been looking for: an unexaggerated, half-stiff dick, in banal lighting, cushioned by sparsely pubed testicles. The pubes had a gingerish hue, and there was a mole at the base of the veined, dun-brown shaft, details that struck Harmony with their specificity. This was a particular penis, belonging to a particular someone. At the same time, it had an everyman quality: average, surely, in both size and arrangement. Consoled by its ordinariness, she wondered how the picture had ended up on the internet, neither disfigured by a rash or waxed for action, but after scrolling through some more of the pages available (*4,590,000 results in 3 seconds*), she realised that men really, really liked taking selfies of their willies, either anonymously or with the rest of them cheerfully, proudly or inadvertently attached.

Sometimes she thought she'd never catch up with the rest of the world. Thanks, Mum. Still, Harmony was more energised than depressed as she carefully deleted her internet history, going back into Explorer to check nothing came up as autotype. After a moment's thought, she tapped in 'po', to fill it in with '-etry competitions', then scrutinised both desktop and trash, in case any wayward porn had floated there to incriminate her. This accomplished, she decided to do a bit of non-cyber tidying before Declan arrived. The house was a mess, as usual; possibly even more than usual. Declan probably thought they lived like pigs. He had Mel's house to compare theirs to, after all. Whenever the three of them came back from Mel and Ian's, Mum had been fond of declaring they didn't live in a furniture shop. Although Harmony knew what she meant, looking round the living room she thought a bit more order wouldn't exactly tip their living arrangements dangerously towards sterility.

After she'd tidied, she went down to the Spar to get milk for the tea she'd finally decided to offer Declan. If anything was going to happen between them she needed to weed out these strange efflorescences of embarrassment. She'd tell him the kettle, which had never been broken, had been fixed. She would also get a packet of biscuits, as though she were the kind of person nonchalantly capable of having biscuits in the house. She chose Hobnobs, nice enough to offer a guest without demanding the remainder be eaten in one lone, secret sitting. Also, not that it mattered now but as a gesture to Mum, because oats. And McVitie's. Unless McVitie's was owned by Nestlé?

Joining the queue to pay, Harmony felt a jolt of recognition at the doughnut bun and green parka of the girl who had greeted her as she walked to Mel's the other week – Chloe or Emily, her tormentor from Severn Oak Academy. She was in front of Harmony in the queue, impatiently waggling a packet of Skips. When it was her turn to be served, Chloe/Emily stepped up, put the Skips on the counter and asked for twenty Carlton Superkings. Harmony realised that although she was now more or less up to speed on cocks, she had yet to smoke a single cigarette. Perhaps that could be her next project.

Since Chloe/Emily paid for her fags and left the shop without looking back, there was no need to say hello or otherwise draw attention to herself. But as Harmony walked out of the Spar, she was the one to be greeted, as before, and just as puzzlingly.

'Oh, heyer.'

Chloe/Emily stood by the side of the shop. She'd lingered to peruse the same graffitied poster that had set Harmony off on her internet dick odyssey. Harmony pulled herself up in her customary head-down stride, as confused by this second effort of friendliness as by the first.

'Hi.'

Katie, that was her name. There had been a Chloe and also an Emily, near-identical cronies giggling behind their hands and encouraging the real bullies to do their worst. But only Katie had those uncanny silvery eyes, fringed now by densely black fake lashes that made her look like a demon doll. The brains behind the brawn. Did she really not remember?

Apparently not. She was waving her hand, still holding the Skips, at the poster. The skin on her face was a matt, uniform orange. A nose piercing glinted by her right nostril. This was new since Year 7.

'Bit weird.'

'Yeah,' agreed Harmony. And then, because she couldn't resist, 'We found her, my auntie and me. Down on the beach.'

'Really?'

'Yeah, in that big storm. She was in the water, like, totally naked?'

Katie pulled a face. She was impressed, but also sceptical. Harmony felt indignant that her integrity was being doubted. It had really happened. She had been there, almost.

'We thought she was dead,' she told her. 'It was freezing out there.'

This detail appeared to win Katie over.

'It was a miracle she survived, they reckon,' Harmony concluded.

'So who do you think she is?'

Harmony shrugged enticingly, as though considering a few options.

'The police reckon she might have come from the caravan park.'

As soon as she said it she remembered that Katie lived in the van park herself, or had done in Year 7, which was probably why that particular location had popped into her mouth. Katie craned forward, induced to scan the picture again. Harmony saw, in the gap left by the huge shawl-like hood of her parka, a delicate line of tattooed dots running up her neck vertebrae. The effect was perturbingly beautiful.

'Oh, God. You know what? God. I think I know her.'

'Really?'

Now who was trying to make herself more interesting? Her own lie had enabled Katie's, rendering it unassailable without exposing herself as equally pathetic.

Katie pulled the plastic off the fags she'd just bought and let the wind carry it away.

'Well, I don't know her, like,' she amended. 'But I've definitely seen her.'

What, with a hairy cock by her mouth, telling the world she luvved spunk? It had been Katie, hadn't it, or one of her lot, who had encouraged the lad behind Harmony to kick the back of her seat whenever she enthusiastically answered Mr Sanderson's questions in English. One day, when she'd gone to sit in her usual place, near the front because English was the one thing about Severn Oak that was making her stick it out, apart from proving to Mum that she could, someone had left a filled condom on the chair. When Harmony flinched away, the lad behind had flicked it up at her with his pen, so that it squelched on to her jumper. She'd flailed it off in hysterical panic, jizz lolling from the ringed mouth on to her workbook before the whole thing splattered on the floor. Everyone had pissed themselves, of course. That was the end of school for her, more or less. And Katie didn't remember a thing about it, she'd bet.

'You should tell the police,' said Harmony. 'There's a special number.'

Katie pulled a face, as though she didn't want to bother the police, out of consideration for how much they had to do.

'Well, it's hard to tell if it's the same lass,' she said, offering Harmony the packet of fags. 'Looks like her, though. God.'

Harmony declined the cigarettes and began to walk off. Enough of this malarkey. That's what Mum would have said. Once upon a time she would have told Mum every word. The thought of this was like accidentally touching something hot.

'See you,' Katie called after her. Her mate Katie.

'Bye.'

Harmony would have eaten the biscuits the moment she

got home, the only way to fill the huge angry hole gouged out by it all, but Declan was already there by the front gate as she turned into their street, chin funnelled into the collar of his North Face, nearly ten minutes early. Oh God, how she loved him. Having him in the world made everything all right. But there were only five more lessons left – four by tonight. Something had to happen. It just had to. And if it didn't, she'd have to make it.

Driving across to Stu's, Mel was annoyed to see that nothing had been done about the felled tree blocking the little green at the top of Warmington Road. It had been there nearly a month now. The council was probably relying on the residents to clear the debris, and the residents on the council; both were hopeless. She'd do some ringing round herself, if she remembered, and if there was still an actual human being left in the council offices. The weather was inching towards spring, and they could count themselves lucky that old beech had been the only casualty of the year's worst storm. Well, if you didn't count that poor girl.

Maybe you shouldn't count her. It must be a terrible thing, not to know who you were, and yet their meeting at the hospital had left Mel strangely buoyant. Edward had noticed her change of mood – the only one at home who did – but then he even noticed when she had her hair done. She couldn't explain to him why she'd started singing along to the radio in the car. Just a good mood, she said.

'Sometimes it just feels good to be alive.'

Stu had promised to be in, but Mel was still pleasantly surprised to see the van outside his house as she pulled up. She couldn't rely on him not finding an excuse to be out. Poor old Stu; she wished he wasn't quite so afraid of her. It wasn't for nothing that she frequently came out with Stuart's name when she meant to call for Edward or Aidan. Everyone assumed he was her younger brother, rather than three years older. Sometimes she forgot and thought so herself.

'I'm bearing lasagne!'

At the door, Stu took the dish from her with a pale, stooped nod; no actual thanks. Mel had made a vegetarian batch, unsure if their household was eating meat these days. He asked if she wanted a brew. Mel followed him through the hall, trying not to take in too much of the disorder on the way. As they waited for the kettle to boil, Stu nervously rubbed the stubbled back of his head, avoiding her eye.

'How are you doing?'

Mel knew his 'yeah, not so bad' would be all she'd get.

'Harmony!'

He shouted directly overhead; the kitchen was beneath Harmony's room. After a second or two came the noise of her muffled, thunderous descent. Appearing at the door, she lumbered into Mel with an ungainly, heartfelt hug. Mel patted her shoulder stiffly as Harmony continued to hang on. She and Stu didn't come from a cuddly family. It was motherhood that had conditioned Mel to like this sort of thing – people would be surprised to know how much, since she was so awkward about it. Abruptly, she stepped back.

'I thought we could get down to a bit of work.'

When Mel, over a year ago, had broached the idea of Harmony being tutored, Aurora had amazed her by immediately agreeing it was a great idea. Should she have been suspicious, then? Great idea for Declan to get Harmony through maths GCSE, Aurora said, great idea for her daughter to find a place at sixth form college or investigate something more vocational. Mel, arguments braced to wrestle grudging consent at best, had assumed this uncharacteristic compliance meant that Aurora was finally regretting her stance on homeschooling – not that she'd ever admit it. Harmony herself had leapt at the chance, which was also a surprise. Mel had been worried, after what had happened at Severn Oak, that the poor girl would be done with education for ever.

Severn Oak. Anyone could have predicted that Harmony was going to have trouble starting at secondary school after no experience of primary. Anyone could, and Mel had, repeatedly. Severn Oak was hardly St Benedict's. When Harmony pitched up in Year 7, the hall had just been rebuilt after a student arson attack a few years before, the building work funded by the school's enforced rebranding as an academy after it was put into special measures. Even Aurora knew, although she didn't confide in Mel until afterwards, that disaster was likely. It had been Harmony's idea, a timid first stirring of adolescent defiance, to confound her mother by embracing the conventional. Mel believed Aurora had actually been pleased when Harmony had had to beat her miserable retreat away from school and back to the familiar wacky isolation of home. Aurora's whole response had been a triumphant 'you see': you see how terrible the world is and the people in it and how right I was to keep you with me, away from it and them for all these years? And now the poor kid was stranded, and motherless to boot.

No, not stranded, not if Auntie Mel could help it. Declan

thought Harmony stood a chance of scraping the maths GCSE. She could get a place in some form of further education with a D in maths, and her English grade was likely to be quite good. Mel had arrived today with an essay in her bag Harmony had written about *The Crucible*. The fiction was that Mel herself had marked it. Since she knew that Stu would refuse either to take on the expense of another tutor for English, or allow Mel to pay for one, Mel had offered personally to see her niece through the syllabus. And this had been her intention, until the most cursory internet investigation had brought home the likely impossibility of Mel, despite her ancient vanity about her A grade at 'O' level, even passing GCSE English, let alone teaching it to someone else. So she had taken advice from Joe's old English teacher at St Ben's, who had agreed to set and mark Harmony's work, for market rates, while Mel acted as her mouthpiece. She was well aware how hilarious Aurora would have found the whole Cyrano de Bergerac arrangement. Mel herself was amazed that so far the deception had worked. Despite a few eggy moments, Harmony didn't seem to have copped on, even to Mel's more floundering explanations of the exam's peculiar, finicking demands. One of the girl's many problems was that she was too trusting by half.

There had been a lapse of weeks, which was Mel's own fault. But today, buoyed by the strange energy that had followed her encounter with the Storm girl at the hospital, she had determined that it was high time for her and Harmony to clear the table at the back of the living room and sit there together to go through *The Crucible*. A fresh start, for everyone.

Harmony, despite the ferocity of her welcoming hug,

looked tired and sullen as she scraped back the chair opposite Mel and plonked herself down. God knows what had been going on. It was cold in the room, as usual, and the girl huddled a vast cardigan around her that Mel recognised as Aurora's: one of her festival acquisitions, rainbow stripes autumnally grubbied, cuffs unravelling. Despite its engulfing size, the toggle-like buttons still strained against Harmony's large and braless breasts, whose graphic outlines Mel found alarming to contemplate, with their pendulous gravity and wayward-pointing nipples. Harmony couldn't start sixth form without a proper bra; it would be Severn Oak all over again.

As they eased into corrections of the structure and grammar of Harmony's essay on the character of John Proctor (had she really never noticed that the neat, red-inked marginal comments weren't actually in Mel's handwriting?), Mel heard Stu leave by the back door. She needed to take the opportunity while he was out of the house.

'I was thinking,' Mel began, 'that we could go shopping together.'

Harmony looked up, wary.

'For a few bits and pieces. Clothes, and things you might need ... is there anything you need?' She bit the bullet. 'Underwear, that sort of thing?'

They looked at each other, then at the essay. 'There's no need to be embarrassed,' Mel said, for both of them. 'I'm a woman too.'

As she said it, it felt like a lie. She hated shopping.

'Or we could do it online,' she suggested. 'Though it helps to try things on, particularly at your age.'

Harmony used her shrug to slump closer to the level of the tabletop. 'I don't mind.'

Right, then. She'd get her near a tape measure if it killed her. 'Good, we can make a day of it. Maybe go to Leeds. There's everything there. Or York's nice. Girls' day out.'

At this, a half-smile lit the cloud of Harmony's face. 'OK.'

'Get you a few bras.'

The sun went in. One of Harmony's breasts, in illustration of the demand Mel was aiming to supply, rested its round chin on the table. Where had she inherited this amplitude? Not from Aurora, for whom bras had always been enviably optional. Harmony folded her arms, crushing her breasts into herself as though Mel wanted to steal them.

'Mum's always said growing girls don't need wire and stuff stunting their natural growth.'

'Well ... you've probably stopped growing.'

They returned to the essay. Ms Mallinson had concluded her comments by advising Harmony to THINK about STRUCTURE, and DEVELOPING her ARGUMENT, instead of writing everything she knew or thought on the topic set. Some of Harmony's essays had been over twenty pages long. Once she started, she seemed to find it hard to stop.

'In some ways she's too sophisticated,' Ms Mallinson had explained to Mel, 'and in others she just doesn't seem to have a clue.'

By the time Mel suggested they plan out Harmony's next essay together ('How does Miller present ideas about persecution in *The Crucible*?') her niece was becoming restless. She tipped her chair and picked at the loose threads at her wrists, as Mel, leading by example, transcribed bullet points: 'Witchcraft', 'Communism' – Harmony didn't appear to have heard of communism – 'Puritanism' ...

'Have you heard any more about the girl? That one on the beach?'

She hadn't, Mel said. There was no need to tell Harmony about her odd detour in the hospital. The news seemed to have gone quiet, she told her. It really was a mystery.

'I met someone who recognised her.' Harmony reached her teeth to her sleeve to snap off a varicoloured thread from the ravelling cuff. 'From the poster.'

'Who?'

'This girl I know, from Severn Oak. She said she'd seen her in the van park. Around, I mean. Before.'

Mel's pulse tripped, although the van park would be a disappointing solution to any mystery. Harmony wound the thread tightly round her forefinger, becoming engrossed in the way its tip engorged. Beneath her elaborate preoccupation, Mel sensed she was waiting for something.

'Has your friend told the police?'

'Dunno. Don't think so.'

Probably not, thought Mel. Many residents of Oceancrest weren't exactly friends to the force.

'Well, what's her name?'

'I can't remember. Katie something, I think?' Harmony flicked a glance up at her. 'Yeah, Katie. Maybe *you* should tell the police.'

Surely the police would be making enquiries anyway? The vans were so obviously close to where Mel had found the girl; it was easy to imagine her being dragged down the cliff path from Brazen Point and on to the shingle, on the assumption that she was dead and would be carried out to sea by the tide, particularly on that godforsaken night. Mel was sure the police were on it. But just in case, she'd give dishy PC Mason a ring. She told Harmony she'd call.

'I'm starving.'

Harmony unravelled the thread from her finger end, the skin scarified with white ridges, purple in between. 'How long does the lasagne need?'

Mel fidgeted her papers. She recalled that essential look the girl had fed her with at the infirmary. She had another duty, long avoided. Lasagne wasn't enough.

'Harmony, love, I know it's hard ... ' She felt Harmony freeze. The words clotted Mel's tongue. 'It's hard for everyone. Stu, me—'

'It's harder for me.'

'Of course it's harder for you. Your mum; of course it is.'

Frantically, Harmony began winding the thread back round her finger. Mel shot out her hand and grabbed the cotton away from her, trying to flick it on to the floor but getting it tangled in her own fingers, inconsequential and infuriating. Seeing Harmony's fright at this miniature frenzy, Mel stilled herself.

'It's nearly a year, so ... I mean, if you need to talk about it – about your mum – you shouldn't feel you can't talk about her—'

'I don't need to talk about her.'

'Well, it might help. You can always talk to me, you know. I know it isn't ideal, with Stu. He's never been much of a talker.'

Oh Christ, she'd got stuck on the talk thing. Harmony convulsed, ambiguously. A shrug of acknowledgement, or disagreement? Mel couldn't tell.

'Just, no one's forgetting, what it must be like for you. I know it must be hard. And you know if there's anything I can do—'

'I'm fine.'

Two words, stones thrown into a vast grey lake. It was all she was going to get.

With trivial relief, Mel finally succeeded in freeing her fingers from the skein of thread. She rolled it into a small, spidery knot and flicked it off the table.

'Right, puritanism ... '

A fresh start, why not? Something more had to be done, and as usual, she would have to be the one to do it. Not for the first time, Mel's sympathy was obliterated by rage. Aurora, Dawn. Bloody Dawn. At least she'd said something, finally. And she'd buy the kid a decent bra. But sometimes she thought it might be easier, for Harmony at least, if her mother was actually dead.

Bare bulb, green wall. Toast in your mouth. Every morning here. The shower, not as warm as your blood, clothes. Teeth to brush, all in a row. Nobody had to teach you that.

They call you Storm. You're Storm, now.

The old woman shouted for hours in the night until she shouted herself quiet. Breakfast has woken her. She fights the teapot, the knives, the stand for her drip. Metal hits the floor as she screams blame for hot tea spilled through the sheet. YOU BLOODY BITCHES, GET OFF ME, YOU BITCHES. Chandra tries to hold her arms, Margaret shouting for bed restraints.

Animal squeal. The veined hand rears and rakes the side of Chandra's face. Blood. Chandra screaming as long pearled nails claw for her eye. You pick up the dish of piss on top of the trolley and throw it in the woman's face. The grey head snaps to the pillow. Shouting stops. Chandra is quiet. All is quiet.

Bare bulb, green wall. Silence. Silence silence silence.

A secret isn't the same as a lie. A lie is what a secret gives birth to, when it mates with speech.

PART 2

'So. Transient epileptic amnesia – it's a form of temporal lobe epilepsy. I think we might have discussed it before. You'd expect it to show up on a scan, scarring from previous episodes ... '

Lennox, scrolling back through his notes, grimaced judiciously, as though Mason had raised some sort of objection rather than continuing to sit in baffled silence. He continued. 'I did *wonder* ... our young lady appears to be right-handed, but when I first examined her – you were present, at the hospital – her semi-voluntary gestures: scratching her nose, picking up the pen I offered – she used her left ... '

The shrink subsided, pondering the pages of his notebook. After a second or two, Dan had to capitulate. 'So that means?'

Lennox nodded, as though fielding a fair point, and resettled the ends of his tie. The narrow bottom tail hung below the fatter part. Didn't anyone teach them how to tie a tie, in medical school?

'It could be an indication of the seizure focus. Ipsilation.'

Maybe he couldn't help it: the jargon was like hiccups. And at least this time Lennox clarified himself without Dan having to admit he didn't have a clue what he was talking about.

'After a seizure, these kinds of gestures tend to be restricted to the same side of the body as the side of the brain where the seizure took place. It's a little tell. You know, a tell in poker?'

'I know what a tell is, ta.'

Which was a relief. Lennox frowned down at his tie, noticing its imbalance.

'So there's that. If it is TEA, typically there's no recovery of lost memory before an episode. But the memory loss is small. I mean, you'd expect to lose a few minutes before, or that morning. You wouldn't expect her to lose her memory entirely. And she'd continue to have seizures, which doesn't seem to be the case, unless this so-called attack in hospital was actually a seizure.'

'And what about the talking?' Mason asked.

Lennox nodded at his notebook.

'Again, TEA might explain it, the effect of scarring. But looking at the scan, there's no sign of physical damage to the centres controlling speech. I have to say I'm stumped. Unless, as I say, this episode on the ward was a seizure.'

'Didn't she go for an old lady?'

Lennox lifted his gaze to the right of Dan, meeting the arrival of a new thought. 'I suppose the hospital might have been looking for an excuse to get her off their hands. I mean, she isn't really ill as far as they're concerned ... and they need the bed.'

Mason disliked having to agree with him, so he refrained. 'Any chance of opening a window?'

The clinic Storm had been moved to was some sort of specialist neurology unit. Residential. It was miles away from Evensand, in a warren of dilapidated Victorian buildings once used, Dan had heard, as a lunatic asylum. The central heating was whacked up to a soporific maximum, maybe for tranquillising purposes. As Lennox grappled with the sash arrangement, it was clear to Mason that it had long been painted shut. So much for education.

While the shrink was working this out, there was a commotion behind them at the door.

'Sorry!'

Oh God, it wasn't. It was. Entering the room fully, Lottie shook out the folded-bat spines of a black umbrella and sprinkled Mason and Lennox, as well as herself, with second-hand rain. Sorry again, and sorry for being late, and still she hadn't noticed him.

'Andy.' Lennox was offering that chiller section hand of his. Dan stood.

Lennox had said there would be social services involvement in the case meeting, but he hadn't for a moment thought it might be Lottie. With the clinic so far away, Mason had been chuffed still to be called on. Evidently psychiatric social services were as overstretched as the police.

'Oh, it's you!'

Lottie smiled at Mason with wide delight, triggering a reflexive answering warmth. It was like bumping into someone on holiday you barely knew from home. Just from sharing an unfamiliar location, your relationship raced ahead a few goes, a double six on the board.

'It was a bit tricky to find ... oh, fantastic!'

On her way to the free chair, Lottie picked up Dan's take-away coffee cup, siphoning a grateful gulp through the lid.

The surprise of this made Lennox bounce a look at Mason. Dan stayed poker impassive. The cup was ambiguously placed, closer in fact to the empty seat Lottie was wrangling than to where Dan was sitting. He'd seen enough of Lottie to know she was the kind of girl for whom the world, and particularly the men in it, did many good turns: it simply wouldn't occur to her that the coffee hadn't been bought for her. But from the quality of Lennox's glance at him, Mason saw he'd added the two of them apparently sharing a coffee to the familiarity of their greeting, and come up with a bunk-up. Good, let him. Lennox had been leading after all the medical palaver. It evened up the points.

Lottie put the cup down, the white lid now branded with her fuchsia lipstick. 'Thanks.' This was addressed to Lennox, for the coffee he hadn't bought her. Tetchily, the shrink removed her umbrella from the table, where it was puddling towards his notebook, and upended it on the floor.

'Sorry.'

For all her sorrys, Mason had never met someone so unapologetic. Why the hell was he feeling embarrassed for her? Lottie reached into her bag for a file.

'Are we really going to call her Storm?'

'It seems to have stuck,' Lennox said.

'Yes, but it's a bit, I mean ... '

'Bit *X-Men*,' Dan offered. Lottie made a small moan of regretful acquiescence. She was funny, somehow. Or maybe that was just him. *Lottie*. Mason hadn't thought about it before, but it must be short for Charlotte. The name made a space in him somewhere, like an animal turning about and about to form its den.

'Well, failing anything better, I think consistency might be a virtue. So let's stick to Storm.'

This was Lennox, reclaiming control. But he pretty clearly had nothing, and Dan would be amazed if Miss Charlotte had much new herself to offer on the subject of Storm. It wasn't the sort of thing she'd be likely to have done a course on, was it? Seeing her lick cappuccino foam from the corner of her mouth, he jumped in before she could get going.

'We had an interesting call yesterday. From Melanie Bale, the lady who found her—'

'Oh, my boyfriend's mo—'

'Yes, I believe you know the lady.'

He didn't want interruptions. Dan reached along the table for his coffee, putting his own lips to the waxy swatch of lipstick. Beside him, he could feel Lottie's shock at this misunderstood boldness. It shut her up.

'Mrs Bale had a tip for us. To the van park.'

Melanie Bale had called the previous morning. Ordinarily Soccolo would have dragged his feet about going back to the park barely a fortnight after they'd been up there to hand round the leaflets with the girl's photo on them. But the Great Ruswarp Hedge Dispute had cashed out in paperwork Soccolo was desperate to escape. Despite its name, paperwork mainly meant filling out online forms, which for Soccolo was an agonising, two-fingered process, his tongue lolling like a Labrador's. So Mason couldn't have timed it more perfectly to mention they'd had a proper tip-off about the Evensand Mystery Girl, as the local press had it. His partner was off his arse and heading for the car park before Dan even had time for a slash.

Even towards eleven there was a sea fret yet to burn off, erasing the horizon. Mason tasted it, tonic and clammy, as he got into the car. Soccolo preferred to drive, always. It wasn't far to the vans, back out of the centre and up from the Evensand road towards Brazen Point. Climbing to the summit of the cliff where the van park stood, next to the Point itself, the fret gradually thickened to fog. Soccolo was forced to cut his speed so he wouldn't miss the turning to the main gate with its snazzy corporate sign, already brined and fading.

When Dan was a kid and for long before, the caravan park had been called Seaview, but about five years ago, under new ownership, it had become Oceancrest Holiday Homes, even though more than half the vans were occupied year-round and their residents weren't exactly on holiday, unless you took a red-top line on unemployment benefit. The new management's first act had been to get rid of visiting stands. All the remaining units were fixed and huge, essentially houses without foundations. Some of them were leased by the council to replace the housing stock that had been sold off in the 1980s and never replaced. Another cluster, overlapping in management but seen as distinct, had popped up shortly after the Oceancrest revamp and become known – local press again – as Little Romania. Emboldened since Brexit, Evensand's UKIP councillor, Carla Gomersley, was leading a wave of increasingly robust opposition to this settlement. She and her followers objected to what they called antisocial behaviour, although from what Dan could see, it was the extreme sociability of the residents that marked them out as foreign – children running from van to van, washing strung out, the keeping of chickens, men gathering outside to drink and smoke, to a background of Eastern European radio. Of course there were fights, usually on Fridays and Saturdays, usually outside the pub the park had rebranded as a 'social hub', but Fridays and Saturdays were fight nights all over the town. And in the summer, there had been a sexual attack on a non-Romanian woman, by, the victim alleged, a couple of young Romanian men. This was yet to come to trial. Relations had been calm for the last couple of months, but it would all get worse as the weather started to warm up and life was once again conducted outside.

Although he had little time for Carla and her Kippers, Mason would have signed the petition against Little Romania if he lived here, no messing. His nan and grandad had had a stand for their Wayfarer caravan at Seaview when he was small, and he had good memories of the place, the living of life in cramped miniature, the trips to the social club to play video games and eat crisps while his grandparents had a drink and a catch-up with the other retired couples and visiting families who made up most of the clientele even ten years ago. Dan could see that the Romanians, the fact of them, were a kind of trouble. But they worked hard, no doubt about it, fruit- and veg-picking and labouring on building sites. God knows what would happen if they were all sent back: even students didn't seem to want to do the agricultural jobs any more. He'd had a summer of it himself in between leaving school and starting his IPLDP, sweating cobs in a polytunnel for minimum wage. He'd never fancied strawberries since, though he had better memories of the girls he'd met behind his then girlfriend's back. He had even, Dan remembered now, seeing the altered landmarks rendered significant by fog, riskily used the Wayfarer as a shag pad once while his nan was at bingo in the club. This was after Grandad had gone, the last summer before Nan got rid of the van. Why hadn't he remembered the girl on the first visit they'd made, just after Storm had been found?

That girl had been Romanian. She might be around still, probably with a kid or two. The thought of that was as spooky as the fog, your own past hanging around like a ghost. Maybe he hadn't remembered the last time because he hadn't wanted to. It had been a miserable shag, rushed and fraught with guilt at desecrating his grandad's memory on the tiny bunk. She had seemed guilty too. Were Romanians Catholic, or anything? Thinking about it, maybe her lack of enjoyment had less to do with guilt than with him. That smell of bodies and mildew, the sheet on the narrow mattress sliding to reveal Edam-yellow foam, mouse-nibbled at the corners. Confused, joyless friction.

'Right, then.'

Soccolo switched off the ignition. They parked up at the back of the pub/hub, its millennial lime-green and purple rendering weathered in scabby patches back to the brick. Dan still needed a slash. Bladder of a bloody woman, according to Soccolo. He stopped to use a piss-stinking urinal in the toilet block next to the hub. There wasn't a soul about. Too early, Soccolo said, for the skivers or old people. Melanie Bale had said the possible witness was sixteen, possibly called Katie, and a long-term resident. Possibly went to Severn Oak. Mason had armed himself with a printout of the photo of Storm used on the flyer. He doubted there would be many flyers still in place from a fortnight ago. The wind up here was never less than challenging.

As Dan's foot resounded on the metal step of the first van in the row, the door above him bashed open.

'Fuck off!'

A toddler repeated himself with all the uncomprehending delight of a parrot. It was a boy, going by the blue Peppa Pig t-shirt gaping over his veined little belly; impossible to tell otherwise. His mum appeared and scooped him up, stepping back to get hold of the door when she saw they were coppers. That was the way it went for several vans, although the toddler was the only one to put the *fuck off* into words. They struck luckier when they got a teenage girl who they'd caught in the middle of straightening her hair – one side was sleek, the other a dark, half-blown dandelion clock. She smiled at them unselfconsciously, apparently delighted to be asked questions, particularly by Dan.

'Oh yeah, Katie. She's up at H16. I think it's 16. A blue door, like?'

She was from one of the Romanian families, with native, broad Yorkshire English. May well have been born here, Dan thought, unlike the lass he'd shagged. She shrugged when he asked if she knew Katie's last name. Never mind.

He and Soccolo walked up to H, which was two quadrants along, both of them choosing to ignore the stench of skunk coming from a van in the far corner of the first quadrant. It was amazing, given the uniformity of the designs available, how much variation there was from van to van: carriage lights and fancy doors, attempts at tiny garden plots staked out with shells and scalloped edgings in the small gaps between standings, prim good maintenance that suggested elderly owners next to the shored-up or strewn plastic tat belonging to young families.

The blue door was one of the heritage style favoured here and there as an extra, with an elaborate brass-effect knocker. The fog had caught in Dan's throat; he hawked and spat before he mounted the steps. They knocked and waited. There was no sound from inside, no electronic indications of life shining out of the door's unlikely fanlight or the open-slatted blinds at the window to its right. Soccolo continued to describe the dinner his wife had made the previous evening as Mason stretched to look through the window.

'Garlic bread. Beautiful. She puts a bit of cheese on it and all. Parmesan, like, bit of mozzarella. Superb.'

Most of what Dan could see was a monster flat screen, switched off; the back of a leather settee; cans and an ashtray on the carpet next to a lurid, abandoned beach towel. The sea was a bit too far and a lot too cold to make it a popular destination. Mason knew residents preferred the soupy indoor pool next to the hub, warm in all weathers, though closed from November to April. Despite the lack of holidaymakers at Oceancrest, this period was still observed as off-season.

'Not here,' he told Soccolo. Soccolo blew his nose with a forefinger, tamping shut first one nostril, then the other. Snot arced into the wet grass. Snail slime.

'Waste of chuffing time.'

They agreed they'd have to come back, preferably at night, when more people were bound to be around. In so many ways, Storm would have been less trouble if she were dead. At least then there would have been a procedure to follow. There'd be teams of them, instead of just him and Soccolo; systematic house-to-house, all the power of forensics and the PNC. Which was fair enough. But wasn't it important, to put the living back where they belonged?

When they returned to the car, a teenage girl was slouched against the bonnet, smoking. It took a moment for Dan to recognise her as the girl with the dandelion head, her hair now fully straightened and some make-up applied, making her look older and less friendly. The girl wanted to know if they'd found Katie. Dan told her they hadn't.

Frowning, the girl aimed her chin up to exhale the smoke

in a vertical jet, as though the fag was a duty she was impatient to be done with.

'You're looking for a lass who's gone missing, aren't you?'

If only it was that easy, said Soccolo. In a way, said Dan. He produced the flyer from his pocket. The girl peered close, holding the fag away from herself with a distastefully extended arm. She nodded.

'Yeah, her. I know her. Well, not know ... I've seen her around, like.'

Not a waste of time then. Romanian, she said, yes. Not sure of the name, though, or which van. Dan ignored Soccolo's sigh of frustration as the girl chucked her fag end, glad to be shot of it. He was taking her name – Timi – when she pushed herself off from the bonnet and shouted over to a tall, dark-haired man who was crossing the back corner of the hub a few metres away, shouldering a rucksack and smoking in quick, covetous drags. A few Romanian sentences and the man approached. Her uncle, she explained.

The uncle, his glowering look now explained as a lack of English, heeled the butt of his fag into the tarmac and, after a brief glance their way that avoided eye contact, took the printout Timi waved at him. The rucksack and his tracksuit bottoms were powdered with plaster dust: a labourer, Dan assumed. He didn't take long with the photocopy. His large eyes were strangely clear; in profile, Dan could see the gap between the domed, copper-coloured iris and the lens. High-shouldered against the chill, he shook his head and handed back the sheet.

'No.'

This was for them. Timi spoke to him again in Romanian, asking a question, but to all of it he continued to shake his head. Another no, both for her and for them: adamant. Timi translated. This girl Timi was thinking of, she was a relative of another family who had left Oceancrest only a few days ago. She'd been visiting for a while to help look after their small children, but it hadn't worked out. She'd gone off somewhere, run away before they left. Timi thought it was her in the photo but Timi's uncle, who knew her better, said it definitely wasn't.

'Tell him that maybe if he came to see our lass in hospital, he could be certain?'

The uncle was shaking his head again before the translation was finished, already walking off.

'Hang on!'

Dan insisted on taking the man's name and phone number, Timi assisting. He was Nicu. Uncle Nicu, as Dan thought of him, watching him stalk off behind the hub, already putting the lighter to his next fag. Dan pocketed his notebook as Soccolo grappled the car door open, eager to get warm.

The sun had finally climbed high enough to melt the fog. As the car swung out of the park, Dan saw the sweep of the sea beneath them, to their left. It was more or less where they'd found Storm.

'Do you reckon he's a bad lad, the uncle?'

Soccolo grunted, as committed to the universality of evil as he was to doing nothing. Dan wondered: there was something about the man that didn't sit right. He'd look him up. They had his surname, his date of birth. It should be enough, if there was anything to find.

'And have you? Looked him up?'

Lottie shot a wary look at the coffee cup, which Dan had been revolving by its corrugated sleevelet as he filled them in about the trip to the vans. Her coffee cup, as far as she was concerned. Dan explained that he'd inputted Nicu's details into their database, but these would only come up with a match if a) Nicu had given them his real name and DOB, and b) he'd ever committed a crime in the UK. Also, it would take a while for overseas records to come up with any match. He couldn't blame her, or even Lennox, for looking so disappointed. He had been just as disappointed himself to discover the hours and days that stretched between the action you were so instantly familiar with from crime dramas. Like him, they'd probably be surprised to learn that nowhere in the station, not even in CID, were there boards with suspect and crime scene photos joined by felt-tipped lines and over-laid with scribbled notes, anatomising a case. When, fresh to Evensand nick, he'd keenly paper-clipped a jpeg printout to a file and used a highlighter to pick out some details in the report he considered significant, Soccolo had remarked that here was another one who thought he was in CS chuffing I.

Lottie swiped her front teeth with her tongue, freeing herself to speak. 'So that probably explains the not talking if, er, Storm doesn't speak English?'

Lennox exhaled. 'She certainly understands it. From her behaviour.'

'Well, we'll see, won't we, if we get this Nicu bloke in. He can have a go in Romanian.'

Lottie wasn't happy with this. What if, she asked, there was some trauma involved for Storm in seeing this man? The way she said *trauma*, claiming it as some special shrink medical word that made Lennox nod in agreement, pissed Dan off. OK, he said, in that case they could try getting a police translator in first. They both accepted this, though he could see how much it pained Lennox.

'I'll have to insist on being present during that.'

'Of course.'

Mason picked up the cup and belted back the last slug of coffee, tepid froth and chocolate. Lottie made another of her comical noises, a startled near whimper, as though she was embarrassed on his behalf for stealing her drink. Progress, then: she was capable of embarrassment, if for the wrong reasons. Dan felt sorry for the lass. Storm, not Lottie. Whatever she was – English, Romanian, an alien from the planet Zog – after what she'd been through out on Brazen beach, she deserved better. The vans were fine for a holiday, but you wouldn't be choosing to live in them full time.

Harmony felt a brief panic when Auntie Mel said the police were going to talk to Katie up at the van park, before she remembered that in this case, it was Katie who had lied. And she wouldn't have told Mel in the first place if she hadn't wanted to land Katie in it, would she? Harmony pondered a scene of glorious karma, delayed by four years: Katie escorted into the back of a police car with that weird head-protective hand clamp cops did, for wasting police time. Even if the truth unravelled to the point where Katie's lie was tied to Harmony's claim to have been there on the beach when the girl was found, Harmony was confident she could style it out. She'd just say she'd said her auntie had been there that night, that she'd been reporting what Mel had told her and Katie had got hold of the wrong end of the stick. Even a homeschooled freak was bound to trump a girl from the vans for credibility. Harmony suppressed the thought that she had used the same lie about being on the beach directly to the hot policeman. It wasn't like anyone had died.

They were in the car on their way to York. Stu had long left for Stoke at bumcrack of dawn when Mel arrived to collect Harmony for their shopping trip. Harmony had actually been looking forward to the shopping part, if not to the company. Apart from the usual feeling of Mel holding back on a great number of things she was dying to say, like a finger on the trigger of a gun that would blast them all to kingdom come if she lost control and fired, there was the agonising possibility that she would make another attempt to talk to her about Mum. The memory of their conversation over *The Crucible* still seized Harmony's guts at random times, as bad as Senokot. The only hopeful aspect was that it seemed to have been just as awful for Mel. It was a relief that they had Storm to talk about instead. That's what she was called now, in the news. Mel agreed that the name didn't quite match her picture.

'Even less when you meet her.'

'You've met her?'

But they were at a crucial slip road for the route, so Mel didn't answer.

Signalling the day's status as a treat, Mel was driving her in the little Fiat Uncle Ian had bought her for her last birthday. It was a mint-green colour and, unlike the Bale people carrier, whose interior was ravaged by rugby boots and the aftermath of dog walks, always pristine. It still smelled new inside, gently chemical and uncompromised. When Harmony stroked the soft leather seat and said how nice it was, Mel's face softened the way it did when people praised the boys. She was wearing a leather jacket instead of her fleece and had put in a pair of dangly earrings, their unfamiliarity marked by the way she lifted a hand from the steering wheel from time to time and pinched each lobe to make sure neither had fallen out. Aurora had said that Mel was really pretty, once.

'D'you know what? Sometimes I just come out and sit in the car, for no reason.'

Harmony said she could see why. Then she spoiled it when they were filtering on to the motorway by hoisting her feet on to the hump of the dashboard above the glove compartment, earning an immediate yelp from Mel. Harmony had actually taken her shoes off, out of consideration. Her socked feet left little sweat blobs on the cream plastic, but that was normal, they'd evaporate. Mum would have taken the piss, or started a row.

'The trouble with your bloody sister is she doesn't have enough to do.'

Mum had barked that at Stu when they were having what Harmony thought of as The Christmas Row. Even said in anger, it had struck Harmony as wrong. Nobody did as much as Mel. So much, so constantly, sweeping up all those around her in her tide of activity: running the dancing school, chauffeuring, baking, going to her book group, her conservation meetings, taking up sea fishing with Uncle Ian so they could spend more time together and winning the season's trophy for best catch (it hadn't taken Aurora to point out how much Ian hated that), camping with the boys, visiting the elderly, doing the Moonwalk for cancer and singlehandedly raising so much sponsorship the infirmary bought a specialist scanner off the back of it. Maybe it was more, Harmony now thought, watching Mel's profile as she drove, her one visible earring swinging with their momentum towards York, that what she did do didn't make her happy. A happy person, she speculated, wouldn't care about invisible sweat patches on car interiors.

Every day seemed to bring more of these kinds of thoughts, as unwelcome and uncontainably burgeoning as her body. Harmony was torn between admiring her own sensitivity and reeling at the abyss adults had built their lives on. They were like the inhabitants of a haunted house who had never seen a horror movie. It would be different for her, she promised herself. Looking out of the window, she tried to think of a happy adult. Mum, who had never cared about marks or stains or being busy: epic fail. Not Stu, either, even before there were reasons, not really. Declan, perhaps, was happy. Not cheerful, which was different. Maybe that was why she loved him so?

Her stomach growled, loudly enough for Mel to hear.

'Did you not have breakfast?'

There had been nothing in, as usual. Harmony had resorted to scooping a dry handful of muesli from the sack left untouched at the bottom of the cupboard since Aurora had gone. Mum's muesli was a thing: she got the ingredients in bulk from the health food shop and mixed it herself. Since Harmony was a little kid, she had witnessed the ritual of her mum sitting at the table running oats and bran and raisins through her hands like some vegan miser. In her absence, the oats had gone rancid. Harmony immediately spat the bolus of dust out into the sink, but it had taken multiple glasses of water to swill the soapiness from her mouth. She could still taste it beneath her toothpaste.

Now Mel suggested they stop at motorway services, but Harmony said she could hang on, which restored the balance of goodwill between them to its state prior to her putting her feet up on the dash. Fortunately it was a swift eighty minutes to York because, as Mel said, they were very lucky with the traffic.

Harmony had only been to York once before, on a history trip early on in her time at Severn Oak. Oblivious to social nuance, she'd plonked herself down in a seat on the coach next to a quiet lad she liked the look of called Adnan. He had begged her, staring fixedly at the gap between him and the seat in front, to move.

'Go. Away. Go. Away.'

It was his terse desperation, his refusal to meet her eye, more than the catcalls and whoops and baying around them that had forced her to get up. She'd had to sit next to the teacher, Mrs Wyndham, who reeked of nylon-wearer's BO and called her Melody.

'So much history,' said Mel now, setting the pace from the Clifford's Tower car park towards the Minster.

'Actually,' Harmony told her, 'everywhere's got history. It's just if the buildings are preserved, and that. You notice it more.'

This was another of her recent insights. Mel didn't appear to understand.

At a café, decided by Mel, Mel said she'd had porridge with the boys and just wanted a cup of tea and a wee. Harmony looked up from the menu for guidance. What would a normal person order? Everything, just about, was bad for you, or exploited someone else in its production. Plus, calories and carbohydrates. As the waitress hovered and Mel started to get impatient, Harmony snapped and ordered a bacon baguette. Brown, when asked to choose, though she'd have preferred white. Mel answered on her behalf when the waitress wondered if she wanted any sweet potato fries: a dismissive 'oh, no', as though the waitress was suggesting something ridiculous.

After the café, Mel clipped Harmony up Stonegate,

past a number of alluring windows into Coppergate, and through the doors of Marks & Spencer. Harmony didn't really mind. Apart from the painstaking trawling of charity shops and car boot sales when a particular necessity arose, Mum deplored shopping, so even M&S was an emporium of otherness. Harmony marvelled as they passed through on the way to the escalator: tuna in caper lime butter; drapey cardigans in dulled pastels; men's primary-coloured polo shirts; all sizes of embellished denim; antibacterial hand gel; matching flannels and towels in every unfaded colour. Inexorably, Mel pressed on to the canyon of the lingerie department. Bras, Mel announced, definitively, charging for a display.

'We'll find someone to fit you.'

Mel cast around, aimed and succeeded in catching the eye of a rigid-haired woman in her fifties with an armful of tanga briefs. And so it was that Harmony found herself being felt up by a dank-breathed stranger with a tape measure, the two of them crammed into a cubicle behind an inadequately occluding beige curtain, a hovering slice of Mel visible in the gap to the outside world. As the assistant leaned forward and lassoed her beneath the ribs with the yellow tape measure, frowning to parse the exact number of circumference, a hot blade of tears gouged the back of Harmony's throat. She missed her mum.

'And one more.' The woman lifted the tape measure to corral Harmony's nipples, as Harmony stared at the small tidemark of grey hair along the assistant's hairline where the auburn dye was growing out.

'Quite a big girl!'

Outside the cubicles, they were directed past many enticing rows to the more limited selection for the euphemistically titled 'fuller figure'. Mel racked through the close-packed hangers, scanning sizes.

'You need three good bras. One to wash, one to wear, one spare.'

Aurora used to call pronouncements like this Mel's Commandments: 'Never Buy a House on a Main Road', 'Naps Make You Tired', 'All Men Like Peas'. Harmony had been there herself for the Sunday lunch of 'All Men Like Peas'.

'And blow jobs,' Mum had added.

It was a family game to make up new commandments behind Mel's back, so Harmony was never sure which ones were really Mel's and which ones Aurora had invented.

There's No Point to a Cat.

If You're Hungry, You're Probably Thirsty.

Jam Doesn't Go in the Fridge.

It's not the Make, it's the Mileage.

You Can't Fancy a Man in Dodgy Shoes. (Mum: 'you can if he's French'.)

Harmony was hopeful of pants to match the bras, but Mel couldn't see the point of this – the lacier items 'didn't wash', apparently. (Lace Doesn't Wash.) She directed Harmony to choose some more basic knickers that would go with the bras, specifying three of each colour (white, black, beigey-pink), and ordering her to make sure they were the right size. Harmony wasn't sure of her size, apart from Large to Extra Large. The meaningless numbers on the labels made her think of Declan. They would be back in time for Declan, wouldn't they?

Of course, Mel reassured her, inserting her card into the machine. In the changing room, she had commanded Harmony to leave one of the bras on. Harmony had chosen the slinkiest, the black, in honour of Declan. Watching her aunt squint and rear back to bring the buttons into focus as she keyed in her PIN, Harmony softened. Mum had always been grudging about Mel's gifts, condemning them as simultaneously extravagant and mean. (*A scented frigging candle – what are we, a health spa?*) But it was basically nice of Mel to buy her all this stuff, and to go to the trouble. Of course, she was loaded, and it wasn't mostly her money, really, but Uncle Ian's. Still. The bra was giving Harmony hidden womanly confidence; she could feel it in the urge to pull back her shoulders and stick everything out in pouting, uplifted display.

Mel, who had bought a stack of items without trying them on – t-shirts and knickers and floppy wads of giant socks for Ian and the boys – suggested they take their shopping back to the car before they continued to the next stage of their day. As she took her bags from the counter, the flick of her eyes to Harmony's chest made Harmony suddenly, hotly aware of herself. She dropped her shoulders back to their apologetic default.

From M&S they took a scenic short cut through the Shambles, where the buttery miasma of fudge production lured them both to stop and watch through the open window of a low-beamed shop. A cloyed brown mass was being paddled into shape by a tall boy in a humiliating boater.

'Your mum's always loved fudge.'

'Mum' hit like a dart between the ribs. Harmony tensed. Was there another awful conversation on the way? Had she been lured in by the bras as a prelude to something even worse? But Mel was getting out her purse. She gestured with some pound coins. Harmony should buy a bag of fudge if she fancied it, she insisted; 'just a small one'. Harmony wasn't about to say no. She entered the shop, instinctively ducking to get through the low door frame. Queuing behind a cluster of solemn Italian tourists being judicious over their flavour selection, she was surprised to be accosted by another boy in a boater. He had very pink cheeks, probably because of the heat from the vats of boiling fudge. Harmony felt the blood in her own cheeks mount in sympathy and confusion. Her newly showcased tits were roughly aligned with the level of the plate he was offering, which contained irregular fawn cubes, whitening to crystals at their corners and each impaled with a toothpick.

'Sea salt.'

The silver piercing under the boy's bottom lip toggled like a floating punctuation mark as he spoke. Didn't work, with the boater. Was he getting pinker? Was it her breasts? Harmony shucked the nearest cube into her mouth, wondering if you were supposed to put the toothpick back on the plate, or if that would be considered manky, like feet on the dashboard.

'Delicious,' she agreed, as the fudge dissolved on her tongue.

He moved on to the Italians, confounding them further, and as they exchanged more seriously couched opinions, jumper sleeves immaculately shawled about their shoulders, Harmony bought a mixed selection already bagged on the counter because it was all bound to be nice and she just wanted to get out of there. She was too much for herself, with this bloody bra.

Outside, Mel automatically declined the proffered bag. Not allowed, she said, then, oh sod it, and rummaged into the corner of the packet for a double square. She moaned in pleasure through the clagginess that she couldn't remember the last time she'd eaten fudge, and Harmony was about to ask her what made her think Aurora liked fudge when she'd never let refined sugar into the house when Mel howled, dropping the clutch of shopping bags and clamping the side of her face.

'Shit!'

Mouth open, Mel pointed and gargled to implore Harmony to take a look. Aware of dispassionate attention from the Italians as they passed, Harmony peered into the obscene, glistening plum of Mel's mouth. She was unsure of what she was supposed to be looking for. Amid increasingly emphatic gargling and pointing, she finally glimpsed a short antenna of wire standing proud of a back molar. The fudge had wrenched out the end of Mel's fixed brace. Mel communicated that they would have to get to a dentist. The wire was very dangerous; it could cut her. This was all said without consonants, since she couldn't close her mouth for fear of laceration.

Mel, ululating 'shit' from time to time on the way back to the car, brightened when they passed a newsagent. With more gargling she urged Harmony into the shop to buy some chewing gum – it didn't matter what kind, apparently. Harmony didn't know about gum, she'd never been allowed it, so she just grabbed a pack near the till. When she returned, Mel commanded her to put some gum in her mouth. Harmony fumbled open the niggling foil and posted a piece towards her aunt's open lips.

'O!' roared Mel, and jabbed a finger at Harmony. *Her* mouth, she meant. Harmony obliged.

'Ooo!'

Harmony chewed, through giggles. What the actual fuck? The gum was stridently minty, a flavour she disliked, but the ferocity of Mel's expression commanded her to continue. It was hard not to feel blamed, even though the fudge had been Mel's idea. A familiar feeling, this. Mel thrust her scooped palm under Harmony's mouth, indicating that she should spit the gum out. Bewildered, she spat.

Harmony watched Mel take the yellow-grey pellet, slimy with Harmony's saliva, and mould it uncertainly into her cheek. Now Harmony got it. The gum would cover the raw end of the brace's wire. Auntie Mel, who didn't even like feet on her dashboard, was happy to wad the chewed receptacle of Harmony's spit into her mouth. Almost as weird was the realisation that even if this hadn't been the outcome of Mel's baffling order to chew, how ready she had been to follow Mel's orders. As Mum used to accuse Stu: *if Mel said jump, you'd say how high.*

In the car, Mel detailed Harmony to call the dentist on Mel's mobile and explain the situation, which she did, grasping what Mel was telling her to say a fraction more easily now that Mel was gingerly confident of closing her mouth a little.

'Why did you get braces, anyway?' she asked Mel, as the motorway flowed past once more. Mel glanced at her, making her earrings swing, and said why did she think? Her teeth were crooked.

'Seems a bit late,' Harmony clarified. Mel gargled a dry, unworded noise. Once again, Harmony felt blamed. That was the thing with Mel: her moods moved so quickly. Once, after a difficult trip to Filey when Harmony and the boys were smaller – Stu and Ian were both working – she remembered Mum flinging herself on the sofa that night with a roar of frustration and relief. Mel had driven them crazy, said Mum to Stu.

'Bloody hell, sometimes I think she's bonkers as fucking conkers.'

Harmony, at eight or nine, had found the phrase an inaccurately round, jolly description of Mel, who was so spiky, with her snapping about finding the best place for a picnic and can't you sit properly to eat on the rug, it's a picnic not feeding time in the chimp house, and shouting at Harmony for luring the boys past the lifeguard's buoy when they went for a swim.

Stu always claimed Mel's bark was worse than her bite. Well, definitely today. Harmony must have smiled at the thought, because Mel glanced at her again, smiling back, mouth askew. Clouds blown past.

The braces were weird. Did Uncle Ian actually want to have sex with Mel with braces in her mouth, assuming that he wanted to have sex with her at all? But when Mel had first had them fitted and Stu said in his mild way that Mel must be desperate for something to spend their money on, Aurora had told him, sharp as you like, that it was Mel's business.

'She's always hated her teeth.'

And Harmony saw then that Mum and Mel had known each other since they were younger than her, when Stu and his world of boys and men weren't part of theirs, the boys enemies and the men irrelevant, and that matters like crooked teeth were a wormhole back to that particular place, which still existed.

The dashboard clock said 2:43.

'Declan's at four,' Harmony reminded Mel. Only three more lessons to go. When it happened with Declan they'd be best friends as well as lovers.

Mel said she could only do her best. Her orthodontist was

in Whitby, on the outskirts, part of a neat suburban row with stark double glazing to shut out the noise of the frantic A road. Inside, the air was trapped and antiseptic, the traffic a murmur against the wasp whine of drilling. Harmony sat, gazing at alarmist posters of gingivitis and decay, while the dentist fitted Mel in. She realised belatedly that there was an antique copy of *Closer* she could have been reading, and had barely started on a Beach Body special when Mel reappeared, the dentist behind her. Or perhaps it was a nurse. Harmony had no experience of dentists, which was down to Mum's policy on sugar.

Mel chatted with the receptionist, her normal speech restored, as they conducted business with forms. Harmony saw, on the display at the bottom of BBC News 24 that played on mute on the TV screen above the receptionist's head, that the time was now 3:27. They could still make it for Declan, just about, if the school run traffic wasn't against them. She stood to encourage Mel towards the door. The pale beech front of the lozenge-shaped reception desk was covered with local posters and ads for Pilates and baby music and guitar lessons, and among these was the poster of the Mystery Girl. Storm.

'You know I found her,' Mel declared. 'I thought she was dead.'

Harmony slunk out into the entrance lobby and pulled the door open, letting the traffic Doppler in over the conversation that persisted behind her. A mean rain met her face. Mel had embarked on the whole story. Who cared?

It got worse. Mel, all excited as they trotted to the car (3:34), had heard from the receptionist that the Mystery Girl had been moved from the infirmary to some kind of special clinic up the road. Wasn't it lucky, said Mel, because she'd have gone on a wild goose chase otherwise? It turned out that the underwear and t-shirts and leggings she'd bought at Marks & Spencer weren't for Mel herself, but for Storm. It made sense for them to drop them off now for her, poor kid. She had nothing, did Harmony realise that? Imagine. Just what they'd scrounged for her in the infirmary. No one to buy her clothes or think of her.

'But what about Declan?' asked Harmony, feeling violent. Mel claimed she'd be five minutes, tops. It was just up the road; Harmony could come in with her if she liked. Harmony declined. Curious as she was about the non-dead girl, her annoyance with Mel was greater.

Of course, the visit was closer to fifteen minutes.

'He'll probably be a few minutes late,' Mel declared, climbing back into the car outside the horrible, depressing clinic. She was now empty-handed. Harmony fought the urge to take her shoes off and smear her feet all over the dashboard.

'He's never late.'

She felt Mel swipe a glance at her away from the road, pinching her earrings to check them before she spoke.

'You could ring him on my phone if you like, to warn him. He's usually OK about rearranging.'

Harmony shrugged, which made the new bra straps dig into her shoulders, and addressed her reply to the window. 'I don't mind.'

She ignored Mel's phone, nested in the cup holder between them. It began to ring as they were negotiating the slipstream of four-by-fours heading back into the east side of Evensand from St Benedict's. 4:12. Mel read the display and fumbled the phone on to Harmony's lap. Declan.

She had no choice but to answer. She muttered a hello

without identifying herself, so he thought she was Mel, and solicitously wondered if she knew where Harmony was.

'This is Harmony.'

A surprised beat. 'Oh. I'm at the house for your lesson?'

Even her voice felt like it was blushing, having to talk to him in front of Mel.

'Yeah, we're stuck in traffic. We'll be there in, like, ten minutes.'

'Very very sorry,' hissed Mel.

'Are you OK to wait and stuff?' Mel flapped an admonitory hand. 'Er, sorry.'

Declan said he was, as long as Mrs Bale didn't mind the knock-on for Edward's lesson. Mel made it clear that she didn't.

Could have been worse, was Mel's verdict when they finally drew up outside the house and she popped the boot so Harmony could retrieve her new underwear. She was right, it could have been. Because when she got to the door, there he was: North Face, hair damp from the mizzle, not in any way ginger. He made everything all right again. Harmony apologised, unlocking the door and waving Mel off after her goodbye double-toot of the horn. The usual excitement of his proximity quelled her self-consciousness about the bra she was wearing and the other bras she was carrying, thankfully disguised by the shopping bag.

She was losing herself in that smell of him as Declan asked, 'Is your mum OK?'

Harmony clutched the bag's handle so tightly it grooved a line between palm and fingers, seeking pain. Mum had never come up, in all the months since Aurora had stopped answering the door, making cups of tea, sorting out his money. She'd assumed Declan had thought she wasn't around any more because she'd got a job, or something equally normal.

'She was at the window.' He pointed towards upstairs. 'I hope I didn't wake her up, ringing the bell. She didn't come down.'

'Oh . . . no.' Harmony knew she was as red in the face as she ever was when she was imagining Declan's tongue in her mouth. Her heart was hammering with shock. Had Stu known Aurora was coming back? Had he forgotten to warn her?

'She's had that bug that's going round.'

There was bound to be a bug going round.

'She's been really ill with it, actually.'

Declan, appearing to accept this, turned his attention to clearing a space at the table and sat. There was no noise at all from upstairs. Perhaps Mum was asleep: when she had been discharged from the hospital she had slept for days. If only Aurora could keep out of the way for just sixty more minutes. She'd managed nearly seven months, after all. Beneath ratio, proportion and rates of change, Harmony implored her to stay out of sight.

Through the unendurable hour, she feared Declan would tear his hair out at the roots. She didn't get a single question right.

'Come on, we've been through this.' His lovely face was pink with irritation. 'It's basic stuff.'

It was worse that he didn't actually lose his temper.

After Declan had finally gone, off to Edward, Harmony crashed upstairs. She wasn't going to give Aurora the satisfaction of rushing into her room, as though she was desperate to see her. Instead, she let her own bedroom door slam behind her, without care. Mum could wake up now. She shouldn't be asleep at this time of day anyway. Either gone, or ill, or sleeping – what was she supposed to say to people, to Declan? How had Aurora seemed to him, at the window: bonkers as conkers? The bra chafed her armpits, suddenly intolerable. Contorting, Harmony struggled herself free from the hooks at the back and chucked the contraption on the bed, launching herself after it on to the twanging mattress. If Declan despaired of her, it was all Mum's fault. Stretched out on her belly, she sobbed ostentatiously at the wall. But from the other side came only a banal, unfathomable shuffling, followed by a cough, before the familiar silence resumed. There was no point. Whatever she did, there never was.

Storm had made it to the national news. Mel hardly watched TV these days, except for box sets, but that morning Aidan had switched on the screen in the kitchen to watch the Champions League highlights over his cereal while she was in the shower and not around to forbid it. The TV was still running, on mute, when Mel got back from dropping him and Edward off at school, and it was the start of recognition at seeing Evensand beach on screen that had her ramping up the volume, stretched across the breakfast bar with the remote, in time to hear the young female reporter, pinched with cold by the brutal wind coming off Brazen Point, say, ' ... *possibility that the young woman may have been a victim of assault.*'

The footage cut to a wide shot of Storm playing ping-pong in an institutional room with a stocky, uniformed nurse.

'*Although Storm, as hospital staff have named her, is doing well, doctors are still mystified by her condition. Without any distinguishing features or property, or anyone who has come forward to report her missing, her identity remains a mystery.*'

Storm, under the supervision of the same nurse, inevitably filled a kettle at a ward sink.

'*Police are casting their net wider, believing the so-called Evensand mystery girl may be a visitor to North Yorkshire who came to holiday or work in the county before suffering total memory loss. In the meantime, police are encouraging any member of the public who recognises the young woman to ring in on the number below.*'

Self-consciously, Storm sipped a mug of tea as the piece concluded, her hands pinned beneath the phone number superimposed at the bottom of the screen. Mel was gratified to see that she was wearing one of the t-shirts she had bought for her.

It was Thursday. Notionally Mel's day off, it always turned into the busiest day of the week. She didn't run classes after school, due to the usurpation of the hall by both Scouts and Brownies. Akela had long been eyeing up her after-school hours, and sure enough, when the lease came up for renewal after its usual two-year term, he had co-opted Brown Owl and pounced. Showing no loyalty to Mel's staunch years of rental, the new vicar refused to intervene. Weak-chinned streak of piss, he was. Mel had managed to distribute the hours on to the rest of the week, with Saturdays bearing the brunt, and forbade Scouts and Brownies the use of the barre, which she'd installed at her own expense. She also made a point of locking up her sound system, which they were far more likely to use. Mel knew which way she'd jump once the current lease was up. Not only did the mosque on the way into town have better parking, it wasn't in thrall to the one-way system. Plus, they'd recently installed a sprung floor in the new hall. She'd unscrew the barre and take it with her, as well, once she'd won the imam round to the innocuousness of Street Dance.

Setting aside the principle of Thursday, it actually suited her to have a day in the week to tackle all her other jobs, personal and professional. Today Mel had in fact hoped to pop in once more on Storm. But Declan had texted her again about Edward, and she realised she couldn't postpone the necessary summit any longer. The tutor would arrive at the house early, before Edward's lesson. Once again, Mel had swapped the time with Harmony. Harmony had been arsey about this, even when Mel suggested she have the lesson at their house and stay on for dinner. Although she agreed in the end, she sulkily claimed it would be difficult. Mel wondered if the difficulty was Aurora. Really, she should have invited the three of them round for dinner, Harmony, Aurora and Stu, but the middle of the week didn't give her enough of a run-up at that particular hurdle. As far as she knew, Aurora was still capable of picking up the phone. And, failing that, Stu certainly was.

Declan was due at 3:15. Mel had settled on a forty-five-minute slot, deciding that half an hour would be too rushed for their chat and an hour awkwardly long – which left her just enough time to get back from the Zumba class she'd started to run at lunchtime, well out of the way of Brownies and Cubs, stop for a food shop on the return journey, stow the frozen goods in the freezer and have a shower. There simply weren't enough hours in the day. This had always been true, except when the boys were babies and the hours had often been far too many, but the feeling was becoming more acute with age.

Age. This was another job undone. Friends – especially, she'd noticed, those who had passed fifty themselves – kept archly asking if they should save the date. For months she had attempted to ignore her birthday, bearing down in her wing mirror. Well, let the bastard overtake, unmarked. Fifty was impossible, an irreconcilable number, despite Fiona Bruce. Perhaps on the day she could just lock herself in the Fiat, which Ian had so surprisingly bought her for her forty-ninth, and howl?

When Ian had presented her with the car last year, she immediately suspected he might have got her age wrong, jumping a year. He claimed not, but he'd certainly set himself a dauntingly extravagant standard to exceed for a landmark birthday present.

Not that she wanted one, or a party. Definitely no party. For one thing, her birthday was barely a week after Aurora's, and anything they organised would surely be rubbing salt in a wound, for Stu and Harmony at least, if not for Aurora herself. Bloody Aurora. As much as anything, Mel resented the loneliness of having to negotiate turning fifty without her. By the time Aurora had stopped being Dawn and hooked up with Stu, the ease of so many of their younger conversations had stalled, but they had always continued to share the bodily common of womanhood: blood, fat, hair, semen, shit, piss, pus. Not milk, because semi-accidental Edward (maybe he'd be a girl! as Mel considered the haphazard pill packet) had been bottle-fed, to Aurora's open disapproval. As the children got older, the two of them had turned their attention to constipation and sagging and general drying out; forthcoming menopause. Mel didn't talk to anyone else like this. Who else would tell her now, without repulsion or dismay, that the three black hairs had re-sprouted on her chin? Since Aurora had stopped being herself, she had to remember to look in the mirror.

Mel gave herself a cursory check as she parked up above the Co-op. There was a bristle, apparently grown overnight. She tweezered it out with pinched fingernails. Should she have known? All the time Aurora had been sharing her skin creeping beneath her armpits and her toenails yellowing into horn, she had said nothing of what must have been happening inside her. When had it started, exactly, her sadness, or wrongness? Perhaps it had just descended, the sky falling in. One morning unable to get out of bed, followed by all the mornings after that. *I've lost my mojo*, was all she'd said at first. *I always hate this time of year.* Then a virus, maybe. A homeopath, acupuncture. Cutting more foods out of her diet. Blood tests, Mel had to hear from Stu; even before their Christmas row Aurora had stopped calling.

Then came that half-hearted walk into the sea, the handful of not very dangerous pills. It had been good enough for the psychiatrists. Suicidal ideation, they called it, and clapped her in hospital until she convinced them she wouldn't try it again. And since then, this limbo of Aurora's times away, friends from Bristol and forays to what she called communities. Nuns, this time. *Nuns.* What would Dawn have said about that, apart from 'wears the soap'?

Still, even with Aurora a ghost of herself, both of them would be fifty. She, Mel, would be fifty. In the meantime, there were Harmony's GCSEs to get through, followed by the culmination of Mel's professional year in her Summer Spectacular, all the while keeping the three plates of the boys spinning: Joseph's wobbling gap year, Aidan's frantic sporting calendar and Edward's stalled entrance to St Ben's. Somewhere among all that, Mel now remembered with a drop, was her wedding anniversary. She had to let go of the trolley and count back on her fingers to calculate, stopping dead in the middle of the world foods aisle. Twenty-two years.

Among all the intimacies she and Dawn bandied, even as teenagers they had never shared much of the experience of sex, as opposed to its effects on their bodies; love bites, cystitis, carpet burn – and, in Dawn's case and just the once, crabs. But once Mel started going out with Ian in her early twenties, she had even shut up about her modest sexual afflictions. Sex with Ian had always been her unspoken superiority, a lucky charm or saint's medal, invoked at the most unlikely moments; walking into the strip-lit school hall for a parents' meeting, or in the passport queue coming back from holiday at some grey, alienated hour: them in bed, the simple success of it. Through pregnancy and weight gain, flu and flatulence, for almost thirty years Ian's desire for her and hers for him had remained enthusiastic and direct. Always.

Though not so much lately. Loading up the boot with bags, Mel totted up the watersheds of abstinence. Ten days, a fortnight, a month. In her marrow, she couldn't accept being fifty had anything to do with the lapse, though common sense told her that she should. Everything she read or saw presented the countervailing message. What if, in her attitude to her own middle age, she was being like Ian with sunscreen? He didn't believe in it, and refused to read any article she put his way, however scientific. Then he'd had that funny mole. Fifty. Perhaps she should consider the evidence.

That dishy policeman, though. Young man.

Pulling out of the clifftop car park, Mel tried to remember the last time she'd eaten Camembert. Honking, runny, redolent of all the bodily effluvia she and Dawn so loved to discuss. Once, on a camping holiday near Aucachan (very hot in August, even Ian wore a t-shirt on the worst days), she'd made herself sick on cheese, she loved it so. It must be years since she'd indulged that pleasure. There was a very good cheese shop in Ilkley, but she couldn't be bothered to make the journey specially. Time, this was the trouble; always time.

As Mel staggered up to the front door with the shopping bags, it was shaving five to three. Conquering these small deadlines always gave her pleasure. Five minutes to shower, two, tops, to get dressed. She bent to the bottom lock. You had to relent minutely from your original pressure on the key to find the fit, a precise degree her fingers knew. After that chunky, satisfying give she stood up to twist the Yale, but when she pushed the door with her hip, it stuck at the bottom. She had just locked, not unlocked, the bottom lock. Strange. As she twiddled the key again, less confident now of her touch and a little apprehensive, a shape loomed in the frosted glass panel. She squeaked in fear. The shape told her to hang on. Ian.

She hadn't forgotten to lock up, then. But where was his car? He explained as he gave her a distracted kiss and took the bags from her, Toothpaste leaping unhelpfully alongside them. A memory stick left behind with plans crucial for a meeting in Goathland; lift from some fitters who had a job up the road and a return lift back to Goathland due from Jonno around half past, because Ian had had a pint and then another half at a posh pub lunch with clients. Mel could taste it in his kiss. She always liked the smell of booze on him. Whisky was her favourite, but beer would do.

The dinky blue memory stick was on the kitchen work-top, next to Ian's open briefcase. Mel scooped up both so that he could put some of the shopping bags up there, out of Toothpaste's way. Taking the offered stick and case, Ian told her she looked nice, aiming another expansive kiss that landed on her temple. Mel snorted. She was dressed for Zumba, in reeking Lycra topped with one of Joseph's old hoodies, hair in a scrappy ponytail. But as she leaned over for the bag she'd packed with freezer goods, Ian put an unequivocal hand on her arse and squeezed.

'Oy.'

She let the freezer bag go and turned, backed up against the island. He put both hands on her hips.

A beery, bloated snog. When she opened her eyes, Mel saw that the doors to the cupboards above the sink were open, which she hated. She closed her eyes and put in more effort. Ian was concrete-hard against her Lycra crotch. He still had his suit jacket on. She slid her hands beneath it and pulled the hem of his shirt out of his trousers so she could get to the warm skin of his back.

'I'm a bit . . . '

He said she was fine. Except, the ice cream would be melting by now and the texture was never the same if you refroze it. There had been a twofer on Ben & Jerry's, the boys' favourite. It must be five past, easily. She stank. But. Ian's fingers scurried to find an entry point in her ancient Sally Gunnell Shock Absorber.

'Bloody thing. Can't you take it off?'

There wasn't time to go up to the bedroom. Declan might even arrive early. The best way . . . Mel removed Ian's hand from her sports bra and directed it down inside her running trousers. He appreciated the initiative, and concentrated. Meanwhile, she unbuckled his belt and delved inside his pants to grip his cock. That was more like it. For shifting seconds they found a rhythm, increased it.

'Come upstairs . . . '

She gurgled no against his mouth and doubled the vigour of her attentions. No time. Mel knelt, a little cautiously (God, her knees), and unzipped him so that she could take him in her mouth. Ian gave a little jounce of apprehension, reliving his caution when she'd first had her braces fitted.

'You sure?'

She mouthed a yes around his cock, lips over her teeth, like a pro. He winced, in a good way, submitted to familiar pleasure. After a second or two he opened his eyes and tugged at her hoody to pull it off over her head. That gone, flung to the tiles and making Toothpaste trot over to sniff it – actually, while they were at it, Toothpaste driven out, the door shut – Ian's hands slithered again to find purchase under the utilitarian bra. He'd always had a thing for her tits, as staunch in his loyalty as he was to Sheffield Wednesday, despite the impossibility of their getting back into the Premier League. Mel crossed her arms above her head and contorted herself free of the bra.

Back at his cock, she glanced up to check Ian's rictus of advancing ecstasy, taking in the electric-blue time on the cooker a few centimetres to the right of his left hand, which clutched the worktop. Just past ten past. She put everything she had into it. Suddenly, finally, Ian convulsed and clamped his hands at the side of her head to still her. His eyes were open, pained. He was warning her he was about to come.

'It's fine,' she broke off to tell him. He moaned a *no*, stroking her hair. He meant he wanted to make her come first. What bloody time did he think it was?

'It's fine.'

Mel resumed, savage now in her determination to extract his orgasm. It was as Ian reared and moaned and clutched, juddering into her mouth, that she heard the tentative 'hello?'

Declan. And again, closer, possibly with footsteps – 'Hello?'

They'd left the front door open. Toothpaste's welcome would at least buy them a few seconds. Swallowing, as she always did, Mel lumbered to her feet (knees, God) as Ian stuffed himself back into his trousers. He at least was fully dressed. Declan wouldn't do more than hover in the hall, surely? She grabbed the balled-up hoody, losing precious moments in disentangling the sleeves, and pulled it on. She wiped her mouth and raked at her hair. There was nothing about her appearance that couldn't be explained by recent exercise. Only Ian's presence would give the game away, and no one Declan's age would suspect a middle-aged couple of having sex. She told Ian to wait a moment and explained who was at the door. He tucked in his shirt, briskly post-sexual, the last few minutes wholly erased.

'Where did you put the memory stick?'

'You put it in your case!' She headed off to intercept Declan.

Five minutes later, Ian gone with Jonno, sitting at the breakfast bar with the tutor and a fresh cafetière to chase the flavourless acidity of her husband's semen from her mouth, Mel spotted, as Declan surely already had, her discarded sports bra hanging rakishly from the corner of the cupboard door open above the sink. She plunged the coffee, ignoring her blush. Beneath the looseness of the hoody, she was very conscious of her uncontained breasts, nipples alert with Ian's recent attentions.

'Edward.'

Declan sighed, clutching his hair at the front. 'Yeah.'

He produced some of Edward's recent non-verbal reasoning sheets and conscientiously explained their flaws. From the previous two boys' entrance papers, Mel was well acquainted with the sequences of arrows and rotated shapes, many of them vaguely heraldic, although you weren't supposed to be distracted by their associations or resemblances, as she knew Edward would be, telling himself some story when he was supposed to be spotting patterns and deviations.

'What's really frustrating,' said Declan, 'is this.' He tapped at the bottom of a paper, dense with monochrome graphics in quadrants, variously reversed. 'Those are the hardest three, and he got them right.'

'Guesswork?'

Declan puffed out a breath of incredulity, releasing his grip on his hair. 'Three out of three? And, the week before . . . '

He produced another paper. The same thing, more or less. Mel was stumped.

'I did wonder.'

Mel encouraged him to continue.

'Well – it isn't possible he wants to fail the exam, is it?'

'Of course not!'

'I don't mean on purpose, necessarily,' said Declan. 'Sometimes kids do things without realising they're even doing them.' He pinched his bottom lip. 'Not just kids!'

Mel stared at the papers, confounded.

'Why would he want to fail? He knows we want him to go to St Benedict's. Like both his brothers. It's a lovely school. He'd be lucky to go there. I wish my parents had been able to send me to a school like that.'

She ground to a stop, aware it was Eddy who needed to be convinced of these reasons rather than Declan. Declan shuffled the papers together and stood them up, shielding himself from her irritation.

'Kids.'

He left it with her. Quite rightly. She didn't know what

would be worse: Edward trying to fail the exam on purpose because he actually wanted to go to a state school (unlikely, given his bogeyman terror of Severn Oak), or being in some way so troubled that he was setting himself up to fail for reasons that were impossible to fathom. Was Declan saying her son was disturbed? She'd much rather he was thick. Much.

The bra dangled. Mel ignored it, although she longed to whip it from the cupboard and close the door.

'He'll be home soon. Harmony's picking him up for me, actually.'

'Right.' Declan armed himself with another sigh and re-engaged his quiff.

Would it be possible, he wondered, for them to follow today's arrangement and have Harmony's final few lessons here, either before or after Edward's, he didn't mind which? It was easier not to have to split the journey, as long as it made no difference to them.

Mel readily agreed, still preoccupied with Edward's mental health. 'How's she doing?' she added automatically.

'Yeah,' said Declan. 'Think she should be all right, just about. As long as she does herself justice on the day.'

And where was the justice in that? Harmony should be the fuck-up; neglected, hopeless Harmony, who only stood a chance at any GCSEs because of Mel, not sturdy, wholesomely reared Edward, for whom Mel would chop off any of her limbs if it would spare him failure or distress. Quelling these thoughts, Mel said she was glad to hear it. Declan, she saw, was blushing, his clear Celtic skin flooded with blood. Was it the bra? Mel commanded herself not to look at it again. She twitched the hem of the enveloping hoody securely under her bum and crossed her arms in front of her on the Corian.

It was only when Edward came home, trailed by Harmony, and Mel saw Declan blush again, that she landed on the non-verbal reason for his discomfort. The t-shirt Harmony was wearing was ripped to display, as never before, her newly supported cleavage. Talking of bras. Also, she'd put on a lot of black eyeliner and done something misguided to her hair. The poor lad. No wonder he wanted to have the lessons at their house. Why hadn't Mel thought? Just because Harmony was a blob didn't mean she didn't have normal teenage urges. Of course the tutoring arrangement had started when Aurora was taking some sort of interest, or was at least around to chaperone … It was all beyond Mel's experience, anyway, as the mother of boys. Poor Declan.

Mel suggested he and Edward move to the dining room, where they traditionally conducted their lesson. She'd bring a cup of tea.

'And biscuits,' said Edward. The look he flicked to Harmony betrayed the sharing of some appalling snack on the way home. There wasn't an atom of of guile in that broad, transparent face. Everyone said boys were easier than girls, because they were more open. And it was true, of all three, but Eddy had always been unusually – Ian would say unnecessarily – communicative. If he didn't tell you something, it wasn't worth the telling. In truth it usually wasn't worth the telling anyway: the entire plot of the CBBC show he'd watched; the banter between him and his best friend Zander; the difficulty of his most recent poo. There was no way he was capable of calculating a tactic to fail his entrance to St Ben's, which meant – if it was true, and what did Declan know, with the wisdom of his twenty-whatever years – Edward was doing it for what Mel could only think of as psychological reasons.

Mel knew she would be best keeping this to herself. To Ian, even children only did things they intended to do. His response to Declan's theory of unwitting self-sabotage would be to dragoon Edward into more practice papers, invigilated by him with fatherly impatience, at best achieving nothing and at worst robbing Eddy of what little confidence he had.

It wasn't that she didn't share Ian's exasperation, but motherhood had forced Mel into accepting the existence of human psychology. Unfathomable. Murky. Edward had always needed her more, even more than the other two. Late toilet-training; sleeping in their bed; that entire year he had to watch the same supermarket DVD twice through before he'd eat breakfast, heavy on her lap with his thumb in his mouth, fondling her earlobe like a security rag as his pupils dilated with the drug of *Fifi and the Flowertots*. Thinking of these things gave her actual pain, low in her stomach.

'Auntie Mel, there's a bra—'

Harmony pointed up to the cupboard. 'What's it doing there?'

Mel told her that she didn't know; perhaps Aidan had been mucking about with Toothpaste, throwing him things to fetch?

'Bit random,' Harmony observed.

Tetchily, Mel unhooked the bra from the cupboard door, noting that her cleaner needed to tackle the fingerprints smudging the paintwork.

'I mean, why was Aidan throwing your bra?'

Mel ignored this as Toothpaste endorsed her alibi by truffling at the bloody thing as she walked out of the kitchen, instinctively determined to rid herself of it. Kneeing the dog away, she stuffed the bra into her open handbag. This sat on a chair in the hall, where she'd dumped it when she'd returned to the house that eventful hour before. Harmony, to Mel's irritation, slouched in the doorway watching this slightly self-conscious performance.

Bolstering her pantomime of purpose, Mel retrieved her mobile from the bag. At the door Harmony loomed, invading her space. Aurora hadn't taught her about that, if you could teach such things. She rested her soft chin against the top of Mel's arm, brazenly reading the display on her phone. Her breath was stridently sweet with whatever she and Edward had been eating. Haribo, Mel shouldn't wonder. Or those revolting sherbet cables. She made the effort not to bridle. She'd noticed, since Aurora's illness, if that was what they were calling it, how much Harmony seemed to need excuses for physical contact.

Mel's home screen was bannered with a series of recent texts. One from Aidan (*getin lft frm doms mum afta footie ok*), and the other three from an unknown number:

Hi Mel its Lottie ☺ *sorry got ur no frm Joe. Can you get him to call me?*

Then, sent half an hour later:

Don't mind how late

And ten minutes after that:

Sorry to bother you x

Trouble in paradise, by the sound. Well, Joe still had a key.

'Shall I put the kettle on? For Declan?'

Mel was agreeing to Harmony's suggestion as her phone rang. For a moment before she saw the display, the logic of the texts made her think it would be Joe, filling her in on whatever was going on between him and Lottie, but it was an unnamed local number.

'Melanie hi, it's Dan Mason. PC Mason?'

Melanie, again. Young *man*.

Almost as soon as he'd put the phone down, Mason was kicking himself for speaking to Melanie Bale. All that impatient bossiness, the whole world her staff. He certainly didn't owe her a call. But something in the way she'd talked about Storm when she'd passed on the tip about the vans had touched him. He felt it in that tender place where Lottie's name insisted on resting.

Shit. He didn't even like the girl, yet here he was thinking about her every few minutes, hankering, as though she was a screen he had to refresh.

Mrs Bale cared, was the point – unlike Soccolo – and filling her in seemed to answer Dan's need to feel he was making progress on Storm's case. As soon as he'd called her about the latest development, an anxiety surged that his breach of confidence might find its way to the press, who they'd been firmly warned not to talk to. He decided to ring her back, even though he hadn't given many details, or, crucially, named names. When the phone went to voicemail, Mason rang off. It would be fine. Melanie Bale was bossy, not gabby. And he'd already said he'd report back after the meeting with Liz Harvey, idiot that he apparently was.

It was all meant to be hush-hush. Liz Harvey's phone call to the Inspector had followed an email no one had had time to reply to, a negligence that had snowballed into this. Mrs Harvey wanted to see Storm for herself. *Due diligence* was the Inspector's phrase, although they all knew it was futile. The man who had killed Mrs Harvey's daughter was in Rampton, serving time for her murder on top of three others, all young girls. He would never be released. He had never confessed, or given information about where the body of Eleanor Barker might be found. But they owed it to the poor woman to let her see Storm. *Respectful* was another of the Inspector's words.

Dan well remembered the photo of Eleanor Barker widely released when she disappeared on holiday down in Devon; he had only been a few years older himself at the time. It was a first school photo, the uniformed little girl beaming out at the lens in startled self-delight. The hair falling in her eyes wasn't so fair that it couldn't have darkened to Storm's shade over thirteen years, and the round eyes themselves were believably brown. Her mother, catching the TV news about the Evensand Mystery Girl, had hoped she was witnessing a miracle. Eleanor, come back to her. Struck dumb by the traumas she'd endured in the years she'd been missing, but alive. You couldn't blame her for hoping.

On the same day the Inspector had convened them to give the due diligence line, Timi, the Romanian lass with the straightened hair, had got hold of Dan through the station switchboard. She told him that the girl she'd thought might be Storm, the runaway, had turned up safe and sound in her home village outside Bucharest. Dan didn't believe her. He didn't say he didn't. He'd thanked Timi warmly for the update and asked for the girl's name, 'just for their records'. She didn't know it, she claimed, but said she'd ask around and get back to him. It was PC Mason, wasn't it?

'Can I get your mobile number, just in case? So I don't have to go through the switchboard and that?'

The shoe had dropped. The Curse of the Uniform, again. Timi fancying him made it less clear-cut that she was ringing just to put them off the trail of this girl from the vans. But people were complicated. Even if she did call him, Mason wasn't going to hold his breath about her coming up with a name. He couldn't get over the feeling that Timi's dodgy uncle had a hand, somewhere, in neatly closing down this line of enquiry.

Lottie had successfully argued for everyone to convene at the clinic for the meeting between Liz Harvey and Storm. Dan had been resistant. He didn't want Lennox there – not that he could give this as a viable reason for getting his way – but after a few emails in which he'd cowered behind the barrier of police procedure, Lottie had let slip that the shrink was about to go on a week's leave. After that, Dan had allowed himself to soften to her point that staying at the clinic would not only be less traumatic to Storm, but potentially to the woman she was to meet. God knows, Liz Harvey had spent more than enough time in police stations, back in the day.

Mason suspected that if Lennox hadn't been away, it might not have been so easy to bring Storm and the Harveys together. Lottie, it was clear when they spoke, was hopeful of the happiest ending. Simultaneously warmed and irritated by her optimism, Dan had tried to warn her. There was no doubt that a face-to-face between Mrs Harvey and Storm was the easiest way to resolve the matter, but even the best outcome was bound to be painful.

Soccolo, who disapproved of the whole business, kept making brutal jokes about how much he could get for the story from the few displaced journos who had already made enquiries at the hospital. But on the day of the meeting, he transformed himself. Dan had witnessed this transformation once before, at the house of one of the twoccers who had died in the RTA, when they had called to inform the parents. Suddenly Soccolo was a solid miracle of compassion, sensitive to shock and silences, the best possible officer for the job. It was the same with Mrs Harvey. Vocal about the *waste of chuffing time* right up to the point when they were told the Harveys were waiting for them at reception, his partner enacted a seamless transition from fretful backstage grumbling to judicious public gravity. Mason was grateful to the old bugger as they escorted the couple out to the car park, Soccolo smoothing nerves with considerately neutral conversation. At the sight of Mrs Harvey, his own tongue had seized up.

Both husband and wife were in their mid-fifties, but Mrs Harvey appeared older, grey-haired and with a blasted look; permanently injured by what she'd endured. Both she and her husband took the change of venue in their stride, unquestioningly accepting Soccolo's suggestion that they share the ride rather than follow in their own car. When Dan held the door open for her, he saw the woman's hand tremble on the frame as she balanced herself to climb in; nerves about the meeting or ongoing debility, he couldn't tell. During the journey she barely spoke, leaving her husband to respond to Soccolo's bluff, untaxing questions. The couple had married some years after Eleanor's disappearance. As was so often the way, Mrs Harvey and the girl's father had divorced, a year after the trauma. Eleanor Barker had been, and remained, an only child.

At the clinic, Soccolo ushered the couple into the empty meeting room and took their distracted orders for the tea he offered. Milk, no sugar.

'Strong, if you don't mind,' said Mr Harvey. He spoke too loudly, as though compensating for his wife's silence.

Dan, strongly wishing himself elsewhere, busied himself with chairs. Their arrangement from the previous meeting suggested confrontation, or judgement: a single chair on one side of the table, six on the other. As he was evening them out to all sides of the square, he heard Mrs Harvey gasp, a gentle, animal noise. Lottie had entered with Storm.

Mr Harvey gripped his wife's hand, white-knuckled, bracing her, but also restraining her from moving towards the girl. Dan willed Soccolo to get back asap with the tea.

Lottie's voice was gentle.

'This is Storm. Storm, this lady thinks she might know you.'

No, no! Not the thing to say, you silly bitch. Because now Storm was regarding Mrs Harvey with her soft, neutral gaze. There was a politeness guarding it that struck Dan as newly acquired since his own introduction with Lennox. Mr Harvey continued to stare down at his wife's hand as she began to weep.

Soccolo made it back with the tea as they were all sitting down. Although Mrs Harvey scanned and rescanned the girl's face as Lottie chattered to cover Storm's silence, Storm betrayed no recognition. The woman removed herself from her husband's grip and pulled her bag on to her lap. It was commodious, halfway to being a briefcase, the chocolate leather of its bottom corners rubbed white with use. She brought out photos of Eleanor and her together with the girl's father, picnics and holidays, followed by a shape in a Boots bag. The tremor of Mrs Harvey's hands rattled the plastic as she pulled the bag away to reveal a worn soft toy: a monkey. Mason smelled the laundry detergent coming off the nubbled fleece as she placed it on the table. She must have washed it for the occasion.

'Mr Nelson. From *Pippi Longstocking.*'

Storm turned to Lottie for guidance. Dan could see she was uncertain whether to take the monkey, wondering if in fact it was an offering she was meant to accept. Don't, Dan was willing her, if you take it she'll think you recognise it; but Lottie's smile of encouragement prompted Storm to pull the creature towards her by one of its long, limp legs. Mrs Harvey trapped her sobs inside her mouth with a clamped hand. Oh, shit.

Mason looked away, at one of the photos face up on the table. Eleanor and a rejuvenated Mrs Harvey, joyful and chestnut-haired, both pretended to prop up a stone column at the top of a hill in sunny countryside, in walking boots and anoraks. Before the murder, Mrs Harvey had been a lecturer of some kind. That sort of life. A nice enough one to return to, if a bit on the wholemeal side.

The trouble was, Storm wasn't Eleanor Barker. The girl's hand still cupped the monkey's plush foot as she regarded each photo presented to her, spending less time looking at each image than she did watching Mrs Harvey's face, gauging its expression for meaning. Did that show, Mason wondered, that faces were easier for her to understand than English, or did she just know that the meaning of people was more complicated than what they said?

150

'... an Easter holiday. North Norfolk. You can see we had – we were very lucky with the weather.'

Mrs Harvey was careful, he noted, not to address Storm as though she were Eleanor. Good. She continued to deal her way through the photos, speeding up along the way. Only the woman's shaking fingers counted the cost to her self-control as she drily captioned the location of each shot. When Mason and Soccolo had gone to the house of the teenager killed in the RTA, his mother had received the news with grief so immediate and incontinent that Mason had almost disbelieved it. There must have been a time when Mrs Harvey had howled and raged. He was grateful not to have witnessed it.

'... in the house in Okehampton. We're not there now, obviously.'

A drop of rain splashed the surface of the print. Beneath, five-year-old Eleanor sat on her father's knee, Mr Nelson on her own lap. Not a raindrop, a tear, for fuck's sake, fallen from Lottie's still-brimming eye. She swept at the photo, smearing the gloss.

'Sorry.'

Storm's gaze slithered to find purchase on Mrs Harvey, or Mason, or Lottie. Soccolo, intercepting Dan's own look of appeal, leaned forward and placed his locked hands on the table, as though a negotiating position had been reached.

'I think we've gone as far as we can, for today.'

If Dan had had a father, this would have been the point to him. It was like hearing Soccolo sing: the unlikely glory of his new voice, its compassionate modulation.

Storm nodded. Even the Harveys seemed relieved. Soccolo stood. In a clinching two-thumbed gesture as familiar to Dan as the smell of his own farts, he swiped the front of his belt beneath his tunic to the buckle and back, releasing his paunch.

'Right then.'

Mrs Harvey began to gather in the photos, overzealously helped by Lottie. For a moment, only the monkey remained, splayed on the table between the woman and Storm, its stitched smile aimed nowhere. Storm picked it up, offering it back. Mrs Harvey stuffed the creature into her bag without bothering to enrobe it in the Boots carrier. To Dan, she appeared anxious to be gone, almost embarrassed by the hope she'd displayed. But when they were in the car, returning to the station, it turned out that he'd got it wrong. She said it was a shame they couldn't have had longer.

'Something might have jogged her memory.'

And again, to her husband, 'Maybe clothes ... '

Mason saw that a locked door must be more bearable than the blasted wasteland Mrs Harvey had been living in for thirteen years. Blaming herself for not using the right key was still a kind of hope, and certainly no crueller than the alternative.

'The DNA, I mean, you'll be able to tell ... '

Soccolo lifted his eyes to the rear-view mirror, still using the gentle voice.

'We'll pass you on to CID for that, Mrs Harvey.'

Dan had hoped it wouldn't come to it. It looked as though it might. There would be no more hope after that.

An hour later, the first pint of Tetley's was nectar as it worked its way through his mood. Even Soccolo remained quiet and unabusive as they drank, like an actor withdrawing from character after a draining performance.

'Shitting awful business. Doesn't get worse than that.'

They absorbed this, in silent agreement.

Dan was on his way for the second, his round, and the last, he'd resolved, for that night as he wasn't made of money and he was starving, when he saw Lottie at the bar, waiting to be served. His heart sank even as his cock rose. There had already been enough difficulty in the day.

'What's the food like in here?'

She always talked to him, Dan realised, as though she expected him to be there, as though they were in the middle of an old conversation. Did she talk to everyone like that? He told her the food was all right, he thought, though he'd never tried it. It looked nice enough when it went by on plates; generous with the chips. They were standing side by side. Lottie's ear and the edge of her jaw looked older than the idea Dan had of her; more definite. Her hair smelled nice. He thought of that fat tear hitting the photo, as though feelings were all you needed and all feelings were allowed.

'You wouldn't recommend the vegetarian special.'

She turned to face him, smile at the ready, giving herself a dare. Dan saw it. She wanted him. She'd decided to want him, even though she wasn't a meat-eater. Why would he say no after the day they'd had?

After he was served, Dan splashed Soccolo's pint in front of him, ignoring his leer, and moved off to join Lottie at her table. When the girl at the bar brought Lottie her goat's cheese tart, Dan demanded a bite to try. She could see his point that goat's cheese tasted like Tupperware, though she was minded to find him funny; the contract had already been struck. She let him help finish her chips. At some point during all this Soccolo made a tactful, encouraging exit. *Go on, my son.*

Lottie, as ever, was forthcoming. She'd broken up with

her boyfriend and had come to the pub after work because he was supposed to be at her flat moving his belongings out. Being her, this was a declaration, not a confidence. He didn't have much at her place, she was quick to explain – they hadn't been living together living together.

'He's younger than me.'

This detail made her falter, that rueful fall in her voice. Dan got it: he'd broken up with her, then, and she hadn't seen it coming.

'Just a bit of fun, eh?'

He gave her that, to salvage her dignity. What young lad in his right mind would break up with a girl as fit as her, good job, own flat? He'd say that as well, if necessary.

She attempted a laugh, at the bit of fun, and said that now it had come to it, and Joe must be well out of the way, she couldn't quite face going back home to be alone. Desolation tethered the attempted lift of her voice.

Dan leaned in.

'Come to mine, then. I'll keep you company.'

Thanks to his nan's will, Dan had been able to put money down for a box of a new build not far from town. Lottie gave him a lift in her untidy little car. Soccolo would scoff if Dan said that he hadn't seen any of it coming, but it was a surprise, truly. Not the sex itself, which was the same old tune with a few different words. He hadn't expected her to go on top, not first off, not without him suggesting. He liked that. She smelled good, all over. Girls did; the smells they had and the smells they added. She came, genuinely, as far as he could tell. But the point when he realised that's what they were going to do, the tipping point, that had been the real glory, there in the pub, over the vegetarian special.

'What a day.'

She hadn't just meant her boyfriend, she'd meant all of it: Storm and Mrs Harvey, her falling tear.

'What if she is Eleanor Barker? I mean, if she never remembers ... '

The emotion of it had torn through his banter about what they put into Quorn.

'Do you think she is?'

Mason had looked away to the blackboard on the bar, unable to bring himself to say no. It must have been obvious, what he felt.

'Then who is she? Who the hell is she, then?'

Dan thought of this good question while Lottie was in the loo and he was listening to the second failed flush from his broken toilet on the other side of the plasterboard. Due diligence respected, he needed to go back to the vans, check out Uncle Nicu. Above the thirsty, short rattling of the handle, Lottie gave a little moan of alarm, probably assuming she'd broken his bog. You had to feel sorry for the lass, her loneliness in her job. At least he had Soccolo. Not a soulmate, exactly; but someone to witness the madness with, so you knew you weren't the one going mad.

When she reappeared in the close-aired bedroom, something had changed. Before, everything about her had been open, that flare of shared laughter as they'd returned to themselves in bed, the way she'd held his neck. Now it was as though she'd given herself some sort of talking-to in the bathroom. He hadn't left a log in there, had he? He would have made a joke to that effect, but Lottie wouldn't look at him. Instead, she fussed around finding her tights on the narrow slice of floor between bed and wall, briskly pulling one of the legs up her forearm and back through itself to get it the right way out, trying to pretend that fucking didn't matter. He was sick of that, to the back teeth.

Dan stretched out, not very far, to take her naked, tight-less hand. He squeezed it, to try and reassure her that he wasn't the tosser she seemed to be expecting.

'Stay, if you fancy.'

Lottie took her hand back, barely polite. Girls. If he'd been a meal she'd be trying to puke him up. She sat on the far corner of the bed and pulled the tights on, frowning at her first hooked, lifted foot, then the second, sheathing them in opaque black. A sniff. Dan liked watching girls get dressed almost as much as the opposite, but Lottie very clearly wasn't inviting him to watch. Standing, the slapstick hike of her tights over her straddled knees to wriggle the waistband up to her waist defied him to find her lovely. She was, still, lovely.

He tried again. 'What's the rush?'

'Stuff,' was all she could manage. He'd thought she was different, but maybe it was the uniform after all. He couldn't regret it, but he missed the way she'd smiled when he'd taken the piss about her being a vegetarian, there in the pub.

Despite Lottie's almost irritable assurance that he needn't bother, Dan stood at the chilly doorway to wave her off. As she drove away, the throat-clearing cough of the clutch told him it was about to go. It was the sort of thing he'd mention, if they were together. What a day. When he crawled back into bed, it was still ambrosially warm, suffused with the scent of her hair. Girls.

The phone, the phone was brilliant, and Harmony would love Stu for ever for getting it for her, but. It was other things too. A tunnel through to the world she'd been missing. A way of connecting when she didn't have any contacts. A golden ticket and a reproach.

'Early birthday present,' he'd said, handing it to her one night when he got back late. She didn't know if he'd got it from a shop or bought it from someone he knew. It wasn't the latest version – Harmony suppressed a disloyal blip of disappointment as she realised – but it was a smartphone, and a billion times better than the antique Mum had passed down. Not an iPhone, obviously, because Apple. There was a proper contract, with hours of data and abundant texts. She knew how much Stu hated any form of admin, so the thought of him wrangling actual forms and payment plans touched her. The specialness of the effort confirmed her suspicion he had known Aurora was coming home, and hadn't been able to bring himself to tell her. The phone was a kind of compensation.

'Thought you could do with a boost, sort of thing.'

Since Mum spent most of each day in bed, there wasn't much difference between her being back and the time she'd spent away. Harmony spent much of her own time in her room, ostensibly revising but mainly on the phone. After a few days of cautious online exploration had emboldened her about her data allowance, she landed on a forum called MySecretHeart, dedicated to unrequited love. The posts enthralled her for hours, particularly those from Beetlebutt, who was a year younger than her and, thrillingly, about to have sex with her piano teacher. She'd been writing on the site nearly every day since early 2014. Harmony spent a rapt afternoon following the thread back to the very first post. Within the last week an older poster, Trujet79, who was in love with her married boss, undemonstratively in life but extravagantly on the site, had kicked off about Beetlebutt's plans, splintering the forum into equally absorbing factions of reproach and counter-reproach, threads of passionately irrelevant personal anecdote and blunt, repetitive trolling. Trujet79 viewed unrequited love as something close to a religious calling. Harmony suspected, along with the trolls, that the only reason Trujet79 had never declared herself to her boss, 'Mr G' (the G was for Gorgeous), was either because she was a) minging or b) a coward. Even more drily discouraging than Trujet79 were the naysayers who pointed out that Beetlebutt was underage and that her teacher (Thel) could lose her job and even be arrested as a sex offender. Harmony was rooting for Beetlebutt, out there in North Carolina. Like her, she was psyched.

Two more Declan lessons to go. Her English papers were first, ten days before maths. English Lit 1 was on Monday morning. She planned to spend most of the Sunday before in bed, going through *The Crucible* one last time. Mel had arranged for Harmony to sit her GCSE papers at St Benedict's, at the back of the hall full of legitimate pupils in their uniformed rows. Although Harmony was familiar with the grounds of St Ben's from waiting in Mel's car while she picked up the boys, and once from a summer fete she and Aurora had been invited along to (oh, Mum's mockery about that), she had never actually been inside the school building.

Auntie Mel had told her that St Benedict's would issue her with a clean copy of the play for the exam. Harmony's own *Crucible* was so overlaid with underlinings and circlings and scribbled notes that trying to read it properly was like attempting a sensible conversation while a toddler shouted at you and tried to climb your leg. Her concentration was meandering from Abigail and Proctor to the lure of her phone, angled near her thigh on a peak of crumpled duvet, when ongoing draggings and grunts on the landing finally enticed her to wonder what was going on outside her room.

Harmony listened as Stu, encumbered, puffed up and down the stairs from his bedroom – their bedroom, his and Mum's. What was he getting rid of? For a wild moment she thought it might be Aurora he was bumping heavily down the stairs. Hearing the back door open, she knelt on her bed to look through the smeared window down into the garden. Not Mum, then. Stu was dragging a cardboard box to join others, along with crammed plastic bags and bin liners, on what would be the lawn if they'd ever mowed or weeded it. Could a lawn be a lawn, untended, or was it just a patch of grass?

She watched, immediately queasy, as Stu upended one of the bags, releasing a cascade of old newspapers. Her window frame cut off the bottom of the view, so there was a small jump each time Stu disappeared to get the next load, reappearing with the contents of another bag or box and emptying them on the mounting pile, adding to the monochrome jumble of posters and magazines.

Not again.

At the next jump, Stu carried an armful of small plastic boxes that he scattered over the papers. The boxes were particoloured, black and transparent, in keeping with the colour scheme. Cassette tapes, or what Stu called mixtapes. Since the elderly ghetto blaster that still squatted in the kitchen as a radio had begun to shred any tape into gibbering ribbons, they had lacked the means to play them.

Next came a slithering cascade of vinyl, 45s, in brittle paper cases. They slid off the mound that was forming and settled at the edges, the unsuccessful icing on the cake. Seeing the records compelled Harmony to stir herself. Stu had a reconditioned turntable for the vinyl which was anally arranged in a corner of the living room, the only notably orderly part of the house. The neatly aligned rows of records were all logged in a little notebook he kept on one of the shelves, so that if one of his mates ever wanted to borrow one, he'd know it was out on loan. That was how precious his record collection was to him. The last time, the Christmas Harmony tried not to think about, it had only been papers headed for destruction.

Down in the living room, the floor was sticky beneath her bare feet. She was relieved to find the shelves of records undisturbed. Harmony slopped on a pair of Stu's old trainers and headed outside. Stu had finished emptying all the boxes and bin liners. Some of the plastic bags took flight in the wind, touching down on the grass before flailing against the hedge, escape aborted. Stu lit a rollie, his own gaze to the sea blocked by the ugly orange panel in the centre of the fence. The one destroyed by the row.

Up close to the bonfire-to-be, Harmony understood. Stu as he'd been about a century ago – well, last century – glared up at her from the pile, skinny and mean-eyed behind an artful triangle of hair, black and bouffant. On the cover of a yellowed *Melody Maker*, this time with the addition of a leather jacket, he defended his balls, his gang sullen behind him. Koolaid Conspiracy. He was going to torch the lot.

The older she got, the harder it had become to believe the story of Stu and his band. According to Mum and Mel, there had been great local excitement when Koolaid Conspiracy had got a record deal while still at school. Stu always liked telling that part of the story after a few beers – the two-record deal. For some years the band had ticked along, although the label had let them go after the second album (*Formica Puppetshow*), with Stu picking up session work and tweaking the line-up until he was the only original member. Harmony thought that when he and Aurora had first got together, Stu might still have been going to gigs and festivals in some sort of playing capacity, although this had transmuted, at what point she didn't know, into flipping burgers at the same venues.

Mum always took the piss about the band, in a way that suggested she had been pleased with Stu's ancient fame. Harmony hadn't understood her heavy jokes about groupies when she was smaller. Groupies seemed as unlikely as Stu's hair, but there were the pictures of the hair facing up at her now to prove it. You never knew.

Stu acknowledged her appearance in the garden by flicking the burning end of his rollie at the fence without moving his hand from his side, a stylish move he had, barely involving the thumb. Admiring it, Harmony recognised a bit of Stu from the poster, followed by another unwelcome insight into the adult abyss: style possibly counted for nothing. Imagine him having all that hair, once.

She turned and ran upstairs. Mum wasn't asleep; no one could sleep that much without being dead. There was a book in her hands as Harmony slammed into the bedroom, although she held it flat on the duvet in front of her, her eyeline dully resting on a point on the wall opposite.

'He's burning it all.'

'Hi, sweetie-pie. You look nice.'

Harmony ignored the hand held out to her and stayed bouncing at the door.

'He's made a bonfire. All the Koolaid Conspiracy stuff. Tapes, records ... '

Aurora dropped her hand back next to her book, blinking to disperse this news into her sedated understanding.

'Right.'

Harmony waited.

'He's going to burn it!'

The last time, that terrible Christmas Harmony thought of as their last Christmas, even though there had been a Christmas since, the bonfire had contained just a small portion of Stu's Koolaid Conspiracy trove, surmounted on that occasion by the framed gold record as its guy. In a way Harmony still couldn't understand, the Boxing Day fire had sparked from the embers of the row started at Mel and Ian's after Christmas dinner. Mum and Stu bickering their way back from Mel's in the dark of Christmas night was as traditional as Mel's donated Tupperwares full of leftovers, and that year's walk hadn't seemed to contain more than the usual level of pissed acrimony. But back home, the two of them opened Stu's Christmas-present bottle of tequila and stoked the quarrel, causing Harmony to cocoon her head in her pillow as the argument flared and roared downstairs. She'd been woken at a bleary, grey hour by Aurora screaming in the garden.

'Right then, OK, let's live in the present! Let's see how you feel about it! Clean sheet, why not?'

'Don't you fucking dare!'

It had been going on all night. Stu and Mum were both still in their Christmas Day clothes, snarling at each other in bathetic puffs of frosty air. Aurora was half-dragging, half-throwing the pile of Koolaid Conspiracy memorabilia Stu kept by his turntable out on to the bald, hoared grass.

'You accuse *me* of living in the past!'

'I'm not accusing you of anything, you mad bitch!'

'You're the one living in the bloody past, Stuart! Look at it! Load of fucking crap!'

Stu watched, helpless, as Aurora ran inside and came out brandishing the framed gold disc, which she dashed from a height on to the papers. It bounced off and landed on the ground, cracking the frame. Up to this point, Harmony had been content to monitor the situation from the relative warmth of her bedroom. But to Aurora's mystification as much as her own, Stu now dropped to his haunches and, instead of rescuing anything from the pile, took his Zippo from his pocket and flicked its long, unwavering flame up the damp newsprint, staring a challenge at Aurora.

'Fuck you doing?'

'Living in the present. That's what you want, right? Let's go for it. Great idea, Aurora. Here and now. Fuck it.'

The plastic at the corner of the gold record's frame started to blister. At this Aurora squealed, as viscerally as though her own flesh was burning. Harmony ran downstairs. When she reached the garden her mother was trying to prise the lighter away from Stu, who blocked her with his shoulder. As Aurora grabbed hold of his arm, struggling furiously for control of the Zippo, Stu, fighting to release himself, suddenly succeeded. The momentum of his freed elbow caught Aurora sharply under the jaw, snapping her chin up, and knocked her to the ground with unintended violence. Before she could regain her feet, or Stu get an answer to his appalled *are you OK*, Harmony, awakened to some atavistic instinct from their time in Bristol, had charged Stu and pushed him over into the barely singed pile, screaming at him to leave Mum alone. Aurora, undistracted, was already skittering towards the Zippo, dropped by Stu in the melee. As Stu fended off Harmony, his hands submissively lifted, Mum scooped the lighter from the grass and arced it triumphantly over the back fence, towards the sea road. Galvanised, Stu struggled up and launched himself with total, illogical anger straight after the Zippo. The fence panel buckled immediately under his clambering weight but he ignored it, his only hope to keep going. Hoisting his trailing foot to hurdle the top, he came down in a perfect *You've Been Framed* pratfall, the splintered silver wood twisted between his legs.

Aurora couldn't stop laughing. Her laughter was far worse to witness than the anger that had preceded it, a genuinely hysterical mixture of the exhibitionistic and involuntary that took minutes to subside. After Stu had stalked off to find his Zippo, he took the van and disappeared for the rest of the day. While he was gone, Mum silently disassembled the bonfire and put all the papers back in boxes, before taking them up to the loft, along with the warped gold record, which had previously hung in the kitchen. For some weeks the gap in the fence stood as a reminder, until they rang a man to come and fix it. He'd reassured them the bright orange wood would weather to match the rest, but over a year on it was still stridently out of place.

Stu, it turned out, had bitten his tongue quite badly as he fell. But that only came out later, because that night, walking through the gap in the fence to the sea, Aurora had tried to kill herself.

'He's burning everything this time,' Harmony told her now, from the door. As usual, the room was heavy with the sweet, fatty smell of the royal jelly hand cream Aurora kept in a tub next to the bed. She had brought it back from the nuns, who kept bees, all her self-care narrowed into the assiduous, constant lubrication of her hands.

'Records, tapes, everything.'

Aurora skewed her mouth, her eyes unaffected. 'That's a shame.'

'Can't you talk to him?'

Mum smoothed her hair behind her ears. The henna had grown out almost to the tips. Since it had got longer, she'd taken to a centre parting.

'Not really. It's up to him, really.'

A desperate angle presented itself.

'What about the fumes, from the plastic? It'll be, like, toxic.'

But even this had no effect. Hopelessly, Harmony closed the door on Mum's assertion that she could murder a cup of tea, if she was making. Back in the garden, instead of talking to Stu about Koolaid Conspiracy, Harmony asked him if he wanted a brew. He said, as he usually did, that he wouldn't say no. He rubbed at the shadow on his chin and neck as though his hand alone might erase it. The days Stu didn't work, he didn't shave, not even the night before, as per the bumcrack ritual.

No milk, of course. One of the things Aurora had once done, apart from everything else, was make sure there was milk in the fridge. Although Stu really wasn't bothered about the tea, he would be eventually. Harmony, feeling the need to offer up some small sacrifice to his misery, found her own shoes and told him she'd be back in a minute. After his gutless ''-kay!', she left him, still staring at the garish patch in the fence.

Harmony bought a Flake at the Spar along with the milk, and another for later. She'd given up on laxatives, a failure even at bulimia. The milk had just been a pretext to get hold of the chocolate, to eat it in secret. Another thought for the abyss: since Mum no longer cared what she ate, and Stu never had, she must crave the secrecy as much as the sugar. It wasn't a thought to stop her. Harmony was barely outside the shop before she was tearing into the packet. One hundred and thirty five calories, so not the end of the world. As with KitKats, there was a technique to Flakes. Biting was a waste, when there could be sucking and crumbling. She stood in the pissy corner not far from the bike stands, wholly absorbed until, with a small sadness, she shook the upended wrapper, with its final stumplet of chocolate and shower of crumbs, into her mouth.

'Harmony, is it?'

She was about to lick her forefinger, which she'd used to blot up the last sweet motes from the packet. It was the hot policeman, the one who'd been to Auntie Mel's house.

'PC Mason.'

'Yeah, I remember.'

Her chocolatey finger felt like a loaded gun. There was another cop with PC Mason, old and large. He was staring at her as though he'd arrest her the moment the Flake wrapper hit the pavement. But as the two of them barely broke their ambling stride while Mason spoke, she saw they weren't actually looking for her; they were heading up the hill, towards the little green.

'I was going to ask your auntie about you. Melanie . . . '

Now Mason stopped. Here it came. Had they already busted Katie? Hot Cop was looking at his partner for guidance. Harmony took the opportunity to shuck the chocolate from her finger, a careless in-out.

'Maybe I can save a bit of time?'

The partner, who seemed to be his boss, sighed, muttering *as if they didn't have enough to chuffing sort*. Harmony began to hear Mason against the panicked throb of her pulse. So, about the night she and Auntie Mel had found Storm, he said, patting around his pockets for his notebook.

'I wasn't there.'

PC Mason stopped with his hands at his pecs, elbows winged.

'The girl, on the beach.'

'Yeah. It was Auntie Mel who found her. She'd told me to stay inside, with Toothpaste. The dog.'

Fat Partner stood with his arms crossed. Was she Wasting Police Time?

'But – hang on. Mrs Bale said – didn't Mrs Bale say it was the dog who found the girl first?'

Harmony nodded vigorously. Not Wasting, but Helping.

'Yeah. I mean later. After Auntie Mel came to use the phone at ours. She told me to stay with the dog while she met the police car. So you'd know which bit of the beach to look on.'

Fat Partner ducked his head and looked up the hill, as though Harmony was making him laugh in a way he didn't find funny. But she could see his sour resignation was aimed at Mason: *I told you so.*

'So you weren't there on the beach at all?'

Mason was gentle; doubting himself before he doubted her. Harmony scrumpled the Flake wrapper into her palm. She couldn't bear it.

'I went out later. On my own. To see if I could see anything.'

She'd wanted to, hadn't she?

'So, right, this was *after* we'd picked the girl up?'

'I think so. I mean, I didn't see her or anything. Yeah, it must have been. It was really dark, and raining and everything.'

'And did you see anything else then? On the beach?'

His optimism renewed, Mason shovelled one hand into his trouser pocket. Fat Partner planted his legs and blew a breath up at the sky.

'What buggerlugs wants to know is did you see anyone else out there, love,' the older one said. 'A *man*. No?'

Despite addressing the question to her, he aimed the sarcasm at Mason like a rock in a catapult.

'Go on, show her.'

Stayed, Mason hesitated in unfolding the piece of paper he'd taken from his pocket. A photocopy. On it Harmony saw half of the blurred dark oval of a man's face, two eyes. But his partner's tone had changed his mind for him. He refolded the sheet.

'Never mind, Harmony. Another time, maybe.'

The old one was already walking back up the hill, bent as though he was fighting a much steeper gradient. Before Mason joined him, more upright, he shot Harmony an under-the-counter smile and winked. The space at the top of her head lifted in relief. He didn't blame her. His grin suggested they should both take the piss out of his mardy-arse boss.

'I did see something!'

She wasn't sure he heard her, so it didn't matter.

Back in the garden, the wind had already rearranged Stu's pyramid of memorabilia into something more lopsided. Stu was still out there, sitting and smoking another rollie, his back against the fence, legs stretched out, staring at the unlit mound. He must have been cold; surprising he hadn't started the fire just to keep warm. Harmony was about to say something along these lines when she saw Stu was crying. The rest of him was normal, smoking, sitting; there was no assistance to his face from his chest or shoulders. She had never seen him cry before. It might, she persuaded herself, just be the effect of the wind in his eyes.

She dismissed the thought of donating the second Flake; it wouldn't cheer Stu up the way it would her. She headed inside and put the kettle on. When she brought the tea out and set the mug on the grass (lawn?) next to him, the crying had stopped, though his face shone with unwiped tears.

'Sorry.'

The economy of her shrug indicated both that it didn't matter and her preference for no further reference to his grief, if that's what it was. 'Grief' sounded like something ripped from your guts, or the sound of seagulls. Every day the torment of them, hurled about the sky. They looked so fucking stupid, you'd never guess until you heard it. Maybe it was different for Stu. He was, after all, very different from her. He wasn't even her dad.

Why had she told that policeman she'd been on the beach?

Looking away towards the smeared kitchen window, Harmony remembered a Sunday afternoon soon after they'd moved in with Stu. That window steamed up by the veg curry simmering on the hob, her, Mum and Stu dancing around to Koolaid Conspiracy's biggest hit – biggest *chart* hit, Stu always corrected Mum – which came on the ghetto blaster radio on Radio 6, thanks to some Eighties DJ. Anyone remember this, the DJ said, 'You're to Blame', Koolaid Conspiracy, and the chords struck and Mum roared to Stu *it's you!* and grabbed Harmony and pogoed furiously, stopping to strike attitudes when the music did, snarling all the lyrics as a piss-take, though she was word perfect, with Stu laughing and only half-joining in as he took Harmony by the hand, so that for the last minute of the track they were a seething, jumping triangle, unironically transported by the pissed-off bass. They'd been happy then, all three of them, each particular happiness reflecting back from the happiness of the other two, so it proliferated endlessly even as it receded: the song, the three of them together, their new life.

Stu thumbed his ash into the grass with a juddering sigh, the only way his unwiped tears connected to his slumped body. Mum used to tease him about his belly, though it was only visible as a mild bulge over the top of his belt buckle, and only when he sat. She used to tease him about everything.

'Sorry,' he repeated.

Harmony had to say it this time. 'It's OK.'

He cranked his mouth into a cheerless smile.

'Two-record deal,' he said. 'Greatest day of my life.'

Harmony waited. Wind stroked the pages of the *NME*s, releasing a top note of mildew.

'Can't remember much about it, to be honest.'

'Drugs?'

Stu looked at her for the first time since she'd brought the tea, the shape of his mouth more genuinely amused.

'No, shit memory. Though that might be the drugs.'

What was the point of making jokes when you never laughed?

'Harmony . . . '

He sighed again, palmed one eye at a time as though it needed to be done and held out his hand so she had to help him. His hand was freezing. He stood with the same grunt he always gave when he got out of a chair, the noise Mum used to say meant he was turning into an old git. He never called her Harmony, usually. Was it ever a good sign when someone used your name to your face? He started to head inside.

'Aren't you going to light it?'

Stu looked back at the relics of his band.

'Fuck it.' He took a wincing slurp of tea. 'Bung it all on eBay. Why not? Might get a few quid.'

But later, when it began to rain, it was Harmony who ran to salvage armfuls before the paper was sodden to pulp, chasing the discs that slid from their packets and rolled across the grass in oily black circles. A spooled tape festooned the bare rose bush, fluttering raggedly through the unpruned branches. She left it there, like a pulled grey party popper, to blow away or not.

PC Mason wanted Mel to go into the police station. When she told him she wouldn't have time before Thursday, he arranged to come to the studio when she had a gap between lessons. She assumed his eagerness to talk to her concerned the 'development' he'd mentioned on the phone, the poor woman who thought Storm might be her daughter. His keenness in keeping her in touch with the case was flattering, although it weighted the umbilical gravity Mel already felt in having saved the girl's life. She was, somehow, responsible.

Mel told the policeman to drop in shortly before four. She had a private lesson before her general classes started, two nine-year-olds she was coaching for a competition duet. Performed to 'Gangnam Style' by an older pair, it had won gold medals on every outing. Now that the original girls had outgrown the routine, Mel had titivated some of what she'd learned to call the armography and updated the music to 'Uptown Funk' for Lola and Kitty Sue. Physically well matched, they were both expressive, lithe little dancers, but it was Kitty Sue's mum's vicarious ambition Mel could rely on to finesse the girls to comp-winning slickness. Edward had tried to make her watch *Dance Moms*, but as far as Mel was concerned it was coals to Newcastle. Monumental and painstakingly groomed, Kitty Sue's mum sat in on the lesson, balancing her mobile in its bedizened case between the tines of her jewelled fingernails to track the girls' every move. With the routine on her phone, Mel knew she would drill them at home to unfaltering perfection.

It was amazing to think that, for a few early teenage years, Mel and Aurora, then Dawn, had formed a similar partnership. Mrs Beagles had forbidden parents access to private lessons, so the two of them never benefited from Mrs Ansholm putting them through their paces to 'Rasputin' by Boney M, even if she'd wanted to. Instead they used to push the furniture back in the Ansholms' tiny living room and practise by themselves. Ignorant of the lyrics, although Mrs Beagles had made the gesture of adorning their disco spandex with rows of vaguely Prussian frogging, they had whirled and flashed across the competition stage; taller Mel hoisting whippety little Dawn recklessly through her legs and up into perilous, limber balances. They had won medals. Over the years, at family gatherings after drink had been taken, the two of them were traditionally persuaded to reproduce some of the more spectacular parts of the routine. This stopped once Aurora and Stu got together. Stu couldn't bear Boney M, even as nostalgia.

For the lesson's half hour, Mel enjoyed the pleasant absorption of four people at work. When Kitty Sue's mum opened the door to release the girls to the changing room, PC Mason was already waiting in the corridor, scanning the trio of Blu-Tacked religious posters above the coat hooks; gospel quotes in italics superimposed on a sunset over tranquil sea, ears of wheat haloed by refracted sunbeams and a clean-jawed father piggybacking a rapturous baby.

Mel ushered the officer into the humid church hall. PC Mason never wore, or carried, either a helmet or cap. Perhaps this was no longer compulsory? Or did he leave it in the car, signifying an unofficial visit?

'When you said studio . . . '

He was right. Mel never thought of the oddity of referring to the church hall as her studio, by virtue of the barre and the tradition bequeathed by Mrs Beagles.

'Thanks for taking the time, Melanie. I can see you're busy.'

For a moment Mel saw their Joseph in the uniform, deploying this democratic politeness. Not that she could imagine him even considering such a sanctioned path to maturity. Since the break-up with Lottie, Joe had reverted to a parody of teenage selfishness, barely speaking, scattering surfaces with the leavings of oddly timed snacks and depleting the airing cupboard of towels, cavalierly abandoned wherever he felt himself adequately dry from his even more oddly timed baths. Mel hadn't felt able to delve into the nature of the rift. Aidan had reported, with a man-of-the-world air, that 'Joe chucked *her*', which was a surprise, if true. She was bracing herself for a conversation about whether the end of the relationship meant Joseph's gap year plans were back on track, although she sensed a delicacy in the timing. Too soon, and she risked Joe opting into inertia purely out of pique at her interference; too late, and his current inertia would become insurmountable. Was PC Mason's mum proud of him? Did he wash his own towels?

Mel offered Mason the stacking chair lately warmed by Kitty Sue's mum. He gallantly indicated that she should be the one to sit, so instead they both stood as he told her about Mrs Harvey and her fruitless journey to stir Storm's memory.

'But you'll be able to tell ... '

'When it comes to it. DNA, and dental records.'

They had, he said, already checked Storm's teeth as part of her medical exam. She had no dental work at all. Not a single filling.

'Someone's been looking after her then,' said Mel.

'Or she's just lucky.'

Mel's face must have expressed her opinion of that.

'With her teeth, I mean.'

Mel pointed out that the little girl who went missing would, at five, only have had her baby teeth. Surely that made dental records useless anyway? PC Mason paused in taking a folded oblong of paper from his pocket. She had a point, he said, merely polite. His unconcern suggested to Mel that he had some other view of where Storm had come from, and it wasn't Devon.

'Now then ... '

The policeman unfolded the paper: had Mel seen this man anywhere? Mel craned back to find her optimum viewing distance. The sheet's upper third contained an uncentred colour photocopy of a passport page. The image, still less than crisp without her glasses, was of a glowering, dark-haired man in his thirties. She confirmed this from the date of birth lower on the page: 1979. Although everyone looked criminal in passport photos, he looked criminal. Obviously he had something to do with Storm. She checked the name: Nicu Vidraru.

'Romanian? Is he from the vans?'

Mason nodded.

Ian used Romanian builders. Although he only referred to

a couple of men by name, the ones who profited from having the best English and who translated for their mates, Mel knew he considered most of the other men hard-working and, to a Yorkshireman, not unsympathetically dour. She wondered about the tax situation. If this man had had any dealings with Ian, Mason might be niggling at the end of a very tangled ball of string.

'Does he ring any bells, Melanie?'

Fortunately, the man didn't. If Nicu Vidraru had been there, skulking away from Storm's body even as Mel followed Toothpaste towards it, she hadn't seen him. She understood what Mason was laying out for her; that this man had dumped Storm off Brazen Point, stripped her and possibly worse; left her for dead. A vicious boyfriend, or a vengeful pimp. But if Mel or anyone else had seen him that night, it could only matter to the police. Forcibly connecting the girl to some horrible or criminal past wasn't the help she needed. If she couldn't remember it, why force her?

'We're wondering if he might know some relatives of hers. Or even be a relative of some kind himself.'

A relative was different. Family was a past that might permit the girl a future.

'You don't think, then, he's – that he was responsible for what happened to her?'

'I wish I could say, Melanie. Obviously we were just thinking, with her not talking – maybe she's not English.'

'I thought that.'

There, she'd said it. He didn't take it the way Joseph would. He agreed with her. He was frustrated, PC Mason explained, that no one in the force except him was prepared to make any kind of effort. The police seemed to have accepted that Storm was the responsibility of social services with a bit of input from the NHS, and to be perfectly honest, as far as he could see she wasn't getting the cream of the crop, doctor-wise.

While he was saying this, Mel's phone, laid out on the stage next to her sound system and bottle of water, knelled an incoming text.

'I blame myself, to be honest. She deserves better than we're giving her.'

Mel, with one eye on her phone, agreed. Mason took her distraction as his cue to leave. His departure stirred interest from some of the mums depositing their daughters for Intermediate Tap; Mel supposed it was the uniform.

The text, unusually, was from Stu. Even more unusually, he was asking if she was around the following day as he 'might drop by'. Mel's small speculation about what could be up halted an immediate reply, and then the Intermediate Taps were streaming in and she was swept up in snaffling culprits for chewing gum and ungroomed hair. After that, Stu's text slipped her mind completely until the doorbell went at home the next day, around noon.

When Mel saw Stu at the door she flinched in belated recollection. Her self-reproach as she let him in was immediately superseded by the shock of him offering her a bunch of flowers. In the countless times Stu had been to their house, both before Aurora and after, Mel couldn't remember him bringing anything other than beers, and those for his own consumption. The bouquet was a supermarket bunch with the price sticker still on. Yellow lilies weren't her favourites, but they were a step up from a garage bouquet and she had the right vase to put them in.

'Those for me?'

She left them in the sink, to deal with later. Given the time, he was almost certainly expecting lunch. She busked by asking if he fancied a glass of wine.

'I'm in the van.'

'One glass.'

She headed for the fridge. Whatever was coming, alcohol might help, on both sides.

'Go on then.'

Toothpaste stood with his muzzle in Stu's cupped hands, eyes narrowed, as Stu's thumbs worked at the roots of his ears. He adored Stu. All dogs did. It might have been the smell of sausages on his clothes.

Mel took out a half-drunk screw-top bottle of Pinot Grigio from the fridge door. Weekday wine.

'You should get a dog.'

Stu released Toothpaste and inched tobacco and papers from the front pocket of his jeans.

'Couldn't, could I? Wouldn't be fair. I couldn't have a dog in the van all day.'

His eyes were pouched and he hadn't shaved. Mel was struck by how much, now, he looked like their dad, though she had always been the one agreed to bear the resemblance. Did that mean she and Stu finally looked alike, now Stu was looking bollock-rough? She always thought of him as he'd been in Koolaid Conspiracy, a wiry stick of liquorice in his black jeans and t-shirt, all that black hair dyed to match. Like their parents, though with pride where they'd felt only horror, she'd watched him parade himself on stage and wondered where he'd come from. Now it seemed very clear that he came from the same place she did.

Roll-up made, Stu took it out into the garden with the wine glass, Toothpaste trotting after him. Mel had no choice but to follow. She'd put the oven on to warm a couple of past-ies sacrificed from the boys' tea and the salad just needed tipping out of the bag. It was freezing out there, though her bulbs were well out, the crocuses a sulphurous yellow she preferred to the chrome of Stu's lilies.

'So, to what do I owe this honour?'

She wished she could stop saying things like that. Stu inhaled and looked down at his feet.

'Thing is. I mean ...' He slid first one foot back, then the other, stamping on each return. He always did that, Mel realised as soon as he did it. He blew a plume of smoke. 'It's over a year, and that.'

So that was it: Aurora. Softening, Mel told him she knew it couldn't be easy. Stu sighed, smoked.

'You know she hasn't really been around much. Thing is ...'

Mel felt her guts drop – was he buttering her up to tell her he'd met someone else? She wouldn't blame him. She wouldn't even mind, particularly. It was purely the dread she felt when anyone did anything surprising. It had been the same when Stu and Aurora had first announced their relationship. Since Aurora's withdrawal had begun to reveal the shape of something damaged and intractable, Mel had looked into her heart and relived the violent emotions she'd endured after that fateful barbecue. Hadn't it been shock, above anything?

Aurora had been the one to tell her they were a couple. Stu didn't dare, his cowardice belying Aurora's blitheness. The story was, they had always fancied each other, ever since school. If so, neither of them had confided this to Mel, who as Dawn's best friend might have been expected to know. The day Aurora broke the news was the first time, school included, the two of them had had anything approaching a proper argument. Mel shouted some strangled home truths, robustly batted back by Aurora, who accused her of jealousy. At this, Mel stropped off, despite the row taking place in the then unconverted kitchen of her own new house, the very house in which she and Stu were now about to eat their pasties. Oblivious, Mel had slammed the door behind her with a dramatic vow not to speak to Aurora again without an apology. When she crept back, about ten minutes later, Aurora had had the good grace to leave.

She turned up the following day cradling a large Thorntons Easter egg, the biggest they stocked. She had paid to have it iced with the inscription 'Sorry I got off with your brother.' It was neatly done, in curled white script. It had taken the woman at Thorntons all her professional effort to fit it on to the egg, and, as Aurora pointed out, at ten pence a letter it hadn't been cheap. She hadn't asked for the full stop, she told Mel, and after a small altercation the Thorntons woman hadn't charged her for it. That was the thing: Aurora did make her laugh, always had, whatever she was called. It didn't occur to Mel until she'd polished off most of the chocolate that the gesture was the apology of someone who wasn't sorry in any way.

Eleven years on, Mel had yet to accept the legitimacy of Stu and Aurora's relationship. Not because they weren't married; even she wasn't that bad. But in the place where she put all the feelings and thoughts too offensive, negative, ridiculous or mad to share with Ian or Joseph – a large and sordid repository, like the wheelie bin behind a dodgy restaurant – she hadn't budged from her original position that Stu was cunt-struck and Aurora needed a meal ticket. And – she delved to the slime at the bottom – she'd been disappointed by what Aurora was prepared to settle for. If Stu was the best Aurora could do, with all her claims on a better life … Was that why Aurora was depressed, or having a breakdown, or recovering from a breakdown? Perhaps getting together with Stu all those years before had in fact been the very first, delayed-action symptom.

Beside her, her brother stamped the ground, devastating the tender spring grass. She waited for him to come out with it. Finally he did. He didn't think Harmony should live at home any more, as long as Aurora remained in her current state.

'It's not like I'm her dad.'

Well, no, said Mel, holding all the buts in a queue. But you're as good as; but she doesn't have anyone else; but what else is she supposed to bloody do? Then, as Stu squinted up at her for the first time, she knew what he was going to say as he took the breath to say it.

'Maybe she can come and live with you and Ian. Just till Aurora sorts herself out. I mean, she might bugger off again, I don't know.'

The early wine sped annoyance through Mel's system. Right, then. Was Stu's uneasiness just in asking the question, or apprehension that they'd say no? What choice did they have? Big house, Joe about to leave, on paper at least … They both watched Toothpaste cock his leg against the birch by the fence.

Stu pointed out that it wasn't Aurora's fault she was suffering.

'It's her fault she refuses to be helped.'

'Come off it, Mel, that's not fair. She's tried all sorts.'

They'd take Harmony, of course. She told Stu over the pasties that she'd have to talk to Ian, but she knew Ian would have fewer reservations than she did. He'd raised the unorthodoxy of Stu and Harmony's situation months ago, shortly after Aurora had come out of the psychiatric hospital and taken to her bed, a phrase Ian himself had introduced that continued to do service for the mystery of what was actually wrong with her. No one had a stronger or more untroubled sense of duty than Ian. He was right; both men were. Harmony needed a home.

Stu ate his lunch in scarcely chewed, frowning bites. Another thing Mel always forgot until she saw it again: the way her brother dealt with food as though it was a problem, quickly solved. Aurora dawdled over a plate, deconstructing pies and disassembling casseroles with careless passes of her fork, more interested in talking than eating. On her return from Bristol one of her holistic affectations had been to claim food that had cooled to room temperature was easier to digest. But even at school, Mel remembered, they were always the last to leave the lunch table. She must have minded, even then. Hanging around for Aurora when she'd have bolted her own meal as rapidly as Stu had just devoured his.

She poured each of them a few bonus centimetres of wine.

'Thing is, I've taken something on.'

This was a lie. The thought of offering Storm somewhere to live had just surfaced, compellingly complete, in the wake of the idea of Harmony invading the spare room. Hadn't gorgeous PC Mason as good as said the police were doing nothing for the girl? And surely the NHS couldn't stump up for ever for this clinic they were keeping her in. Presumably at some point the only option left would be to put her into social housing, with or without some kind of medical support.

'But this is your niece we're talking about,' Stu objected. 'This other lass is a complete stranger. And some sort of ... mental case.'

'She's not a mental case. She's just lost her memory.'

'Lucky her, eh?' He threw back the last of his wine like he was doing shots.

Anyway, said Mel, they had room for both. She promised she'd talk to Ian. At the door, she thanked Stu for the flowers in the only way possible: ironically. Stu's grin acknowledged the lame manipulation of his gesture. Looking down to scrub the top of Toothpaste's head goodbye, he told her that settling Harmony with them would allow him to leave Evensand altogether. 'Fresh start,' was the phrase he produced.

Mel tasted reawakened dread. 'Where?'

It struck her that Stu's business partner, Craig, lived in Selby. That wouldn't be the end of the world. They'd been talking about expanding the business, getting a bigger van. But how was Aurora meant to fit in with this grand plan? Mingled with Mel's irritation at her brother's ready selfishness was the frisson of possibility that such a radical gesture might give Aurora the boot up the bum she needed. Or failing that, just a boot up the bum.

'Maybe Australia? If they'll have me. It's tricky, all the applications.'

Australia, for God's sake. No wonder he'd brought her flowers. He didn't dare look up from the dog.

'Might be too old.'

'Course you're too old!'

Stu recoiled, his eyes as wounded as a child's. Mel wouldn't have said it without the wine. She hugged him to make up for it, suckering his ear in an aggressive, misaimed kiss.

'I suppose you never know, eh?'

She waved him off. That was Stu; not fifty-three, but perennially fifteen. Ready to form a band, imagine himself somewhere else, get together with Aurora. All these changes people made, to disguise the ways they couldn't change. Sometimes it felt like she and Ian were the only people on earth who didn't live in a fantasy world. Back inside, she woke up her laptop. The rhythm of thuds and door slams from upstairs indicated Joseph was finally stirring. If he didn't get a move on, he'd be late for his shift at Scoffs. She wouldn't interfere. She hadn't interfered about Lottie and that had ended happily. As far as she was concerned, anyway. Blowing a pasty crumb from the keyboard, Mel nerved herself to google Elizabeth Harvey and Eleanor Barker. What if that was where Storm truly belonged? Perhaps it was the happy ending the girl deserved. It didn't mean, of course, she'd get it.

Dan had had to give himself a talking-to, to sustain Storm's dilemma as his default preoccupation. Like getting out to the gym, it took just a little effort, and as with the gym, he'd benefited from upping his reps. Without the discipline of this self-imposed investigation, time, which stretched so glutinously when he was waiting in the car or writing up statements, inclined him to aching thoughts of Lottie. But it flowed properly again whenever he encouraged himself to check out Nicu and the question of what he might have been up to the night Storm appeared on the beach, trawling the database for any incidents to do with prostitution or trafficking in the area. Nice Claire in the office probably assumed Dan's requests for paper files were footwork he was carrying out for CID, which in the end he may well be doing, sparing them the arse ache of this stage of enquiries.

For the moment, though, it was an exercise purely for his own good. Soccolo's response to Dan's attempt to question Harmony Ansholm when they'd encountered her outside the Spar on Warmington Road had flagged up the idiocy of letting his partner glean even a small part of what he was up to. So Mason kept his counsel as he helped Soccolo grumble his way through the other Storm-related approaches that had continued to trickle in. The deluge of mismatched runaways had almost dried up. They had put in a request for a better jpeg of a Dutch girl thought to have taken off from a trip to London to go and join a cult, but as Soccolo said, peering at the Interpol scan, if it was the same girl he'd eat his own ballsack. To their mutual relief, Liz Harvey had been passed on to CID and the bad news awaiting her from the swab taken from Storm's mouth.

Still, every time Dan logged on to the PNC, he could hear Soccolo point out that their job was to respond to *reports* of a crime and pursue possible *perpetrators* of crimes; in the case of Storm, no actual crime had been reported. Why Mason wanted to make work for them both, given that they had calls and paperwork coming out of their ears, arse and nostrils morning, noon and night, Soccolo would be at a loss to fathom. Unless Dan was brown-nosing his way into CID?

Perhaps he was. But despite his efforts, he hadn't been able to build much of a case on the shadier side. Prostitution in Evensand was restricted to a contained street trade of familiar junkies near the old bus station, a building perennially reprieved from demolition by a pointless preservation order and the locus for what little crime the town had. On top of that were a few brothels run cosily in houses and a solitary massage parlour, its street façade and accounting impeccable. Vice got more ambitious and chaotic towards Whitby, but Dan was nervous about encroaching that far in case his investigations sparked interest from out of his jurisdiction.

What Dan really needed was something to tie Nicu solidly

to vice, and then to Storm on the crucial night. Only then was there a possibility of CID taking Mason's theories seriously. He thought of Nicu as Uncle Nicu, because of his relationship to Timi, but also as Drac. The Drac thing was because of Whitby, home of the Count, and the Romanian's aura of lugubrious menace. Romania, Transylvania; they were close, weren't they? Weren't they even the same country?

As close, probably, as Whitby was to Evensand. So, completely different. Nicu was officially a plumber, the kind who worked on building sites rather than the kind who came and sorted out your ballcock. Installation, not repairs. He was on a big job at the edge of Goathland, where a new estate was popping up with unreassuring speed. It was being built by the same company responsible for Dan's house. Dan was currently acquainting himself with the gaps – some of them literally gaps – between the dream of the show home and the reality of what he was paying his mortgage for. Only that morning, the handle to the bog had come off in his hand while he attempted to force the lax flush. He had been surprised to see that the handle was white on the inside, plastic sprayed silver, though the flimsiness of it should have alerted him. When he tried to reattach it, the cistern itself, with an alarming though self-limiting heaviness, had shifted down the wall a few centimetres. Dan had no idea about that sort of thing, how to restore the cistern to its proper angle. Never had a dad to teach him. Maybe Nicu himself was responsible for the faulty installation.

Lottie knew his toilet didn't work. She also knew the size of his cock, which did. Dan had tried a few texts after their night together, keeping it light. It was fairly clear from her stone-cold lack of response that she wanted nothing to do with him.

In the patrol car, with Soccolo segueing from *Game of Thrones* into his review of Mrs S's Wednesday-night tagine, Dan resisted checking his phone for its lack of messages from Lottie and went at the problem of Storm the other way. He dearly wished he could put the girl in a room with Nicu, to see if he sparked any recognition from her. But he had no grounds yet for taking Nicu into custody, and even if he had been able to persuade him to turn up to the clinic voluntarily, which was unlikely, there was Lennox to bar the way. The shrink had been furious to come back from leave and find out about the meeting between Storm and Liz Harvey. Soccolo's contempt for the email Lennox had sent to Hildebrand, about Dan and Soccolo 'crassly overstepping the mark with a highly vulnerable patient', had been balm for Dan's soul.

'Chuffing nutter himself, if you ask me.'

Pre-shag, Dan would have been able to exploit Lennox's wankery over the Harvey meeting to get Lottie onside about putting Nicu and Storm together. But that was a no-go, all ways round.

After a tetchy morning on patrol, they returned to the station, where Soccolo went from being out of sorts to being stricken with the shits. So much for Mrs S's famous tagine. Or maybe she'd finally clocked that he was shagging about and taken revenge: laxatives in the lamb. Soccolo conducted a shaky conversation through the toilet stall door. He was apologetic about the stench, which was extreme, as were the sound effects. He'd have to sign himself off sick. Gratefully, Dan saw his afternoon open out. Without Soccolo there, he could accommodate his own investigations around any call-outs.

But Dan immediately regretted Soccolo's absence when the first call came: the latest instalment in the Ruswarp leylandii saga. A trip to the magistrates' court had calmed both parties down, as Soccolo had predicted, but as he had also predicted, this was temporary. Yesterday the neighbour had rung in to complain that the hedge maniac was failing to observe the undertaking of keeping the hedge at a maximum of two metres. And now Hedge Man was calling to report damage to his property; the hedge trimmer had conducted another raid to lop off the offending centimetres. Dan wasn't jumping for joy about tackling either of them solo.

'Now then.'

Twenty minutes later, Mason stood at the door of Nathan Latimer, grower of The Hedge. Soccolo's counsel had been to talk to him first. Apparently, of the two unreasonable parties, he was the less unreasonable. Latimer had grown the leylandii to monster proportions in response to the trimmer, Laurence Andjati, going high-handedly batshit about its existence in the first place, a point Latimer himself made to Dan on the doorstep.

'I only grew fucking hedge because he was on about noise fucking dogs were fucking making all time.'

Latimer didn't send out ideal neighbour signals, given the neglect of the front garden, the weathered St George flag draped from an upstairs window and the duo of baying Staffies that strained on their chains as Latimer answered the door. But Andjati's repeated calls to the station and his assiduous filming of his neighbour's comings and goings – hedge-related or not – had understandably wound the other man up. Latimer had an assault conviction from nearly ten years back, but Andjati didn't know that. Of the two, Andjati alone had faith in the police, despite them finding him a colossal pain in the arse.

At the door, Dan was careful to emphasise that he was there in response to Latimer's own call about damage to his property.

'Constable!' This was Andjati, already rounding the boundary, out of his door like a missile launched by the arrival of the police car. Dan turned to him, standing firm.

'I'll be with you in a moment, sir.'

'Seven centimetres over the limit!'

'Fuck off!' Latimer addressed the neighbour, not Dan. 'Cunt!'

The dogs, hoisted by their collars, scrabbled the air frantically, desperate for a taste of uniform. Dan raised his voice against their volley of barking to suggest he come into the house to talk about it. He attempted, with a twitch of his head, to indicate his aim was to escape Andjati, who was waving a metal tape measure extracted to display the offending seven centimetres.

Latimer, surprised, shut the dogs in the kitchen and invited Dan in, no further than the hall, its floral wallpaper flayed up to dog level. But the tactic worked. Dan's presence calmed things down, until next time, or the time when Andjati might provoke his neighbour to the point of violence and he or Soccolo would come too late. A punch to the head, a kicking. It was funny, until it wasn't.

It was only back in the car, lungs ballooning a breath twice the capacity of any he'd taken for the last half an hour, that Dan realised how anxious he'd been, weighing in without backup.

People were nuts, that was the trouble. And so much of their unpredictability came from predictable addictions; in Mr Andjati's case, to being right. Dan's months in the job had opened his eyes to a world fundamentally divided, not between right and wrong, as he'd have told you when he started training, but between stress and boredom. It was medication of one or the other that generated the raw stuff of his working day, which itself travelled along that spectrum. But while Mason hated his own boredom, he didn't like it when the stress came either. Hedge Wars, in combining the two, was truly the worst of all worlds.

The journey back from Ruswarp took Mason right by the entrance to Oceancrest, the eroded optimism of its sign more dismal than ever in the unfiltered spring sunshine. He slowed the car. Timi? She was a way in, but Dan knew that route too well. The yellow foam mattress, the guilt. He didn't have the heart for it. Turning away from Oceancrest, it was barely a diversion to the crescent adjacent to Brazen Point: Whitecliff Road. Dan only allowed it to occur to him as he parked that his arrival at Malcolm White's house might clash again with one of Lottie's appointments. They must stop meeting like this, in the way they hadn't since their night together. The smell of her hair, animal and sweet. Lottie, now she was definitely more stressful than boring. When he saw her car wasn't on the street, he felt a jarring drop of disappointment. He encouraged himself onward, professional.

The Whites' porch, as Mason waited for someone to answer the Big Ben doorbell, was close and dewed with condensation, the geraniums dry in their margarine tubs, silted with dead leaves. Dan prepared himself for Malcolm, but the door was answered by an elderly man. His hand as it appeared on the wood, knobbed with arthritis, made sense of the fumbling delay. He was a dapper old gent, eye whites ringed yellow with age, but wearing an ironed dark green shirt and with some Brylcreem slicking back and darkening to toffee a few strands of hair still the same butterscotch shade as his son's.

Mason's explanation of who he was and why he was there travelled slowly, due either to deafness or senility. After a delay, Dan saw the moment when understanding lit the old man's eyes.

'Do you have any ID?'

Their public information campaign about cons on the elderly was clearly reaching its target. Mason was in full uniform, topped off by a high-vis gilet bannered with 'police' and his radio strapped to his jacket. Taking this in, Malcolm's dad still didn't budge the door a centimetre. Dan pointed to his car.

'That do you?'

As the old man blinked in the words, Dan feared he might be in for a long wait, but a smile belatedly lit the tortoise face and he stepped back to open the door wide to him.

In the musty living room, Mr White made no move either to open the blinds or switch on a light. After some increasingly irritable shouting upstairs ('It's the police! The police!'), Malcolm made an appearance, his pudding bowl hair feathered up at the back and his face bleared with sleep, though he was fully dressed, in what looked like the identical clothes to Mason's previous visit. The three of them stood in an anxious triangle, Malcolm at its apex, twiddling his fingers and looking between Mason and his dad for a cue.

Dan decided to go loud and slow as he recapped what Malcolm had said about the girl being put in the water.

'She's lost her memory,' Mr White told him.

'That's right.'

'Not a stitch on her,' he added, unsalaciously.

'No.'

'They took her clothes away.' Malcolm's speech jerked out through his teeth.

'Did they?' Mason leaned in. 'Who?' Malcolm glanced at his dad, looking for the answer.

'We don't know if they did!' Mr White's tone with his son was far more emphatic than was warranted. Exasperation seemed to be his factory setting.

'Did you see anyone taking clothes away, Malcolm, down on the beach?' asked Dan. Malcolm now looked very worried indeed.

'You haven't done anything wrong.'

Malcolm jerked an arm. 'I were in me bedroom.'

Did he mean just now? Dan recalled the confusion about his mother's death. Lottie, again.

'You mean the night of the big storm?'

Malcolm looked again to his dad.

'Speak up, lad!' shouted Mr White. 'He wants to know if you were in your bedroom the night there was that big storm. When the satellite dish came down.'

Malcolm wrung his clasped hands, washing them of distress.

'Can't remember,' he said finally. Dan didn't believe him, which was quite exciting. He asked if it might be possible to see the bedroom. Although he told Mr White he could stay downstairs, and would have preferred it, since he seemed determined to jump in and answer any question aimed at his son, the old man insisted on toiling up with them, hoisting himself stair by stair with a doggedly advancing grip on the banister.

Malcolm's room stood above the living room, and shared

its astonishing view of the left scoop of Evensand beach as far as Brazen Point. The house must be worth a bob or two, with a view like that. Dan was interested to see a cheap pair of binoculars on the windowsill, the kind you might get as a free gift. As he moved to the window, his feet dislodged narrow strips of newspaper, arranged over the carpet in an unfathomable pattern. Untorn papers waited in a stack by the bed, a double-page spread fanned on the carpet in readiness. What was that about? No doubt Lottie would have been able to explain, what with her module.

'Bloody mess in here.' Mr White kicked aside the paper strips. But the bed was made, Dan saw, its faded pink duvet pulled up to the pillow. Both were indented, as though Malcolm had been sleeping above the covers. When Malcolm joined him at the window, Dan took in a breath of his unwashed clothes.

'Not fit for visitors.'

Mr White stooped to pick up the newspaper, his warped hands ineffectual against the subtleties of paper and carpet.

'Tears them up . . . '

'Nice pair of bins,' said Dan. 'Mind if I take a look?'

Malcolm shook his head. He almost smiled. Next to the binoculars stood a framed photograph of a thinner, adolescent Malcolm. He was flanked by a round-featured middle-aged woman who must have been his late mum, and a small sprite of a girl, presumably a sister. Both hugged up to him, the girl pulling a distorting face at the camera.

'He likes looking at the birds!' Mr White exclaimed, from halfway to the floor, as if birdwatching was his son's surmounting eccentricity.

'You're in the right place then, eh?'

Lifting the binoculars, Dan calibrated the crude focus

sitting at the bridge of his nose. His brain took a moment to make sense of what it was seeing: the indignant eye of a gull; then, with a swoop, the buff and white feathers of its wing. The bins' magnification was better than their appearance suggested. Dipping them to check the normal view, he saw the bird alighting on a rock at least a hundred metres away, out where the tide was starting to turn.

'That's where they found the other one,' Mr White informed him.

'What other one?'

'Damn thing.' The old man righted himself, abandoning his attempts to tidy the scraps of paper. He regarded Dan balefully.

'There was another girl, wasn't there? Just after the war. There were still Yanks up where the vans are. GIs, you know. Darkies and all sorts.'

Mason's nan had told him all about the GIs. She'd had a good war.

'They found her down there, dead as a doornail. Strangled with her own stocking. She'd have got that from the GIs and all ... they reckoned it was a GI that did it. It was still round her neck. Nylons ... '

'Did they catch him?'

Mr White planted a wavering hand on the edge of the bookcase next to Malcolm's bed, launching himself to join them at the window.

'Did they heckers like – they'd all buggered off back to America!'

He pointed to the outcrop where Mason had focused the binoculars.

'That's where she was. He'd put her in the sea but the sea washed her back.'

The empty waves skimmed in, ebbing back up the beach. Going even as they came. Despite a lifetime next to the sea, tides did Dan's head in. Watching the sea for any length of time was like walking up the down escalator.

'She was no better than she should be, if you get my drift.'

This, as though shielding Malcolm from dodgy sexual realities. Given that Mr White was roughly the same age as Dan's nana, Malcolm must be at least as old as Dan's own dad. Wherever he may be.

'I were a Bevin Boy.'

Mason had no idea what this was. Some kind of youth club, or something to do with the war? He raised the binoculars again. There was no doubt that if Malcolm had been at his post the night of the storm, he'd have been able to see what happened to the girl, despite the weather. Whoever had taken Storm on to the beach must have used a torch, or at least the torch on a phone.

Dan reached into his breast pocket, beneath his crackling handset, for the photo of Nicu he'd got off the PNC. It was the same blurred screen grab of Nicu's passport image he'd shown to Melanie Bale, and tried to show to Harmony. It didn't particularly look like Nicu once you'd met him, but it was enough for a rough idea, age and size and hair colour. Dan startled Malcolm by holding the printout out to him.

'Have you ever seen this man, Malcolm?'

Malcolm's focus yo-yoed between Dan's face and the sheet of paper, assessing what he was supposed to say. Before he could speak, his father tugged the sheet off him to get a better look.

'What's this in aid of?'

'Hang on, Mr White, I wanted to see if Malcolm had seen him.'

'Why would he have seen this feller?' Then, accusingly, 'Have you seen him, lad?' Under his father's glare, Dan saw Malcolm's confidence dwindle from imminent speech to bewildered silence. Excluding Mr White with a turn of his shoulder, Mason made an effort to speak gently.

'Did you, Malcolm? It doesn't matter, one way or the other. You've not done anything wrong.'

'You've done nothing wrong,' Mr White echoed.

Malcolm nodded, unsure. Dan tried to look as neutral as possible.

'You did see someone?'

Another nod, less tentative.

'They had a row.'

'Did they now? Where did you see them?'

Malcolm's eyes cannoned from Dan to his father. Asperger's, Lottie had said. But wasn't that autism? And didn't autism mean no feelings? Malcolm seemed to Mason to be a mass of feelings, trying to attune themselves to those of others. If anyone was bloody autistic it was the dad.

'Down there,' Malcolm said suddenly, crooking an arm to the view.

'Right. When was that?'

Malcolm hesitated. Just as Dan could feel Mr White summon the next command to squash him into silence, his son managed to push the words past his teeth.

'February the twentieth.'

No one had put that date in his mouth.

'You're sure? February the twentieth, out on beach?'

Malcolm nodded. February the twentieth was the night of the storm. Malcolm White, you little beauty. It was all coming together, thanks to no one but Dan.

The morning of the English exam, Harmony's brain was awake and racing well before both the alarm clock and the alarm on her phone. Mel still rang an hour before she was due to pick her up to make sure she was getting ready. She was, just about. Good, said Mel, because she needed to drop her and Aidan off early and would be there in five minutes. She made this change of plan sound as though it was Harmony's fault.

'Have you had breakfast?'

Mel asked this in the car; another accusation. She had been too nervous for breakfast, Harmony lied, adding truthfully that Stu had brought her a cup of tea before he took off for work. Mum, naturally, was still asleep when she left. She was actually feeling a bit sick. The previous night she'd eaten a family-sized Dairy Milk and a packet of shortbread. She didn't even like shortbread much. She'd bought it precisely to stop herself eating the whole packet, imagining herself dawdling over a finger or two like a normal person. But as usual, after the second biscuit it was like the shortbread was trying to eat her.

'You can get something in the canteen. Ade'll take you – won't you?'

Aidan, bedheaded and drowsy, nodded from where he was slumped in the back, nursing his kitbag.

At St Benedict's, keen to avoid the scrum of four-by-fours already churning gravel further up the drive, Mel shouted good luck from the open car door, leaving Harmony with Aidan at the gate. Harmony was relieved to see her go, although she was grateful for Aidan's insouciant escort through the purposeful blazers heading up to the school building. St Ben's was Hogwarts, basically. Hogwarts with a glassy new wing stuck to the back that had been declared open by an Olympic gold medallist the previous year. Inside, there was a strong smell of tinned soup, which Harmony identified, after moments of confusion, as boys. St Ben's, unlike Severn Oak, only got girls in the sixth form.

Aidan led her through the corridors to the canteen. Sliced from the outer edge of the modern wing, it resembled the café of an art gallery. Here, though, instead of the conventual atmosphere remembered from outings which she and Aurora concluded by sharing a hushed scone and a pot of tea, the noise resounded to the ceiling, just like the canteen at Severn Oak. Beneath the din, amplified by the airy glass, a few girls shuffled trays of yogurts and fruit alongside the variously sized boys loading up on cooked breakfasts. Like dolls, the sixth-form girls came in a range of colours, but all appeared produced from the same mould. Hair glossy, limbs long, skin clear. Is that what was meant by a selective school? Seeing these girls, so chosen, Harmony wished herself elsewhere, but it would have been weird to duck out now, weirder still to explain it to Aidan, who was handing her a tray and joining the back of the queue.

He told her the sausages were pretty good, so that's what she had, with scrambled egg. At least he spared her, or himself, from sitting among his friends. Instead, the two of them took the end of a table with a view out on to the many playing fields, some occupied by boys and teachers sacrificing their preschool hour to sport. As Aidan forked up a sausage and halved it in a bite, he raised one hand and slapped it back against the passing hand of another boy who was tearing messily into a croissant. In the same year as Aidan, he must have been at least a year younger than Harmony, though he looked older; not just because of his height, which equalled Aidan's, but from the manly set of his features. Rugged, you could almost call him, if a 14- or 15-year-old boy could be rugged. A crag of a brow, full lips. Shoulders.

'Fuck were you, bro?'

Aidan shrugged. 'Mopper.'

A teacher, Harmony presumed. Unless it was slang. Aidan waved a fork.

'My cousin and stuff, Harmony. Finn.'

'Hey.'

Finn, already on his way, peered back through chaotic black curls that reminded Harmony of Koolaid Conspiracy. St Ben's boys always wore their hair long, in contrast to the brutal barbering popular at Severn Oak.

'Dude!' Aidan called after him, redundantly. He returned to his plate. Harmony was very aware that she and Aidan had never eaten a meal together without the rest of the family present.

'So, tell me about yourself, Harmony.'

He was taking the piss, acknowledging the same awkwardness. She did love him. The thing about Aidan, which was so much not the thing about her, was that he was going to be all right. He took everything in his large stride.

'Not much to tell.'

What would he say, Harmony wondered, if she told him about Declan? She busied herself with the resiliently textured egg.

'Did you win?' she asked desperately. 'Your . . . match the other day?'

She wasn't sure if it was football Aidan played at this time of year, but he was bound to be involved in some kind of sport. This kept them going for a while, as Aidan detailed the complicated position of the school team in the league. Harmony was still unclear by the end of his account if this was actually a football team. Silence ensued. She could see Aidan straining after some subject of common interest, which seemed fair enough. It was his turn.

'So, Mum's gone off on one—'

This brought mutual relief. Mel was fertile ground, conversationally. Harmony knew what his mum was like, Aidan said, through glimpses of chewed toast. She loved a project. Now she was talking about them taking the girl in, the one Mel had found on the beach. Like, literally giving her a home. That's why she was quick off the mark this morning, going to the clinic to see her. Aidan shook his head, like Toothpaste wicking off a puddle.

'Insane.'

A bolus of sausage clagged Harmony's mouth. Clearly Aidan knew nothing about Mel's arrangement with Stu. Stu had broached it with Harmony a couple of days before, juggling his words as though they were too hot to hold in his mouth. How would Harmony feel, he'd wondered, if work took him away for a bit – just a possibility – and it was OK with Aurora and he'd have to check – don't mention it to her, yeah, nothing was settled – about going to live with Mel and Ian? Just while she went to sixth form, or whatever? Only if it suited her, obviously, she didn't have to agree to it straight away ... But Harmony had already caught the suggestion two-handed, before it could cool. Yes, she'd said. *Yes*. The prospect of moving into Mel and Ian's spare room was like opening the window on to a vast view that made you realise you'd been living with the curtains shut. To be in their house, away from Mum, or the lack of her, far from Stu's sadness, with meals made and clothes clean and life decided for you. To be told what to do every day, instead of having to make yourself up. She couldn't wait.

Now Aidan was telling her Mel and Ian didn't want her, just her. She'd had an image of herself and the boys and Toothpaste sprawled on the sofa together, eating popcorn and watching *Strictly*, Eddy casually including her in his rota of goodnight kisses as he was sent off to bed. But it wouldn't be like that at all. It would be the two of them, Harmony and this mystery woman, girl, whatever she was. Storm. Waifs and strays. Mel offering Harmony a home was the kind of charity Stu so roundly rejected for himself, although apparently it was good enough for her. Or ... The egg was sulphurous, repulsive. Since Aidan didn't know about the plan for Harmony to move in, perhaps Mel was intending to replace Harmony entirely. Outside, boys chased a ball into the distance. It wasn't fair. Life isn't fair. That was Mum, when things went wrong. If she was OK with that, why couldn't she get out of fucking bed?

Aidan belched, smiling with pleasure as he extended its coda into speech. His plate was clear.

'Exam time!'

He left her in the heart of the old building, at the open door of the richly polished hall: dark panels, lighter parquet, the soup smell ancient and pervasive. He pointed out the teacher she needed. Harmony was slightly surprised to see it was a woman. Of course, she realised, the boys were allowed to have female teachers, just not actual girls. The teacher was up by the curtained stage at the far end of the hall, consulting with an older man of forbidding authority. Aidan, with the excuse of getting to his form room on time, left it to Harmony to approach them.

'Don't fuck up!'

In the car, Mel had demanded an assurance from him that he'd take Harmony exactly where she needed to go, and although Aidan had observed the letter of the law, Harmony couldn't help feeling he'd bottled his last duty. With a protective arm across her bosom, she approached the teachers and introduced herself, surprised her voice made a sound they could hear.

The way the woman, Ms Mallinson, said so *you're* Harmony, suggested she'd had some other, pre-existing notion of Harmony. Perhaps this was just the effect of her name. Harmony knew from Severn Oak that it created an impression she didn't live up to. She was ticked off a list and taken to a desk towards, but not right at, the back. Alphabetical, the teacher explained. The other exam-takers hadn't appeared yet. Each desk accommodated an exam booklet and a pristine copy of *The Crucible*, as promised.

'No looking!'

Harmony busied herself arranging her pens, three, just in case, as well as a pencil and rubber, all supplied by Mel. It would be all right. This was a good thing to be doing. From somewhere deep in the building an electric bell resounded and, after a short delay, released a wave of boys into the hall. As they surrounded her, Harmony, head bowed but intensely conscious of the looks and, from more than one direction, stifled laughter, dearly wished she'd not been included in the alphabet. Why couldn't they just put her at the back?

The boys soon settled under the practised, weary sarcasm of the male teacher.

'I'm sure you all have the self-control to contain your bladders for two hours. But in case of emergencies, kindly put up your hand and an invigilator will have the dubious honour of escorting you where you need to go.'

Since the day was unseasonably warm, the teacher concluded, with pointlessly acid emphasis on *unseasonably*, the boys were all allowed to take off their blazers. In the ensuing flurry of blazer removal, the boy in front of Harmony revealed an enormous wall of back beneath his thin white shirt. Harmony tried to decide if she could bear to take off her rainbow cardigan. She was feeling quite warm herself, but breasts. She decided against it.

The teachers watched the clock on the wall until the second hand jerked up to the hour, releasing the command to open booklets. As Mel had advised, Harmony read the whole paper through twice, choosing her questions. Then she read the chosen questions through again, to make sure she'd understood them. Around her, many of the St Ben's boys were already writing. It was all going to be fine, she reassured herself. She began.

Perfectly, just before the halfway point, Harmony finished her question about presentations of belief and started to contrast the characters of Proctor and Abigail. The boy to her right was using a fountain pen with a furiously creaking nib. In front of her, the sheet of white-shirted muscle played at the shoulders of the big boy as he wrote and wrote, his free hand jammed in his hair. Like Declan. She wrestled her concentration back to the question.

Three sentences into her introduction ('*It is indeed the case that in presenting the characters of John Proctor and Abigail in his play* The Crucible, *Arthur Miller is showing us different attitudes to truth*'), something prodded her bum. Harmony stopped writing. Not just something, something belonging to someone was pressing deliberately and luxuriantly into the flesh between her coccyx and anus. The pressure released, then intruded again, as though whatever it was was trying, without much urgency, to burrow into her arse. For an aroused, puzzling moment Harmony allowed this, as in a dream of contextless violation. Then, in belated outrage, she turned and saw that the boy behind her, gangling and concentrated, had stretched one long leg up on to the back of her chair, where his foot, reaching the gap above the seat filled by her overspilling backside, treadled, oblivious, in time to his speeding hand. Ms Mallinson had seen Harmony turn. She hurried up the row of desks.

'Is there a problem?'

Harmony was unsure if she herself was allowed to whisper back. But as soon as the teacher reached the desk, she saw the boy's bridging leg and tapped it down with a whispered admonition. The boy, startled and apologetic, retracted both feet beneath his chair, as Ms Mallinson waved her irritably alerted colleague away from joining them from the front of the hall. Harmony's radiating blush awakened the rest of her body, around the point Gangly Boy had probed. Had he meant it? He didn't look like he had. But she knew from

Severn Oak the bully's expertise in feigning innocence. A broken-voiced giggle from the next row suggested collusion. The male teacher shushed the hall back to silence while glaring at her, blaming her differences. The worst of it was, she'd half-liked it. Her body, more than half.

She struggled herself back to Proctor and Abigail. She hated Proctor, and felt passionately sorry for Abigail. By the time the command came to stop writing, she was just a brain again.

As she left the hall, Harmony was touched to see Aidan waiting before he, bowed over his phone, saw her. He stood opposite the wide doors, leaning against a tall plinth surmounted by the pugnacious bust of St Ben's founding headmaster. The prominence of the bust's ears was emphasised by a sunny brightness that contrasted with the rest of the head's grimed bronze. Aidan had told her the ears had been polished by generations of exam-taking boys, seeking luck by touching them as they streamed past. She hated this story while loving it, and the sculpture itself seemed to embody this ambivalence, with its coexisting sheen and dullness, the way you had to contemplate the rough scoops from the sculptor's impatient fingers in order to see the founder's irascible, unhandsome head.

Seeded by whatever he was looking at on the screen, Aidan's face bloomed in a grin. Harmony havered, delayed by the current of boys crossing between them, which included Finn. Passing Aidan, he apprehended him with a loose fist bump meant to seal some arrangement. Without looking up, Aidan demurred, cocking his head to the hall: talking about her, still unseen. Finn called something back to him and Harmony's blood chilled as she understood, in the rueful shake of Aidan's head, his reluctant laughter, that it was almost certainly some comment about her. Some obscene, clinching diss. She waded into the stream of boys. The laughter hadn't quite ebbed from her cousin's face when he spoke to her.

'Mum wanted to make sure you knew about the buses.'

His tone was careful with duty. By the door that joined the old wing to the new, Harmony saw Finn hoist his chin at Aidan, urging him towards somewhere he wanted them both to be. Heathcliff-on-Sea, five divisions out of her league. Not fair.

She told Aidan he didn't need to bother about seeing her to the bus stop.

'My boyfriend said he'd pick me up. He's got a car.'

'Cool.' Surprise buffeted her cousin's face. But he was too nice, or uninterested, to doubt her. His phone buzzed a text. From the door, Harmony saw Finn bent to his own phone, his expectant grin mirrored by Aidan as he read whatever his friend had written.

'Seriously, go,' she said.

They were boys. Five years ago Finn would have been shouting the story of that week's *Doctor Who* episode to Aidan as they loped away. Declan, unlike these two, was a man.

Harmony took out her own phone to chaperone her through the crowds of roistering boys, the cold-eyed gaggle of girls sifting out cronies by the door. Aidan had an iPhone. She bet Finn did too. That unblemished girl she passed, showing her clone friend something hilarious on Instagram, had one of the big ones, cosied in a case with blue bunny ears. Mum thought Apple was like Nestlé to the power of ten. Dead Chinese factory workers, landfill, the minds of a generation. But Mum didn't live in the world, and Harmony had to. Oh, God. And there was only one more lesson left with Declan.

The stop for the Whitby bus was on the road that skirted the playing-field edge of St Benedict's grounds. Harmony was briefly anxious that Aidan might spot her waiting and wonder what had happened to her boyfriend, in which case she would say that he had asked her to meet him in Whitby, where he worked. What as, she wasn't sure. Perhaps he worked in the music shop? When the bus came, apart from a couple of sixth-formers who paid her no attention, she was relieved by the lack of St Ben's kids who got on. The lower school wasn't allowed to leave at lunchtime.

Harmony searched her phone for the location of Storm's clinic, or what she was fairly confident was the clinic, from its proximity to Mel's dentist on Maps. She couldn't remember its actual name, if it had one. While doing this she saw that Mel herself had sent her a text, hoping the exam went well. *Think so*, Harmony replied. She didn't much care, now, if it had or not. That toe, though, up her bum.

The bus reached the outskirts of Whitby. Harmony was so anxious about missing her stop that she got off too soon and had to walk for nearly ten minutes before her trajectory as a pulsating blue dot was endorsed by real-world recognition of the surrounding streets. Once she passed Mel's dentist, she relaxed slightly. She was going the right way. Sure enough, she soon rounded a corner into a street that contained the drab huddle of buildings behind its unassertive NHS sign. It occurred to her that she was hazy enough about visiting times and rights in a proper hospital, let alone a clinic. What was the difference? Just one more thing to add to the pile of things she didn't know. Anyway, she was relying on Mel being long gone since her morning visit. That much was crucial. She and Storm needed to be alone.

Inside, the proscenium of the reception desk was deserted. No one was waiting, either. To the right of the desk, a sign screwed to the wall commanded: 'Please ring the bell for attention'. Despite this promise, the whole building felt forlornly unpopulated. For a moment, Harmony considered ignoring the bell and proceeding through the inner door to whatever lay beyond, but she didn't know where to go. She pressed the button. It was a normal oblong white doorbell stuck to the counter, greyed with use.

Waiting, Harmony relived the interlude in the exam hall, that bizarre intrusion into her body. If the boy had meant it, was it a way of fancying her, or just a joke? Her lack of certainty felt fundamental to anything that might happen with Declan, or any other man, ever. Either a joke or an object of desire: she might even be both. If she had complained to that teacher, it would probably mean she had no sense of humour, and she had no idea who else to complain to who could have made it any better.

She was about to press the bell again when a nurse appeared, not in the vacant area behind the desk, as Harmony was expecting, but craning her head out from behind the mysterious inner door. The nurse's expression was irritable, as though she was seldom summoned in this way.

'Can I help?'

Harmony began an explanation of her relationship to Mel, and Mel's association with Storm, but the nurse was already bracing the door open for her with one arm and waving her through with the other, staring beyond her into the empty reception, apparently on the lookout for someone more essential or interesting. Silently, but at speed, she led Harmony through a series of doglegging corridors until they reached a lift.

'Third floor.' The nurse, who was shorter than Harmony and quite young, reached past her to press the call button. As her thumb held the dulled silver circle, she heaved a vast, visceral sigh.

'I'll leave you to it.'

Harmony saw that the nurse wasn't pissed off, or even particularly impatient, just extremely tired. It was so easy to get things wrong. Like the toe up the bum. Or being wanted by Mel and Ian. Wanted by anyone at all, ever. Playing fields, hair, attention. Fair trade, sex, carbohydrates. Proctor and Abigail. None of it was fair, but the very least you could do was try to make it fairer.

The lift door opened. Alone, Harmony got into the empty cube of air and ascended, up to where the blank girl waited, for nothing and no one, yet with everything coming to her.

Your own room, with nothing of yours. Light in the window, beginning to stale. A girl comes who isn't a nurse.

You know the days, like a card game. You know a card game. These things they bring. Clothes and books. The cards. Mr Lennox watches to see what you might choose from these unchosen things. You choose nothing. Wear the clothes that are clean. Read none of the books. Play patience. In the room he looks for any changes you've made. There are none.

King, Queen, Jack. Deal the days out. A phone rings downstairs, on and on, never answered. Patience, patience.

Mr Lennox hates you. Ace of Spades. Mrs Bale loves you. Queen of Hearts.

But this girl, new. What does she bring? No clothes, no care. Unchosen flesh. Anger, like air. Good. Questions, untethered by the anger. DO YOU THINK YOU WOULD EVEN WANT TO LIVE AT MEL'S? I MEAN, HOW OLD ARE YOU? WILL YOU BE ABLE TO DO A JOB? CAN'T YOU REMEMBER ANYTHING AT ALL?

A secret isn't the same as a lie. A lie is what a secret gives

birth to, when it mates with speech. DO THEY THINK THEY
CAN TEACH YOU TO SPEAK? MAYBE YOU HAD A BOY-
FRIEND – MAYBE YOU WERE MARRIED?

Its father's child, as well as its mother's. DO YOU THINK
YOU'VE GOT A FAMILY SOMEWHERE?

It's time now. She's the one. You choose.

PART 3

Mel had to see Aurora. She hadn't been in touch since Aurora's return from the nuns, and at the very least they needed to discuss Harmony. The guilt twinged like tooth-ache, although there was some excuse for negligence with the Summer Spectacular looming. While relishing competi-tions, and facing the grind of exam sessions with something that secretly verged on enjoyment, Mel purely dreaded the show. She knew the audience was the very besotted opposite of critical. Parents loved watching their children perform, or at least filming them. But afterwards, despite the bouquets and cards and shyly offered toiletry gift sets, nothing, not even relief the thing was over, could blot out Mel's shame. It was as though she'd exposed a humiliating desire to several hundred people; inviting them, under the auspices of some deliciously wrought burlesque, to watch her flash her disappointing knickers.

It's not me, Mel wished she could say. *I didn't mean it.* But for a week or so, not only would she have to field the response of Evensanders encountered out and about, but every time she passed the civic centre, the upbeat cursive on the banner outside remained to taunt her until it was pasted over for the next event: 'NYDA presents "Summer Spectacular: Classic Broadway"', or 'Summer Spectacular: The Beat is On'.

Unlike Mel, Mrs Beagles had loved putting on shows: a legacy of her time as a Bluebell Girl in Paris in the 1950s. As well as the Summer Spectacular, she had enthusiastically mounted a 'Winter Wonderland' each Christmas. Mel had phased out 'Winter Wonderland' easily enough during the interregnum when she still operated the school under the aegis of the Berenice Beagles Academy of Dance. Then, after Mrs Beagles' death, and Mel's rebranding of the school as NYDA – North Yorkshire Dance Arts – she had invoked a new rigour towards exams in order to attenuate the Summer Spectacular into a biennial event. In this way, the agony was at least restricted to every other year. A false economy, she had discovered. After a year of freedom, here it was again, the agony doubled.

Part of her extended bad mood over the run-up to and aftermath of each show was the loneliness of torment by something everyone else considered so trivial. Although Ian was stoically supportive, and contributed scenery and labour for every Spectacular, Mel shared as little of her working world with him as he did of his. The boys couldn't care less what she did, as long as they were fed. Aurora, perhaps taking her cue from Stu, had never displayed the least interest in Mel's work. She and Stu had only ever attended one Spectacular – from Aurora's mouth 'Spectacular' oozed irony like fat from a chip – in the year Harmony had had a go at tap. This had been some time ago, just after her failed venture into Severn Oak. As with school, Harmony and tap had lasted a single term. Neither Aurora nor Stu had attended any subsequent Spectacular. Mel wished no one had.

Routine by routine, each remorseless day as she drilled her girls, her desperation rose. It wasn't the threat of their incompetence that startled her awake in the night from dreams of nakedness and crumbling teeth. Nor was it the customary anxieties over the family, or even Storm. It was the show. Mrs Beagles had always used a central conceit to thread the very disparate elements of each Spectacular into a whole, staunchly recycling a limited store of concepts: time travel, a circus coming to town, a trip around the world, a magic toyshop that could also be a magic television and even – Mrs Beagles' swansong, rendered in cardboard – a magic computer. All relied on two of the school's most competent junior dancers (ideally a boy and a girl, when there was a boy) to hang around downstage and express wonderment while the routines were being performed, then cover entrances and exits by enacting linking bits of business between. Mel had herself done time as a 10-year-old who clapped her hands in synthetic delight at the circus. Now she was stumped. She couldn't think of a new twist on the formula. Her brain didn't work that way; it never had.

Kitty Sue and Lola were expecting the nod, she could see. And in the meantime there was Edward, and whatever was going on with Joseph, and Storm, and Stu wanting to leave the country; which brought her back to Aurora. Abandoning the Spectacular, Mel got in the car. As ever, the avoidance of more painful tasks underwrote the currency of getting things done.

Aurora had once cared about the garden, but Stu never bothered. To reach their front door, Mel now waded through fronded stalks of cow parsley that were taller than she

217

was. Sneezing as she waited for an answer to her knock, Mel considered the likelihood of Stu having discussed his plans to abandon Aurora, with Aurora. It wouldn't be the first time he'd left Mel to do his dirty work. When Koolaid Conspiracy had gone off on tour in 1982, she had been the one to break it to their parents that Stu wasn't taking up his engineering place at Manchester. He had also, as far as she knew, never actually told them that he'd broken up with Lisa. Months after Stu and Aurora got together, their dad had buttonholed Mel to ask, in intense discomfort – 'your mother's been wondering' – if Harmony was Stu's child. It must have been obvious to them that Harmony's real father was mixed race; or 'exotic' as Mum had settled on, after years of being told her other euphemisms were offensive. And yet, so bamboozled were Colin and Hilary Ansholm by the expectations and realities of modern life, exemplified by their son's wayward path away from a full grant into indie rock stardom, that they were prepared to think anything was possible. Mel's parents had lived their whole lives in Evensand, apart from her dad's National Service, which had taken him to Northampton. To his dying day he had referred to Northampton as if it was the Punjab.

Harmony came to the door, looking freshly woken and cross about it. Although she still lumbered in for a hug, unusually she was the first to detach herself. Stu was at a car boot, she told Mel. Mel said that was fine, because it was Aurora she'd come to see. She didn't want to be detained by discussing Harmony's future with Harmony. Ignoring the warning that Aurora would probably be asleep, she knocked twice on the bedroom door and opened.

Aurora wasn't asleep. To Mel's surprise, she wasn't even in bed, but sat cross-legged on the rug beside it, sorting through a pile of old clothes. She wore a sludgy t-shirt and leggings that may have been nightwear, her hair haphazardly gathered into a ponytail. Before Mel's eye adjusted to the familiarity of her aspect, she saw how old they both really were. Then time was gone, a smear of the eye blinked away: Aurora was just Aurora, and Dawn, with her particular points at knee and elbow and that elfin set to her chin.

'Heyer.'

But not the same. This was why Mel hadn't visited. She hated it, the murderous violence with which she wanted to shake life back into the husk of her friend, the desire both to rage and weep. But releasing your own feelings into the room was like peeing in the sea: a small contamination quickly assimilated into a much vaster pollution. Soon, the hopelessness closed over your head.

It's lovely once you're in.

When Aurora had walked into the sea that Boxing Day, Mel had considered it no more than an exhibitionist paddle. She'd been wrong, hard as that was to accept. Not necessarily wrong about the feebleness of Aurora's attempt to kill herself, but in her impatience with the cliché she had misread its genuine message of despair. The gesture had seemed more like irritation, or pique, pointedly aimed at Mel herself after their confrontation over Christmas. Mel hadn't been ready to forgive her.

Knowing that Christmas was always a flashpoint between them hadn't stopped it being unusually bad. It began, as ever, with Aurora's traditional offer to bring a vegetarian alternative. Stu and Harmony tucked into turkey with the rest of them in a way that gladdened Mel's heart, as did Aurora's mealy exclamations about their annual eating of flesh. Mel's martyred refusal of Aurora's offer to provide her own nut roast was equally traditional. Then came the cursing of the making of the thing, always home-made, never bought, halfway to stuffing so really not much extra bother, Mel protested. After this, a week or ten days before, came the predictable threat of Aurora and the gang not coming for Christmas at all. Aurora usually rang to announce she or Harmony had a bug/cold/virus and didn't want Mel's household to get it/wouldn't feel up to it. Or there would be the possibility, just as suddenly declared, that she and Stu might book a winter sun holiday at the eleventh hour in order to get a bargain (*'If you fly on Christmas Day you save literally hundreds of pounds'*). This never happened. Once, Stu's frozen shoulder. Sometimes, Stu's work, in the years when German Christmas fairs took off and it became a busy time for him – *'he's so knackered I think we might just lie low and make it a quiet one this year'*. But Mel always dragooned the three of them into joining the celebration in the end, resentful of the extra effort expended in persuasion at a time when every atom of her energy was spoken for.

It had been a double whammy. Harmony had succumbed to a gastric thing at the beginning of Christmas week, which Mel robustly batted back with the assurance that the boys and Ian had had something similar and it was over in forty-eight hours. And then, on Christmas Eve, as Mel had locked herself away in the bedroom to confront the last of the hated wrapping, Ian brought the phone in, eyebrows raised, and made off with the scissors. It was Aurora, tearful and furious after a row with Stu. Mel continued to wrap, the phone clamped uncomfortably in her shoulder. It would be impossible, Aurora claimed, for them all to play happy families after everything that had been said.

'Stu can come. Honestly. Harmony and I can just have something here; it's not like we enjoy the meal. Honestly Mel, I don't want us to spoil it for everyone else. There'll be an atmosphere.'

If there was one thing Mel knew from twenty years of hosting family Christmases, it was that the forced mixture of escalatingly pissed people and excited children was a great diluter of individual atmospheres. But Aurora resented dilution.

'It was a bad one, was it?'

Mel taped the corners on Stu's present as Aurora elaborated. By the time she was looking around for the scissors to cut the paper for her father-in-law's box set, the worst of Aurora's indignation had blown itself out and the day was back on. It was then that Aurora made her mistake.

'Listen, Eddy's OK with money, isn't he?' She was talking about Edward's Christmas present. 'I looked for that kit thing but they didn't have it anywhere.'

Mel knew this was a lie. She would have known even if she hadn't herself seen the castle construction kit in WH Smith in Whitby – not even a gift shop, not even an obscure gift shop – a few days before.

'They had it in WH Smith. I thought I said.' She had, she'd said.

'Oh, WH Smith. I didn't want to get him something from *there*.'

Rage fizzed up against the top of Mel's skull. 'But it's what he wanted.'

Edward's birthday was the day before Christmas Eve, and Aurora had never once bothered to mark it with a separate present. Years before they had agreed to winnow out the adult Christmas gifts and concentrate on the children, so Aurora hadn't had that much to do – not even make a bloody nut roast. If she'd known, Mel would have got Edward the castle kit herself since he so dearly wanted it, but she'd been foolish enough to cherish a small fantasy of Aurora redeeming herself from years of tedious fair trade offerings (the dreamcatcher, the African-print juggling balls) by finally giving the poor kid a present he could get genuinely excited about. She'd even selected the cheapest item on Edward's Christmas list out of consideration for Aurora and Stu's limited budget.

'Anyway.' Aurora's tone had become querulous, as though Mel was the one being unreasonable. 'I'll put the money in his card and he can spend it on that if that's what he really wants.'

Mel knew this was what Aurora had always intended to do, if she'd given it any thought at all. Aurora coughed out a metallic little laugh.

'It's a bit clinical, to be honest, being told to buy a present to order. Spirit of Christmas.'

'As opposed to putting ten quid in a bloody envelope? Yeah, Charles Dickens'll be creaming himself over that one, Dawn!'

Mel didn't hang up. She just put the phone down on the bed and went to retrieve the scissors. When she came back, she was being commanded to replace the handset and try again. As she'd said to Ian in bed, towards three, after all the presents were wrapped, they'd had a row about the lost scissors and finally filled the stockings, Edward's castle kit was bad enough, but the thing that really drove her crazy was Aurora wanting Mel to absolve her of her own laziness. To say, as ever, that anything Aurora did was OK.

On Christmas morning, the atmosphere between Mel and Aurora hadn't been diluted by company, alcohol or the day. So it had been hard not to think that the Boxing Day suicide attempt didn't lie in some way at Mel's own door, however unfairly. It was only in the months since that the real damage had revealed itself, suggesting a different, more complicated incitement.

Now, sitting on Aurora and Stu's unmade bed, forcing a smile, she spotted a depleted card of pills on the bedside table, along with bottles of vitamins. Antidepressants, Mel presumed. Aurora said she was just sorting through a few things, which seemed like a sign of slight improvement.

'Stu's at a vintage fair.'

'Car boot, Harmony said.'

A shrug. Same diff. Mel knew she'd have to plunge straight in.

'Has Stu spoken to you at all? About Harmony?'

Aurora's response was to camber slowly up on to her knees, reaching to the bedside table. With two fingers she hooked a scallop of pale pink cream from an open plastic tub, and, lowering herself back into her lotus position, began to work the cream luxuriantly into the backs of her hands. The smell was pleasant: beeswax, roses, a touch of camphor.

'Harmony's spoken to me.'

Aurora worried the cream into the webbed piece of flesh between thumb and forefinger. Right, said Mel, irritated, dangling. About … ? Aurora made her wait, finishing the job with a few languid, two-handed Uriah Heep passes from wrist to fingertip. Moisturised, she raised herself again and reached for the bedside table. Mel waited. Not more hand cream, thank God, but a letter-sized piece of paper, folded in half. Aurora offered it to her. It contained two words, written in characterless capitals: PRUNELLA WEBSTER.

Obviously, Mel didn't have a clue what this was. Harmony had been to the hospital, Aurora told her; clinic, she corrected herself. Mel realised they weren't talking about Stu at all, but Storm. Aurora nodded at the note.

'She gave her that.'

'Harmony gave Storm—' Mel looked again: PRUNELLA WEBSTER. 'Why?'

Impatience rendered Aurora briefly normal. She jinked her chin. 'Not Harmony. Storm gave it to *her*. She wrote it down for her.'

Mel contemplated the words, the oddity of the name they apparently formed.

'Storm,' said Aurora, as critical of that other name as if Mel had been responsible for it.

'They had to call her something.'

But maybe this was the girl's real name. What kind of name was Prunella, in this day and age? And hadn't PC Mason said she couldn't write, as well as being mute?

'What was Harmony doing, going to see her, anyway?'

Aurora retrieved the sheet of paper and replaced it on the bedside table. Her greased fingertips left two translucent marks at the top of the page. She didn't know, she said. And then added that Harmony had mentioned Mel was thinking of practically adopting the girl, woman, whatever she was. Maybe she was just curious to see what Mel was taking on.

Languorously, Aurora took up a faded green t-shirt, which she began to fold. Mel quelled her urge to escape what needed to come next. Clearly Stu had said nothing. She watched Aurora's familiar, slender fingers tuck one sleeve, then the other, towards the shirt's centre. A million years ago, Dawn had had a job as a Saturday girl at Skelton's. As Mel approached the possibility that Harmony might stay with her and Ian until Aurora was feeling more herself, Aurora, taking her time, shook out the shirt and started again. It was just, Mel explained, a temporary measure, until Harmony could – Aurora aligned the bottom hem, meticulous. The t-shirt was too far gone for a charity shop to take. A section of the hem was frayed.

'Until she can what?'

'Stand on her own two feet.'

Aurora, palms flat, slowly smoothed the worn cotton along her thighs. 'She can't.'

'No, she can't.'

Mel had promised herself she wouldn't get angry. 'Which is why we'd like to help.'

Aurora turned the hem up to the neck and, with agonising care, folded the shirt left to right to form, once more, a neat square. All her nimbleness had thickened since she'd been ill, as though the drag of normal air had to be fought. She said she'd have to think about it.

'Well, you've got plenty of time for that.'

Aurora's head came up, as if for bait. Mel knew she would have to go before she bludgeoned her with the bedside lamp, or told her about Australia. She got up from the stale bed.

'You're very twitchy. What's up?'

'Stuff to do, you know. The Spectacular.'

Mel quelled a flashback to her explosion of stress in Junior Tap the previous day. As she started 'Jitterbug Boogie' on the CD yet again and counted everyone in, one cohort, made skittish by her bayed instructions, had launched themselves two bars early into a travelling run of tap-step-ball changes, cannoning into the obediently static group in front, who, spooked in their turn, barged into the next, triggering a catastrophic domino effect that advanced row by disintegrating row. Amid a cacophony of mistimed taps and the giggling thump of falling girls, Mel killed the music and ranted. As she released the harrowed, sweating kids, ten minutes late, she had been well aware it wasn't the routine that was the problem.

'Sorry. I know I'm an old cow sometimes.'

The bunch of Aurora's mouth, borrowed from Stu, acknowledged that this was the case.

Maybe the linking kids could be aliens, watching humans? Green face paint, funny costumes. Mel strained after a title: 'Out of this World'. Her eagerness dropped. Her first remembered Beagles Spectacular, around the time of the Apollo landings, had been danced around a listing tinfoil rocket.

'It stresses me out,' Mel heard herself say. 'The Spectacular. Having to think of a story.'

'Can't you just use one of the old ones? I mean, no one actually cares.'

Seeing that Mel found this comment unhelpful to the point of insult, Aurora added that maybe Mel's problem was using Mrs Beagles' so-called stories at all. Why did she even need to bother? Of course she needed to bother, snapped Mel. Aurora pointed out that, apart from everything else, the cod story made a long evening even longer. Mel couldn't disagree. Spectaculars were usually over two hours, which, on a warm June evening, could feel endless. Cutting the links between one dance and the next would be a godsend.

Between them, Mrs Beagles struck a raddled Bluebell Girl pose, fishnets and green eyeshadow.

'People expect it, though.'

'Oh, sod Mrs Beagles,' Aurora said. 'Why do you have to do what she did? It's all so fucking fake.'

Fake. Yes. That was the problem. Mel believed in Zara

Patel tapping her little heart out to 'Alligator Crawl'; she even believed a bit in the nubile proficiency of her Grade 5 Moderns gyrating to 'Back to Black', but she couldn't believe in the pretence that it all connected. For some reason this dead gesture to stories no one believed in was precisely what soaked her with that uniquely shameful shame. And yet, from beyond the grave, Mrs Beagles waved her ostrich fan, showcased a well-turned ankle.

'People need breathing space,' Mel said. 'And the kids need a bit of time to get on and off.'

Aurora nodded. She was taking Mel seriously.

'How about colours?'

A thematic link, she explained, drawing down her top lip parodically, so Mel knew she would readily disown the seriousness if challenged. Just put them in the colours of the rainbow, clump a few dances together with the same-coloured outfit, like, all the ballet red, all the tap orange or whatever, and when you need a gap, get a new kid to bring on the colour – some kind of banner – so that at the end you have a rainbow on stage.

Mel saw it, perfectly. No pretence, just dances. Sloth-like, Aurora was already stretching to retrieve the smirched piece of paper bearing PRUNELLA WEBSTER. She used its blank side to sketch out a pattern for the rainbow banner. The strips could Velcro together, she explained, to build up the climactic prism, formed of parachute silk.

'Parachute silk?'

'They use it at festivals. Stu can ask for you.'

Downstairs, Harmony was nowhere to be seen; either out or locked away in the bathroom. Mel would talk to her about this Storm business when she came to their house for her last lesson with Declan. Lightened, she let herself out.

As soon as she opened the front door, the humid afternoon hit her like a brick. Perhaps it was her age, this sensitivity to temperature. She sat in the parked car, blasting away with the fan, until she saw Aurora staring out of the window, wondering why she hadn't driven away. Mel gave an appeasing wave and cranked back the seat, allowing the cold air to chill her face and toes. A minute or two could do no harm.

The babble of the radio filled her newly tranquil brain. A rainbow of dances. In the way only Aurora could, she had blundered into the darkness of Mel's soul and, finding herself in a place she considered merely dingy, turned on the light. God knows, she could still love Aurora for that.

For Mason, there were better times Harmony Ansholm could have chosen to turn up at the station. He and Soccolo were starting a week of mornings. Having sat on his Malcolm White news for a few days, Dan had decided to pay his partner the courtesy of telling him about it first thing. It was best, before he got CID involved. Biting sideways into a dripping bacon bagel, Soccolo listened and, eventually, swallowed. What were Malcolm's 'difficulties' exactly, he wanted to know? How reliable could he be considered as a witness? And if he had seen Nicu on the beach, so chuffing what? Mason gabbled through the shape of the case as he saw it – Nicu pimping Storm, either casually or in some more organised way; the girl cutting up rough about it, possibly threatening to go to the police; a row where Nicu attacked her and, thinking he'd finished her off, dragged her on to Brazen beach ... The tolerant vacancy of Soccolo's face recalled Dan's mum when he'd recounted exciting dreams to her as a little kid. He ran out of momentum.

Soccolo's mouth birthed a yellow worm of bacon rind. He laid it on his thin, ketchup-smeared napkin. Here was the thing. If the girl couldn't remember owt, so what? She was fine otherwise, wasn't she?

'But if he's trafficking up there, if there's trafficking going on ...'

The more Dan said *trafficking* the more it sounded like a rush hour problem on the A174. Soccolo wiped his mouth and tossed the balled paper.

'If there is, don't you think CID lads might be on to it?'

'Fuck's sake.'

Dan strode off, before he lost it. At the end of the corridor, he gave his walk a point by turning into the civilian office, where a water cooler stood by the door. Still pissed off, he pulled out a cup from the dangling stack, placed it inattentively below the spigot and pressed the button. The jet of water hit the misaligned cup's flimsy rim, knocking it off the draining tray and wetting his trousers at the knee, before splashing his shins and shoes on its way to the floor. Claire, without looking away from her screen, wondered what he was like. Then she remembered there was a lass waiting to see him.

'What lass?'

'Harmony Ansholm?'

Harmony Ansholm was slouched in a chair at the front desk, thumbing at her phone. More make-up than previously, Dan noticed. He hoped it wasn't in his honour.

'Not at school?'

Aware of the polyester of his uniform trousers sticking clammily to his knees, he led her through the lifted hatch in the sergeant's desk and into their realm. The girl explained she was homeschooled, adding something about exams he didn't catch. Mason glanced into the first interview room and, finding it occupied, took her into the second. The clock over the table where he and Harmony sat showed 9:10. Lottie would be starting work.

'So, what can I do for you, Harmony?'

It was Storm, she said. He'd said he wanted to know anything Harmony had seen? Dan nodded encouragement. Suck that one up, Socco. Another witness in the bag after Malcolm White would be impossible to ignore, even for him. But this time he needed to nail it, and Harmony had caught him on the hop. Proper procedure meant showing her a folder with a fair mixture of random shots they had on record, mixing Nicu in with likely local bad lads to see if she could ID him from the night the girl was found. He'd have to go through that formality with Malcolm White as well at some point, which might have its difficulties. It wouldn't take him long to get a folder together now, though, for Harmony. He asked her if she'd mind a short wait, as long as she didn't have to be anywhere? She said she didn't mind. Before he'd reached the door, she was back on her phone.

By the printer, Mason kept an edgy eye out for Soccolo. Given his partner's view on the futility of his investigations, Dan's mind was a blank about any possible alibi for his current errand. But luck stayed on his side as he assembled the file. No one even came to hijack the printer. He glanced at the clock: Soccolo was probably taking his morning dump. He tucked the sheet with Nicu's glowering passport photo into the middle of the pile, fourth out of six. More than fair. As he returned to the interview room, the phrase 'cracked the case wide open' played in his head on a compelling loop.

When he opened the door, Mason was dismayed to see his

partner's monumental navy-blue back screening Harmony Ansholm from view.

'We were just beginning to wonder where you'd got to.'

Soccolo bared his teeth, glancing at the file Dan was holding. Soccolo was allowed to join the interview. It was normal. But Harmony's face, once Dan could see it, was lividly sullen, refusing eye contact. In Dan's absence, Soccolo had barged in and made something happen.

He adopted a tone of breezy enthusiasm, to blow them all past the awkwardness. 'Have I missed summat?'

Summat and nowt, said Soccolo. Dan saw how very much he didn't like Harmony. Soccolo wasn't keen on young people. They grew up into all the other people he didn't like.

'Harmony and I have had a little chat, like.'

The girl wouldn't look at Soccolo, but just about managed to dart a look up at Dan – 'sorry' she said – then back at her hands. Soccolo wondered theatrically if she'd like to tell PC Mason what she'd just told him. No?

'Harmony's been telling us a few fairy tales, haven't you, Harmony?'

The top of the girl's head nodded, shaking the high brown cloud of her ponytail. All this time, said Soccolo, she'd claimed she'd been on the beach the night of the storm, when she'd been safely tucked up at home, looking after her auntie's dog.

'Yeah, she said' – Mason appealed to her – 'you said, you were looking after your auntie's dog. You went out later, on your own.'

Harmony picked at the skin beside her thumb. Apparently not. And that was just for starters, said Soccolo. As if intuiting the contents of the file Dan was now holding under the table, he took pleasure in telling him that Harmony had been responsible for sending them on a wild goose chase, back in March. There had been nothing going on at the vans, had there? She mouthed a chastened 'no'.

'It was Melanie Bale who tipped us off about the vans,' said Dan, back to Soccolo, cajoling. 'She said it was that lass who lives at Oceancrest. Katie.'

Soccolo wriggled, making the legs of his chair squeal.

'That was Harmony putting her oar in, weren't it, Harmony?'

Harmony nodded. 'Sorry.'

'But . . .'

Dan didn't know what to think. Now that he'd won, Soccolo's tone was dispassionate, almost gentle. 'Just got a bit carried away with the excitement of it all.'

His better self. Soccolo scraped his chair back and stood, scything his waistband to free his paunch.

'Right then.'

Mason curled his file into a scroll. It could go straight in the bin. He too stood. Wait, Harmony said, weren't they going to ask her why she was there? Without looking at each other, both men were in agreement that they already had. But the girl was searching her phone. Apparently she was here on other business.

'I wrote it down.'

She flashed the phone at them, insisting. From the screen, Dan read PRUNELLA WEBSTER.

Harmony couldn't see why they wouldn't believe her story that Storm had passed her a note. This was what she had wanted to tell Dan, she insisted, nothing at all to do with a man on the beach. She'd been to see Storm at the clinic, for real, and Storm had written down the name for her. Dan jumped in to ask before Soccolo could: why didn't she have this note, if it existed? Her mum had it, Harmony said, as though Mason was being unreasonable beyond all imagination. Apparently, her mum had written something on the back of the piece of paper which she needed, chinny reckon.

'Right. Was anyone else there when Storm wrote this note?'

No one, apparently. Soccolo was holding the door open, as much for Harmony as for them.

'It's true!' Tears unbalanced the girl's voice.

'OK. Did she say anything to you?' asked Mason. 'Storm?'

'No.' This, as though Harmony couldn't think of a more ridiculous question. 'She can't talk, can she?'

Soccolo barked a laugh. 'Come on, let's be having you.'

Harmony didn't shift. Weren't they going to write it down? Dan promised he'd remember it: PENELOPE WEBSTER. She was fierce then in her demand that he write it. As he scribbled on the slippery file cover with his still-damp knee hoisted as a desk, Mason was struck by the possibility that Harmony might at least be telling the truth about this. For all he knew, Storm could have started communicating in writing. Lennox would hardly bother to let him know. In fact, Lennox would love keeping that sort of information to himself. Dan's pulse surged. The only person he could ask was Lottie. A legitimate enquiry.

Out in the car with Soccolo, Mason texted her: *question re Storm, can you call me? Cheers, Dan.* Before sending, he amended this to *development in Storm case, please call. Dan x* Too late, he regretted the kiss. Oh yes he did, that.

Soccolo drove, as usual. Why did he always get to drive? Dan still felt narked enough by the morning's disappointments not to make conversation as they crawled through the streets of the one-way system, negotiating the overspill of shoppers from the narrow pavements. Soccolo didn't notice his silence, as Mrs S had tried him on a South American ceviche the previous night and he was in two minds about it. Lime, chilli, halfway between raw and cooked but not as slimy as he'd been expecting, he wouldn't want it every night and it was more of a starter than a main course, as he'd told her, but it made a change, quite fresh, like ... A woman stepped out into the road ahead. Soccolo trod the brake, more heavily than their speed warranted. They both whiplashed back as the woman dropped from view, a clear metre from the bumper. Drunk, Mason thought, as he got out and rounded the front of the car. They hadn't touched her.

A second woman had broken from the crowd and was attempting to pull her friend off the road. Their high-pitched altercation wasn't in English. The collapsed party, heavyset, with extravagant blond hair and a made-up face slick with tears, refused to budge, gesticulating and shouting as her mate tried to pull her to her feet, one of which was missing a shoe. Not drunken exuberance, Dan saw then, but the extreme, promenading climax of a drama.

'Is there a problem, ladies?'

Soccolo had stayed in the patrol car, leaving Dan to do the heavy lifting. Dan weighed in to help the friend, a brunette version of the blonde, as she shouted and dragged at the distressed woman, who seemed determined to stay where she was. Behind them the horns of blocked cars blared, further provoked by Soccolo beginning to reverse; Dan wasn't sure why. Even with the friend's help, hauling the woman up to her feet was like trying to inflate a punctured balloon. She kept collapsing back to the ground, which she smote, biblically, shouting imprecations directed at the two of them, which her friend glossed vainly in the same slurry of alien language. The gist of it seemed to be a violent husband or boyfriend who had turned up and threatened or attacked the wailing woman, taken her phone and fled. The victim seemed simultaneously in fear for her life and desperate for revenge – wanting Mason both to stay to protect her and take off in pursuit of her nemesis.

'Trust me!' she shouted, her only words in English. 'Truuuust meeee!' as though everyone was doubting her story, or her hoarse distress. Shoppers gawped, fresh from the Co-op.

'Let's just get you out of the way.'

Finally, Mason and the companion succeeded in half-stumbling, half-hauling the blonde woman off the road. As she sank on to the pavement, plump knees frogged open, the file of pent-up traffic accelerated past, uncomfortably close. Where was Soccolo, with the car? Dan squatted down to the distressed woman's face. This near, he breathed the vaporous non-smell of a spirit, possibly vodka, but her eyes were undulled. She was younger than he'd thought, under the make-up: thirtyish rather than fortyish.

'Are you all right?' asked Dan. 'What do you want us to do?'

It came again – 'Trust me!' Her palm was up, supplicating. Somewhere, he saw, she was enjoying this. People did; the operatic immersion in their own drama.

'I do. I do trust you. But if you don't tell me what the matter is, we can't help you.'

Her friend pointed back along the promenade. Romanian, Albanian, possibly Polish. Still talking, mitigating, she shook her head at Dan, unaggressively shooed him off, backhanded. I'll deal with this, the gesture said. You can be no help to us.

'You're sure you're all right?'

The blonde woman wailed, her chin to the sky. Feeling foolish, Dan went to find Soccolo. Back round the corner, his partner bipped the horn from where he'd pulled up on the pavement outside Oxfam, as tersely as if Dan himself had been the source of the hold-up. Lazy bastard. Dan got in the car. Soccolo's only intervention, once they'd cruised past the two women, was a shouted warning back to the brunette that she'd better keep her mate off the road or they'd have to take her in as drunk and disorderly. Since neither woman understood what Soccolo was saying and weren't even looking his way, he called this out mainly as a sop to the surrounding shoppers, many of them disapproving and elderly.

On their way to Sandsend, Mason finally had to say it.

'Think they were from the vans?'

Soccolo paid bland attention to the road. 'Put it this way – don't think they'll be selected for county cricket, do you?'

'On the game?'

'Change the chuffing record.'

Dan released his window button. The air he let in smelled of spunk. This two weeks, the ditches and hedges teeming with white blossom, the countryside was like a teenage boy's bedsheets.

'Here's the thing, lad.' Soccolo only called him lad when he felt he had something genuine to impart. In itself it was almost an apology. 'Way I see it, what we do, uniform, majority, like? Basically, it's domestics. Junkies, prozzers, Queen of chuffing Sheba – it comes down to the same thing. Either buggers winding each other up or taking things that belong to other buggers. Like stupid bloody kids. Like this bloody business with the hedge. And those women, it's no different. Row with the boyfriend, all kicks off. Just cos we can't understand what they're saying doesn't mean there was *trafficking*. And even if it were, yeah? Even if it were, it's not kiddies or owt. Handjobs to pay the rent, jumps for sad fuckers who can't get it for free. It's not a chuffing crime syndicate, it's human nature. See what I'm saying?'

Dan did, almost. The language barrier, or the fact of being foreign (hadn't that word come up on a course?) was like the uniform again. When you became a thing, instead of a person. Human nature, to do that. Because if you didn't, you had to live life as Malcolm White, fighting every day against a baffling infinitude of human differences that threatened to overwhelm you. So there had to be rules. Did this mean that he and Soccolo were in agreement after all? Or was Soccolo calling him some kind of racist?

'Watch *Thrones* this week? Tits were out.'

Dan shook his head. But, but, but … Why had Soccolo reversed round the corner, out of sight of those two women, when there was an empty disabled bay right outside the Co-op? Unless he didn't want the women to see him, or for Dan to witness them seeing him. *Trust me* … His partner wasn't a complex organism. Yes, he operated from the impulse to do as little as possible, but Dan wasn't making more work for him. If vice was an issue at Oceancrest, CID would do the work. But Soccolo didn't want Dan to go to CID. He didn't want CID to know about Storm and the vans and Nicu. About vice. He'd been quicker to get in that interview room with Harmony Ansholm than he was to investigate the new civvy officer's boob job. Why was he so keen to discredit what the lass had to say?

Dan's phone vibrated, flashing Lottie's number, but he was too poleaxed to pick up.

What if Soccolo was a bad lad?

Posters on MySecretHeart were speculating about what had happened to Beetlebutt. It had been over a month since she had disappeared from the site. TruJet79 trotted out her pet theory whenever a regular poster wondered where Beetlebutt had gone: that it had all ended in tears between her and The1. This is what happened when you declared your secret love, she wrote. It caused emotional and actual damage. Each of Trujet79's messages ended with the automatic tag: '*I have spread my dreams beneath your feet. Tread softly, for you tread on my dreams.*'

'You don't know that, she might just be happy,' typed Harmony, as she had a number of times, in a number of ways, under her username SandyChick1. Trujet79 responded promptly, despite the time difference in Waterloo, Ontario.

Trujet79: You're entitled to your opinion.

'I have spread my dreams beneath your feet. Tread softly, for you tread on my dreams.'

SandyChick1: Thanks. Sorry I think a couple of your dreams didn't make it I'm a bit clumsy lol

Once more, Harmony read through all of Beetlebutt's staling posts, hoping against hope that by the time she reached the most recent, Beetlebutt would have updated the MySecretHeart community on the final instalment of her love story. TruJet79 might not be able to bear a happy ending, but Harmony knew. It had happened for Beetlebutt, and it could happen for her.

She had sat her English Language paper at St Ben's, and was facing maths in a week. Her last Declan lesson was two days before the exam. Harmony was finding it hard to do any maths revision, even harder than with English. Lolling on the bed, the room stuffy even with the window open, Harmony put her hand to the piebald wall. The sameness of her room, the purple paint she'd chosen when she was ten, its piggled archipelagos near the bed, worried at over so many unstimulated hours, was a waking dream. On the revision sheets, all the numbers turned to ice cream. A mint Magnum. At Mel's house, they kept boxes of Magnums in the freezer for anyone to have when they fancied or remembered. Harmony bet they weren't thinking all the time of the Magnums the way she was now, the thick crackle of the chocolate and the soapy toothpaste sweetness of the ice cream. She scrounged around her room for change and came up short – she might need two, or maybe there was a deal going on a whole box. There were bound to be pound coins scattered around downstairs. Stu, currently at work, was careless with his pockets.

In the living room, she knelt by the low part of the settee where Stu preferred to sit and pincered bounty from the gap between the seat cushion and the frame.

'Lost something?'

The surprise of Mum's voice triggered an involuntary scream, jerking the coins from Harmony's fingers.

'Just, needed money. For the bus.' Harmony reached for an escaping pound before it rolled all the way to Aurora's foot. 'I'm off to the library.'

Aurora was wrapped in a towel, fresh from the bath. Since her return she rarely bathed during the day, let alone came downstairs. What was going on?

'I'll come with you. We can walk, can't we?'

Yeah, said Harmony, course. As if this was a casual announcement. How long since Mum had been for a walk? How long since she'd left the bedroom, for any length of time? Harmony tried not to flinch as Aurora touched her head. The points of contact tingled from the strangeness, as though her hair had nerves.

'Birthday in a few weeks.'

Her fifteenth had come and gone with cake and cards from Mel and fifty quid from Stu, and Mum in bed, asleep.

'Sixteen,' said Mum.

'Yeah.'

Aurora got dressed; a 1980s dress she'd either had since the 1980s or picked up at a vintage fair. It was all Vs and angles, mustard chevrons on navy blue. It used to suit her. Now you could somehow tell it was ages since she'd worn proper clothes. She reminded Harmony of the way Auntie Mel looked in her Christmas outfit: as though someone else had done up her buttons.

'Looks warm out there.'

But Mum put a cardigan over the dress, and shivered into it as they set out. Green mohair, also vintage-looking, though it was one she'd knitted herself, that year she'd sold a few pieces at the fairs and talked about getting a website.

Outside, Aurora walked slowly. She reacted nervously to cars that passed, staring after each one as though she'd forgotten about cars. Could they cut on to the beach and take the town steps up the promenade? Course, said Harmony. She would really have to go to the library now, she saw. She hadn't gone near it for months, not since her humiliating expulsion over the KitKat the day of the massive storm. Mum wouldn't come into the actual building with her, surely. As soon as the coast was clear she'd be able to duck out and get her Magnum.

It was very close, the sky above the sea crammed with mardy curds of cloud, threatening rain. Mum stopped and watched the sea come in, the colour of milky tea. She still hugged the cardigan against her, for protection. Closer to the town steps, an elderly couple walked their dogs, pursued and preceded by their wandering tracks on the sand.

'Might be enough for one day,' Harmony said. 'You don't want to overdo it.'

Mum, watching the waves, murmured a noise that meant she'd heard her, but not that she agreed.

'I'm glad you're feeling better, anyway.'

This came out of Harmony's mouth like a lie, although it must be true. What was going to happen with Declan if Mum was feeling better? She would have to adjust her plan. She couldn't see how. And – she minded this less, because the future beyond Declan was a white wall – if Mum went back to normal, would it mean that she wouldn't be allowed to live with Mel and Ian, if they were still offering?

'I used to think Evensand was a shithole,' said Mum, 'when I was your age. But it's quite pretty. This bit, anyway.'

Harmony tried to see. Brazen beach was like her

bedroom, so familiar she couldn't see it, put it into a frame. The Spar, the precinct, the library, the entrance to the golf club ... One day she would live in beauty, and it would be like the new wing at St Benedict's. No poxed concrete, no rusted metal. No Oceancrest. No fat. She would be beautiful herself, then.

'I mean, don't get me wrong. It's still a shithole.'

It really was Aurora. Tears ignited from the lump that had sat in Harmony since the Christmas row with Stu, sparking her eyes and throat. She swallowed them down.

The shingle behind them churned. The old couple had caught up, advancing to reach the bar of dark, packed sand where she and Mum were standing. Watching their dogs frolic ahead, in and out of the small waves, Harmony looked up and caught the high, tiny figures of walkers moving along the edge of Brazen Point. There were no fences. Anyone could drop like a stone into the sea. She thought of Storm, on that night, pushed and pulled like the rubbish collecting before them at the tideline, until she was dragged free by Auntie Mel. The drop would have killed her. She hadn't dropped.

Prunella Webster. Were the police even doing anything? Harmony could see they wouldn't believe her, that Storm had taken a pen and printed those clear letters as Harmony tried to talk to her in her drab room at the top of the clinic. Knowing Storm couldn't talk hadn't prepared her for the provocation of the girl's silence. Talking at her, trying to explain why she was there, asking questions, was like pelting pebbles against a window. As Storm's eyes scanned her face, Harmony had had a powerful feeling that the house wasn't empty. Someone was in there, holding the door shut. That lump in her flared.

'I know you can understand what I'm saying! Are you, like, mentally ill? Cos you shouldn't be going to Mel's, they'll put you away somewhere, you know, worse than this.'

And then it was all coming out, her desperation to live with Mel and Ian, the cousins, how shit it was at home with Aurora either taking off or in bed every day and Stu miserable, her weight, Nestlé, the impossibility of being normal. Storm stood. Going to the table under the window, she moved some stacked paperbacks to reach a sheaf of paper, taking the top, blank sheet. A pen, held left-handed. The writing. And during this, Harmony saw a new and different energy, as though . . . what? Storm had become, not someone else. Someone. All her blankness abandoned in the simple intention of forming two words. PRUNELLA WEBSTER. Authority in the way she'd handed the paper over, her eyes suddenly acute. A particular gift, for Harmony.

On the beach, Mum stretched a toe to prod at the scurf of tideline debris: seaweed, the plastic webbing from packs of cans, sticks, an ancient Yazoo bottle. In the old days, she would have said something about contempt for the planet, or made Harmony help her fish out the worst contaminants (plastic webbing, because sea birds). Today she seemed content to look at them, entranced, even, by each thing she saw, as though discovering beauty.

'Have you looked her up? This Webster woman?'

It was just as long since this had happened, Aurora weaving into Harmony's thoughts as though they'd been having a conversation. Stu used to joke she was part witch. She knew who it was when the phone rang and was uncannily good at finding anything lost. Once.

Harmony hadn't looked up Prunella Webster. The name

was Storm's. She was relying on the police to put it into their computer. She was an idiot.

'It rang a bell,' said Aurora. 'I said.'

'You didn't say.'

'Didn't I?' Arms folded, Mum looked at her feet, then Harmony's.

'What size are you now?'

'Seven. What kind of bell?'

Aurora shook her head. 'You'll need to look it up. Something from . . . '

The sea provided no answers. 'They won't grow any more,' said Mum, about Harmony's feet. A few dots of rain landed, stippling the sand. Mum considered the sky.

'Maybe I will go back.'

She asked Harmony if she minded coming along. Harmony saw how the short journey daunted her, the crossing of the road. This relapse into frailty opened up a new sinkhole of disappointment. For so long Mum's inertia had led Harmony to expect nothing. How stupid was she, so quickly restored to thinking that life might have started again? But as they walked back to the house, another, more shameful hope bloomed. If this was just a one-off, Harmony would be able to make it work with Declan after all.

She left Aurora sitting at the bottom of the stairs, urging her back out on her mythical trip to the library. As penance for her fungal ill will towards Mum's recovery, Harmony walked all the way into town, as if it really had been her plan all along. She didn't even stop at the Spar for a Magnum; Aurora's burst of activity had made her superstitious about eating forbidden food so close to home. The library, when she got there, was closed. For good. There was a sign outside telling everyone to go to Whitby if they wanted to borrow a book. A big, rounded logo decorated the sign, belonging to the company that had taken it over. Its circle was formed of what were meant to be interlocking hands or cradling arms, but to Harmony their rounded intersections looked obscene, like squid fucking. If squid even did that. The squid were going to turn the library into a Community Creative Space. Portable metal barriers had been set up across the wide Edwardian portico, as though thwarted book-borrowers might storm the building.

Harmony sat on the steps and ate her Magnum. Almond; the Co-op in town hadn't had mint. As she sucked the nub of chocolate that anchored the last of the casing against the stick, the taste of wood tanging her mouth, she clicked out of MySecretHeart – still no update from Beetlebutt – and tapped 'Prunella Webster' into Google. Waiting for her phone to load, she looked up and saw Finn, Aidan's hot friend from school. He was mooching by the top of the precinct over the road, the neck of his white shirt open, hands in pockets, St Ben's tie and blazer probably stowed in the backpack slumped at his feet. Aidan had told her that they all did this to avoid being beaten up on the bus, though it was obvious they were St Ben's boys, not least because no one from Severn Oak bothered to remove parts of their uniform.

Seeing Finn glance her way and give a desultory chin lift of acknowledgement, Harmony waved across the road, eager and alarmed. He remembered her. As the beaming 'hiya!' rose to her mouth she saw, too late, that Finn's greeting was directed to a Severn Oak lad – his identity clear from the sharp edges of his haircut as much as his purple tie and blazer – approaching from the zebra crossing between them. Harmony killed her speech, mortified on her own behalf.

Finn, though, hadn't noticed her at all. He was already hoisting his backpack to one shoulder, not planning to stick around now his mate was on his way. The two boys performed the standard fist bump, heads averted. It ended in a hand clasp, during which the Severn Oak lad expertly palmed over a little bag of weed. Finn bungled the catch and the bag dropped to the ground, where he squatted – Harmony could see the shape of the *fuck* in his mouth – to pick it up. Severn Oak was amused, both were unconcerned. Finn stood, pocketing the weed, while from the other pocket he took a banknote (ten or twenty, Harmony couldn't see: was weed really that cheap?) that he uncrumpled with a few clumsy swipes before handing it over. Harmony felt the adrenalin of transgression. Here in public, outside the library, even if it was closed.

Be normal. Just be normal. She scrutinised her phone: *Results for Prunella Webster.*

'Hey, Harm!'

Confused, she turned. Did Finn actually know her name? Of course not. The 'hey' had come from behind her. It was Aidan, on his bike, huge knees bare in fluorescent-yellow shorts, round cheeks pinked by the ride from school. As he sat up to coast the few metres before he braked, he hailed Finn, matter-of-fact. Severn Oak lad was already loping up Court Street back to the sea, in the opposite direction from Aidan, who didn't give him a glance as he landed one foot to balance the bike. Astride, he waited for Finn to approach. Finn's greeting, chiding Aidan for lateness, indicated Aidan was meant to be part of the transaction Harmony had seen. Stu and Mum were known to enjoy a spliff, or had been, in happier times. But she knew Mel's outrage, if she found out what Aidan was up to, would be off the scale.

'What's up?' Aidan called to her from across the road.

Harmony gestured behind her, to the locked library doors. 'Didn't realise it had closed.'

'The fuck.'

As ever, Aidan was affable. Since they were heading Harmony's way, he invited her to join them. Why not? She chucked her lolly stick and crossed the road. After a grunted hey, Finn restricted his animated but mainly incomprehensible conversation to Aidan, who sat on the bike between the two of them, propelling it along with lazy strokes of his feet. A blue carrier bag full of aerosol cans swung heavily from one handlebar. They were going tagging on The Walk, Aidan explained.

The Walk was a disused railway branch line that had once lured tourists up the coast from Whitby. Abandoned in the early 1960s, it had decayed for twenty years, until a local group claimed it as a conservation area. They stripped out the vandalised track, creating a walkable channel bordered by imperilled varieties of rampant greenery, which butterflies and bats and rarer bird species had since been coaxed back to colonise. Three large Victorian railway bridges punctuated the four-mile stretch, every brick of the arches and pillars below occluded by the unnatural metallic sheen of spray paint.

Aidan's enthusiasm for tagging was news to Harmony, although she knew The Walk well, from the days when Aurora had fancied nature study as part of her education. Aurora didn't know many plant names, but had encouraged the younger Harmony to pick and poke and bring things back home in jars to die. A happy time. Even then there had always been a couple of taggers hard at work beneath the arches, surrounded by a sweet fug of weed. Although The Walk was popular with dog owners, Mel wouldn't be persuaded that the route wasn't a refuge for flashers, drunks and addicts, as it had been in her childhood, and she refused to use it. In all ways, the place was perfect for Aidan.

The rain made another half-hearted effort as they neared her house. Harmony realised how little she wanted to go in, back to either the predictable boredom of revision or the unreliable burden of Mum in her newly lively state. Careful not to look up, she continued to walk with the boys. They seemed prepared to tolerate her presence, saying nothing as the three of them left the beach road behind. Apparently she was with them now. By the time they reached the brambled opening that led to the top of The Walk's first section, the rain had given up again, releasing the pencil-lead smell of damp dust without washing it away. Finn told Aidan he looked a total tool in his kit. Aidan told him to fuck off, but pulled his school trousers from his backpack and climbed into them, over his yellow shorts.

Both boys rejected the first bridge, for reasons she didn't understand. Aidan pedalled ahead to recce the second, leaving her alone with Finn. The two of them walked in parallel, along the ghost path of the train tracks. Harmony had been rationing her looks at him all the way from Evensand. His unbuttoned white shirt, the tails hanging; his black hair sprung to curls from the humidity; his full, raspberry-red mouth with its scant moustache of fine black hair moodily agape over his glinting braces. He was just so . . . large. She got out her phone, as did Finn.

Do you mean 'Prunella Webber?'

Dismissing the suggestion, Harmony scanned the results. *Prunella* was a twilled woollen dress fabric, whatever twilled was, which got its name from the colour of prunes. Harmony skipped through the page of variations on this information, cited to Webster's dictionary. On the second page, Prunella Webster was highlighted in the stub of a Wiki article. She tapped the link.

'It's calm.'

Aidan squealed the bike to a stop across their path, scuffing dirt. He had judged the second bridge acceptable. To Harmony, it looked much the same as the first, but Finn agreed. The boys stood back, surveying the competition. On one side of the arch, the tags spangling its expanse were dominated by a huge line of pneumatic gangsta letters in pearled green and purple, reading 'GROONZ'. The whole tag was thickly ringed in silver, tripled with silver dashes at one bottom corner to give a cartoon bouncing effect. Working quickly, Aidan took out a can from the plastic bag and began to spray a fuzzed red outline over the shape made by his predecessor.

'That's a shame.'

Aidan turned, killing the spray.

'It's really good.'

She could see he hadn't even looked. Shrugging, he aimed the nozzle back at the line he'd started. She couldn't imagine her cousin would achieve anything nearly as good as Groonz. Edward was famously the artistic one in that family. But the main point, possibly, was to obliterate what had come before. Taggers were boys.

While Aidan worked, Finn sat on the scrubby verge that rose off the bridge, long legs stretched, and began to build a spliff. Passing beneath the arch, Harmony walked up to the derelict platform beyond. *Calm.* Who knew how easy it could be to walk into another world? Making sure she could still be seen, especially by Finn, she sat in what she hoped appeared as artless nonchalance on the mossed concrete.

Cross-legged, peering down with the semblance of profound yet sensual thought into the lush weeds filling the drop below, a muddied flash of red caught her eye: an abandoned sweatshirt, or jacket. Harmony leaned over the platform edge, delving for a ribbed portion of what looked like cuff.

Too late, she recognised the serrated, spear-leaved weeds matching the height of the concrete. Sitting back on to the platform, she endured the agony of the nettle stings fizzing along her fingers and up her wrists, hoping Finn hadn't noticed. She saw he was preoccupied, working some origami with a Rizla. The jumper flopped beside her, sodden. It was filthy, unsalvageable; it must have been there for months. She toed it back down among the nettles and refreshed her screen.

The Wiki entry was about a man called Anthony Laurence Minton Frome (*b 1916 d 1977*). Harmony skimmed the article, looking for Prunella Webster, passing Mass Observation and Sociology en route. She backed up to a sentence that ended '. . . *in association with Prunella Webster*'. The entire sentence read:

From 1943–45, Frome conducted pioneering fieldwork in coastal North Yorkshire, publishing his findings in 1948 as 'Evensand: a seaside town', in association with Prunella Webster [citation needed].

There was no further mention of Prunella Webster. Harmony thumbed back, to check. Nothing. The name wasn't underlined, so she couldn't pursue it to another link. Harmony pondered, against the hissing of Aidan's paint can and the shrilling of the restored birds. Evensand, though. Inspired, she googled 'Anthony Frome Evensand'.

There was a lot about him.

From the lack of repercussions, Mel could only assume any plans Stu was making about going to Australia were still being conducted in private. When she rang to ask him what was happening for Harmony's sixteenth birthday, he immediately passed her on to Harmony, worried perhaps that she might probe the other matter. Harmony, it turned out, had very clear plans for her day. It fell, conveniently, on Thursday. Could Mel take her to the Frome house, she asked? Mel had no idea what this was. Some sort of restaurant, she assumed, which sounded a nice idea. She offered to book a table for the evening, resolving to sweep Stu and Aurora along in the arrangement. No, Harmony said, the two of them would have to go during the day. There were opening hours, ten to four. And it was a house, not a restaurant. It wouldn't take them long, but you definitely needed a car.

'It's like, a historic thing?'

A stately home. Far easier than corralling everyone into a restaurant, and actually quite enjoyable. Edward was the only one of hers keen on that sort of thing, and he'd be at school. It was just the right time of year, if they were lucky with the weather.

Another jolt of guilt buzzed. It was weeks since Mel had been to see Storm, for all her giving out to Stu that they were prepared to offer her a home. Not entirely to her surprise, Ian hadn't been keen when she'd broached it. Harmony was one thing, he said, but a complete stranger ... He had agreed with Mel that it was all very sad, what had happened, but should they really be taking any sort of responsibility? What about the boys, with Aidan facing public exams next year and Eddy starting at St Ben's? Mel hadn't disabused him of his notion of Edward's prospects. Edward would be starting somewhere next year, St Ben's or no. Thank God the entrance exam wasn't until the autumn. Perhaps Ian was right, and a change beyond their cousin coming to live with them would be disastrously unsettling for the boys. She hadn't offered anything concrete to Storm at her last visit beyond raising the possibility of a room in their house, but the thought of confronting her face to face now contained the discomfort of this offstage decision. She would go to the clinic once she wasn't quite so busy.

Aurora, after helping her to the epiphany regarding Mrs Beagles and the Spectacular, had further amazed her by not only goading Stu into providing a supplier for the parachute silk, but offering to sew the rainbow banner herself. Then the phone calls had started. Wanting to know which colours would correspond to which dances, Aurora jibbed at Mel's choices. How could 'Back to Black' go in the blue section? Wouldn't the infants look odd in purple costumes? Surely the music for 'Clair de lune' – *for fuck's sake, Mel, it means moonlight* – was the opposite of orange. This was annoying enough, but Mel was fighting a war on two fronts.

Mel's exhilarating plan, following Aurora's suggestion about cutting the tedious spoken links in the show, had been that each banner would simply be brought on stage by two of the correspondingly costumed dancers, who, after sticking their colour to the rainbow, would then assume their places with the rest of their class and begin their routine. But following the lesson when Mel announced this innovation, Kitty Sue's mum had taken Mel aggressively to task, accusing her of trashing her daughters' dreams. Lola and Kitty Sue, as the best junior dancers, had earned the mantle of responsibility for the show. Unmollified by Mel's assurances that the girls would have their moment in the sun, Kitty Sue's mum had begun to stir up dissent among the weaker mums, muttering about Mrs Beagles and cherished traditions. Mel was terrified that she might withdraw Kitty Sue from the show entirely. And if Kitty Sue went, Lola would surely follow. Mel relied on both girls to marshal the less talented members of their groups, like sheepdogs nipping at the heels of straying sheep. Without them it would be chaos.

She conceded. Kitty Sue and Lola, in special rainbow unitards, were to run on with the banners for each dance, Mel promised Kitty Sue's mum. She gave them bits of business, a few linking steps which she encouraged them to improvise. The girls resorted to the traditional pointing and hand-clutching, which Mel feared Kitty Sue's mum would have coached them to ramp up to stage-school level by the night of the performance.

Passing the civic centre, her minimalist poster reproached her: 'NYDA presents: Summer Spectacular'. Escaping the tyranny of Mrs Beagles had been a dream, all too brief.

It was all right for Aurora; she wouldn't even come to the bloody show. Mel recalled the one performance Aurora had attended, the year Harmony took part. Her silence afterwards had seared Mel with her disapproval, even as Mel fielded the praise of parents claiming, as some did every year, that it was definitely the best show ever. In the lobby of the civic centre, Stu, equally mute, had darted away to the bar to get Mel an unwanted white wine, fleeing his obvious dismay at what he'd been forced to witness. It had all added to the familiar, soaking wrongness.

Well, she had other things to feel ashamed about at the moment. Her failure to offer Storm a home, for one. Why did Aurora need to know which dance corresponded to which colour, anyway? It was just a bit of sewing. This much she could moan about to Ian.

'Good Aurora's feeling a bit better, though.'

This mild remark, uttered as Ian craned to scan the open fridge for a beer, skewered her. Of course: Aurora was feeling better. She must be. The sewing was one sign, but her arsiness was the clearest one. She should be celebrating this improvement instead of deploring it, like the carping old hag she evidently was.

Had Stu noticed the change? It couldn't be relied on. The public interest taken in Stu in his late teens and early twenties meant he hadn't been forced to develop his muscle of interest in other people. He was like a tennis player with one massive forearm, unnaturally trained to serve himself. Or maybe he'd always been like that, which was why he'd accepted his early success with such blank aplomb. Mel remembered him getting off the phone and standing at the door of their childhood living room to tell her the news of the Koolaid Conspiracy two-record deal, as offhandedly as if he'd heard a distant relative was getting married. Although that might have been shock, rather than aplomb. It was difficult in their house to do justice to big news, or any news at all. Mel recalled her 13-year-old self at the tea table, excitedly announcing a school trip to France, which no one in their family had ever visited. There had been silence from both parents, before her mum's heartfelt, sighed 'oh dear'.

Amid all this personal murk, the clarity of fulfilling Harmony's wish for her birthday outing shone as a beacon. This, at least, was some simple good she was able to do. The weather on Thursday morning was fair; no rain, at least. Before she left the house, Mel ransacked the drawer in the spare room where she kept all her pupils' Christmas and end-of-term offerings. She and Ian were going to give Harmony money, with the promise that Mel would take her to York or Leeds or even Manchester to spend it if she liked. But Mel recognised the importance of having something to unwrap, along with the improbability of Stu or Aurora having bothered. Unable to choose between high-end shower gel and a scented candle, she wrapped both. There was a card, signed by Ian and the boys and the traditional fake paw print from Toothpaste, and she'd made a cake Harmony could share with them all when they came back from their outing.

When Mel parked outside the house, Aurora was first to appear, billowing parachute silk. She was dressed, Mel noted, and had eyelashes, which meant she was wearing mascara. Definite progress. Ian was right.

'I think you should have a look.'

Reluctantly, Mel got out of the car. Aurora demonstrated the size so far of Red Orange Yellow, draping the Velcroed strips over the boot, their ends trailing.

'It's not going to be too big, is it?'

It didn't look like it, to Mel. She had given Aurora the

measurements, adjusted for the back of the civic centre stage. Aurora promised she'd followed them, to the centimetre. As she twitched at the seams, trying to spread the strips to be seen to their best advantage, Mel saw what was really needed. It was unusual, in fact possibly unprecedented, for Aurora to want her approval. Could it be a side effect of the antidepressants?

'It looks great to me. Just right.'

'I've just basted the side seams, it'll be neater, obviously – and I can always come in a bit on the ends. It'd be good to see it in place ... '

'Can't wait to see it finished!'

Aurora gathered in the fabric as Harmony appeared from the house, looking surprisingly presentable. Perhaps things were looking up all round.

'Now, what about blue? Which dances?' Aurora asked. 'You're not trotting out "Rhapsody in Blue" again, are you? Don't tell me – "Blue Moon".'

Not only was Mel trotting out 'Rhapsody in Blue', as part of the same section Tyler in Infant Ballet was appearing as Little Boy Blue, encircled by blue-sashed toddler shepherdesses. She said she couldn't remember without her list, and diverted into giving Harmony a birthday kiss. A shame, she added formulaically, that Aurora wasn't coming along on their outing. As Aurora shook the silk from the boot, it hovered above them for a moment, a sunset canopy.

'Not sure I'm wanted.'

Harmony reared a look at Mel, of surprise and dismay. 'Course you're wanted!'

'Course you are, you silly mare!'

The silk, sharing Aurora's delayed gravity, alighted at last into her gathering arms. Mel said there was plenty of room, and Harmony definitely didn't mind sitting in the back. Aurora didn't appear to believe them. Mel continued to insist, opening the passenger door, but Aurora, folding the banner ever smaller, shook her head. Her mouth was a resigned, infuriating curl, a private joke she shared with her sewing about their insincerity.

'Dawn, bloody get in, will you?'

Mel really meant it now. Aurora looked up, shaken out of her communion with the beginning of the rainbow.

'Next time.'

Mel saw that this pantomime of not being wanted was preferable to ownership of her own aversions. Bloody people. But before she got in the car she kissed Aurora goodbye, which she never did. When Dawn had come back as Aurora, she had started that: hello and goodbye, one on each cheek, French-style. It still made Mel giggle with surprise, and if she saw it coming at an opened door, she made sure to step back and avoid it. But now she leaned in and smacked Aurora a proper kiss, clamped her in a hug. She breathed the medicinal, honeyed rose of the hand cream. Poor bloody people.

'Definitely next time. And I won't take no for an answer.'

Harmony reinstated herself in the front seat. Mel hadn't had time to look properly at where they were supposed to be going, but Harmony said she had it on her phone. It was a few miles north of Brazen Point, on the Goldsborough road. A house lived in during the war by a writer or politician Mel had never heard of.

'Your mum seems a bit better.'

Harmony murmured an acknowledgement that also indicated her reluctance to discuss Aurora.

'Has Stu talked to you at all?'

He had, though not, it became clear, about Australia. Mel decided to steer Harmony away from the possibly volatile subject of living with them. It was meant to be a special day. Instead, she asked her what she thought she might like to do next year – try for sixth form college, or have a look at some other courses, or think about getting a job? At this, Harmony's engagement dropped. She gazed out of the window, *mmn*-ing meaningless, blanket acquiescence at whatever Mel proposed.

'There's ages,' she said, finally. 'I haven't even done my maths yet.'

'I know it can seem it,' said Mel, 'but you've got to think ahead. I didn't, when I was your age. I got a bit stuck.'

'Stuck?'

This at least hooked Harmony's goldfish interest. She sat straighter, turning to look at Mel as she drove, expecting a story.

What to say? It wasn't a story. Although Harmony might have been surprised by how desolate Mel had felt when Dawn had buggered off to do her degree at Keele. International Studies, pretty arcane in 1983. Mel assumed Dawn had no interest in International Studies, or even a degree, and was just doing it to be different. Mel's teachers had suggested she herself apply to university, but without sufficient enthusiasm to pile through either Mel's assumption of their underlying apathy or the actual apathy of her parents. She had thought Dawn, so much less conscientious than her, had felt the same way. She had been wrong.

By the time Dawn left for Keele, Mel had been working all summer at a care home in Ruswarp (which was still there, part of a franchise now), making what felt like a lot of money from shifts and night shifts and double shifts she had had the stamina, at eighteen, to take on. In the gaps, she continued to take lessons with Mrs Beagles. After Mel had run out of children's exams to pass, Mrs Beagles had begun to train her and a couple of other girls for their professional teaching exams. This was less a decision than an unchallenged continuum.

All this time, Stu was off being a rock star. Mel wondered now if she had stuck so close to home to calm the troubled waters of their parents' panic about him abandoning his place at Manchester and the guarantee that came with a degree, in those days, both of a grant and a job at the end of it. As a boy, Stu's unprecedented trajectory towards further education had been a source of pride, as opposed to what the Ansholms saw as the mystifying redundancy of a degree in their daughter's case. Putting some of this into words for Harmony, it boggled Mel how readily she'd accepted the status quo. It hadn't felt like that at the time. The buoyancy of her mum and dad's baffled, gentle pride in everything she'd ever done, from passing a tap exam to driving on the motorway at night, always kept her afloat above the rock bottom of their low expectations.

And also – she saved the words for this – it had suited her. She had hidden even from herself the convenience of her parents' lack of aspiration on her behalf. Instead, in a fit of worthy one-upmanship provoked by Dawn wanging on in the pub about International Studies, Mel had declared a desire to do a physiotherapy course, for which she wouldn't receive a grant. As she shaped it self-righteously for Dawn, the work at the home was aimed at sensibly shoring up her savings so that her mum and dad wouldn't have to fork out, which they couldn't have done in any case, being unable to afford it.

She hadn't really wanted to do a physio course. It just sounded better, having a plan, and the course seemed tenuously connected to working at the home, and even dancing. On the day she and Dawn stood in front of the school noticeboards, searching out the paper strips attached to their names spelling success or failure, leaving Evensand had seemed as impossible and reckless as walking off the top of Brazen Point. She couldn't tell anyone that, not even Dawn. Especially not Dawn. Mel had got better grades (two Bs and a C; Geography, Biology and Maths), but Dawn's were more than good enough for her Keele offer. They'd loved her at the interview, and only wanted two Es. That night, along with the rest of the sixth form, Mel got pissed on Pernod and black at the Salutation, toasting the future everyone seemed to want except her.

Now, in the car, she attempted to impart lessons learned.

'It's always good to know your own mind, to know what you want.'

'I know what I want,' said Harmony.

This was surprising to hear.

'Well, good.'

When she and Ian started going out, more than two years after school, Mel was still working at the home. She had become deputy manager in all but name, and was also, with associate teaching exams in ballet and stage under her belt, Mrs Beagles' principal assistant. Her bank book, a real book in those analogue days, was filled with pages of neat cashier's ballpoint totalling the cheques she'd been socking away every week. This meant when she and Ian came to buy their first place – an ex-council bargain not far from where Stu and Aurora lived now, part of the first wave of the sell-offs – Mel had paid the whole deposit: five thousand pounds. Ian's parents, who had been braced to stump up the cash, were amazed. Mr and Mrs Bale thought Mel was a lovely lass, but they were dispassionate Evensand snobs. Since Ian had been to St Benedict's and grown up in a detached house, it was clear he was better than Mel. The money, in destabilising this assumption, actually made them like her less.

The relief, though, when she and Ian decided to get married. No more pretending, even though everyone apart from Dawn had stopped asking about the physio course ages before. Mel had passed her teaching exams and was fully qualified to teach tap, ballet, modern and stage (nobody taught stage). Mrs Beagles' knees had continued to deteriorate. Stu's second album had tanked. The present ate up the future and shat it out as the past.

'You've done OK,' said Harmony now.

Mel couldn't disagree.

'Well, it was more luck than judgement, is what I'm saying.'

Mainly luck, if that's what you were calling the ungraspable accident of time and place. Even if their Joseph made it to university, he wouldn't be able to earn enough to put a deposit down any time soon. Though he was lucky that Ian would be able to sort him out with one of his starter homes if the time came. Not an outright gift, because they didn't believe in silver spoons, but a bit of help. Would he even get a proper job, the way he was going? God knows if any of the boys would.

Harmony was still floundering in the gap between luck and judgement. 'What if you have bad luck?'

'Well, yes.'

'No, but what if you do? You can't do anything about it, can you?'

'Yes you can.' Mel watched the road. 'Because if you've planned ahead, you'll have . . . contingencies.'

'Contingencies? Like . . . savings?'

'I'm not really talking about money, Harmony.'

Harmony twisted a strand of hair around her forefinger, bored or in disagreement. A look of Aurora huffed her mouth. She thought they might have missed the turning. Surely they would have passed one of those brown signs, said Mel. Harmony said she wasn't sure it was that kind of place.

Incredibly, back when the past was still the future, it was Dawn who had tried to take Mel on about the way her life was going. They'd been in the Sal. Mel was paying. 1985. Dawn, with a confrontational haircut, was back on her last vacation before finals.

'You can't enjoy it, changing people's nappies.'

Mel had told her countless times that dealing with incontinence was a very small part of her job at the home. She hadn't told her, yet, about Ian.

'Don't you want to get out of here?'

'Not particularly.'

The Salutation, still going strong today under shades of Farrow & Ball and a gastro menu, had been their regular since O-level year. Then, it was overwhelmingly brown and crimson, kippered by a million Benson & Hedges. A sour, reassuring stench of spilled ale emanated from the carpets, and there was always a fire. Coal, not wood. It was like drinking inside a dog.

'Rather you than me, mate.'

Mate was a new thing, acquired at uni. It hadn't occurred to Mel till then that Dawn wouldn't come back after Keele. She felt a little foolish even asking her what she was thinking of doing, what job she'd be getting. And then alarmed, as Dawn burst into tears.

She was pregnant; ten weeks. She knew exactly because it was a lad at a party. She and her boyfriend always used condoms because he was petrified about her getting pregnant, even though she was on the pill, so it definitely wasn't him.

'But . . . you're on the pill.'

It happened, said Dawn, especially when you were a bit, shall we say, hit and miss about taking it. Mel marvelled. Hit and miss? There were even days printed on the packet.

'Anyway, it makes me feel weird.'

Two days later, Mel drove Dawn down to Scarborough in her new car. A tomato-red Panda, secondhand, her pride and joy. She was still nervous on the motorway, particularly at roundabouts, but Dawn didn't notice. She hadn't learned to drive herself, and had complete, incurious faith in Mel's competence. The tiny gap of rolled-down window Dawn sporadically used to smoke out of admitted a blast of air that buffeted the car's tinny chassis, increasing Mel's already considerable anxiety. Dawn turned up the Smiths tape she'd produced from her bag far too loud for Mel to concentrate on the road, and when Dawn insisted you had to listen to The Smiths loud or not listen to them at all, Mel turned them off. They weren't nice to each other, that morning.

The abortion clinic wasn't at all clinical, but run out of a terrace flanked by seaside bed and breakfasts. The waiting room felt far too much like a living room for Mel's liking. She had anticipated surroundings that corresponded to the self-important maturity of their mission. Dawn just took the piss. From the armchair next to Mel, she kept up the manic jokiness she'd maintained all morning until the moment the nurse called her in, when all the blood left her face, making Mel feel suddenly sick.

Blood. Following the nurse's instructions, they'd stopped on the way back to stock up with maxi-pads. Dawn, silent about her interlude beyond the three-piece suite, resumed the jokes, light with relief and adrenalin. Mel let her put in *The Queen is Dead* and play it as loud as she liked, one side after another and back to the beginning, all the way up to Evensand. To this day, even if she was in a shop and heard that unprecedented opening chord, it sprang from her body the nauseous dynamic of wet motorway traffic surging past as she tried to get her and Dawn home: here, uncanny; suddenly gone. A thrilling announcement of sex and death.

A week later, Dawn was off to do her finals. When Harmony was born, nearly fifteen years later, Mel hadn't even known Dawn was pregnant. Scant communication had become the norm between them, but taking in the postcard announcing Harmony's birth – the black and white Mapplethorpe shot of Patti Smith looking like a degenerate nineteenth-century boy which she recognised from Stu's copy of *Horses* – it struck Mel then that Dawn's gesture of announcement, as well as the inclusion of a very un-Dawnlike exclamation mark, suggested the overcoming of an obstacle whose existence had never been acknowledged by either of them.

'Life's complicated,' she said to Harmony, for all of this.

'Yeah.'

As if the girl could know, at her age. Well, perhaps more than many at her age. Mel probably still had the Patti Smith postcard somewhere. Joe would be all right, just about, and Aidan was never a worry, but what would happen to Eddy?

When they found the Frome house, after locating a farm track next to a private road that briefly diverted them on to a false trail, Mel understood what Harmony had meant by it not being the kind of place to merit a brown sign. She'd been expecting elderly attendants to usher her into a swarded car park, where they would press her into offsetting the cost of her visit against National Trust or English Heritage membership. Instead, she stopped on a rutted verge beside a barred gate. Pulling in behind a battered blue Berlingo, Mel thought uneasily of doggers.

'Where did you say you found out about this place?'

'Online. It said you have to walk from here.'

Mel was reassured to see a weathered yellow footpath sign by the gate. Harmony said it wouldn't be far. Shutting the gate behind them, they crossed the field beyond and came out of an identical gate at the far corner.

'That must be it.'

In front of them, across a track, stood an unpicturesque red-brick cottage. It was the kind built for tenant farmworkers over a hundred years ago, a gabled square divided into two halves, with a door on either side. Mel's paternal grandparents had lived in half of a similar house, if not in such isolation. What had drawn Harmony here?

'Are you sure?'

Harmony was sure, though she appeared a little disappointed. There was a moment of confusion as she decided which door to knock on. Getting closer, a marked division was visible between the building's two sides: the paintwork and path of one dilapidated against the fresh maintenance of the other. Harmony chose the smarter, powder-blue door, which lacked a doorbell. Tapping the knocker incited barking from inside the adjoining cottage, but nothing else happened for long enough to give Mel hope they might be able to abandon the visit entirely and find somewhere nice for lunch. Harmony herself was stepping away when the door was opened by a young woman. The delay had prepared Mel for unfriendliness, but she greeted them enthusiastically; an embarrassed compensation, perhaps, for having been in the loo when they knocked. The woman was in her twenties, opulently plump, with vivid, Hispanic colouring. She was dressed like a land girl in a red print tea-dress, lips clashing scarlet and black hair tucked into a yellow print bandana. Mel liked this look, though she was uncertain of its context; if the clothes were simply the woman's style, as seemed to be common among some sections of the young, or whether she was meant to be in the 1940s, because of the house. Harmony had mentioned something about the war.

'Did you make an appointment?'

As a further disorientation, the girl's accent was American. Harmony said she hadn't made an appointment. The curator, if that's what she was, immediately reassured them that it wasn't necessary. She could fit them in, although there was someone coming at two. Not exactly rushed off her feet here, she added, waving them inside. The low warmth of her voice invited them to share the ironic gap between its educated modulation and the rest of the world. Mel felt reassured.

Inside, the house smelled damp, preserved, of paper and upholstery and woollen clothes that had become wet and been inadequately dried. A smell of the past. The 1940s, Mel decided, definitely. Facing them, three steps ahead, was a steep staircase, and just before, in the tiny hall, a door on either side, one open and one closed. Counter-intuitively, their guide led them to the left, closed door, darting back first to close the door to their right. Mel glimpsed the zombie glare of a laptop screen before the door shut. The young woman opened the other door.

'Here you go . . . '

It was one step down into a mean-windowed, dim living room with an unlit fireplace. Mel recognised original wallpaper, swathed with basketwork and ribbons faded to urinous yellows and sepias. Her grandparents had had something similar. She also recognised the corrupt sweetness that thickened the musty smell of the room: ancient pipe smoke.

'So. I'm guessing you know a little about Anthony Frome, since you're here?'

'Nothing at all.'

The girl blinked.

'I know a bit,' Harmony intervened.

'Don't mind me,' said Mel.

'Well, OK, so background . . . Tony Frome came to Farm Cottages in 1940 after he was invalided out of the army with TB? Tuberculosis. The farm at the time belonged to the father of an old school friend of his, and Tony rented the cottage for a peppercorn rent of ten shillings a year.'

Mel wandered around the room as the girl continued to speak, her chocolate-sauce tones coating the words so deliciously she felt no need to pay attention to the dullness beneath. The furniture was arranged and accessorised as though this man who Mel had never heard of had just popped out for a paper nearly eighty years ago and never returned. Sure enough, she noted a pipe on a low table near the fire. It sat next to an open notebook, weighted to stay at a particular page by the placement of an uncapped dark green fountain pen. The handwriting was thick and spikily untidy, its ink faded from black to rust in patches. The proximity of this arrangement to a low-seated armchair suggested a favourite working position. By the chintz frill on the bottom of the chair sat an abandoned china cup and saucer – Mel's bird's-eye view took in the ivory interior of the empty cup, crazed with eggshell cracks – and a veined grey marble ashtray. Nothing in the room was either old or beautiful enough, in Mel's opinion, to command interest, though she felt a tiny excitement at the tobacco tin also on the table, her grandad briefly brought back to life by the murky Gold Flake gold and red.

'What about Prunella Webster?' Harmony was asking.

'OK. So Prunella Webster was originally billeted a few miles away from here, in Evensand, and she worked with Tony, conducting some of the original field interviews but also writing up his reports and generally liaising with the Ministry . . . Tony wasn't so much about the admin.'

'Was she, like, his girlfriend?'

Prunella Webster. Mel struggled to see the shape of the bell this rang.

'It was kind of complicated? They were lovers, for sure. She moved in with him here.' A complicit sigh, as though they all knew what was coming next. 'But he was married, and also liked men, she was into men and women and was engaged to someone else. . .'

Harmony rang the bell for her. The name on the note Aurora had shown her, she muttered. The name written by Storm.

The American girl had turned away to fetch them a black and white photo, which she removed from its place on the mantelpiece.

'Here they are.'

Mel recognised the front door of the cottage, behind the man and woman. The man, Tony, was a spare, Brylcreemed figure. His horn-rimmed glasses reflected white circles of light, rendering his face unknowable, although the wiry assertion of his stance exuded energy. He stood next to a tall young woman in a print dress that hung awkwardly above her long bare calves, inches too short. She held a cigarette, her other arm high across her body, a cupped hand supporting the elbow of her raised smoking arm. As if in amusement with the person taking the photo, or a good-natured reluctance towards the whole enterprise, she was looking down, fairish hair blown towards her smiling mouth. Everything about her suggested a not unappealing deficit of the self-assurance in which Tony evidently abounded. Square to the camera, he had his arm around her, as though bracing her to the taking of the shot. Perhaps the picture had been his idea. When Mel bent round Harmony, who was scrutinising the photo centimetres away from the protective glass, she saw that the hand of the man's embracing arm didn't emerge at the woman's waist, but at the underside of her breast, where it puckered the fabric of her dress.

'Yuk.'

So Harmony had also noticed this. A moment, accidental or intentional, trapped seventy years before. Revealing not just itself, but the high bulge of Prunella Webster's belly straining against the frock's blurred print.

'There's another ... I'm Lara, by the way.'

The young woman, Lara, led them to a walnut side table which contained an arrangement of clouded drinks bottles, their shoulders furred with dust; whisky, gin and French-labelled vermouth. Next to them was a framed studio portrait of Prunella Webster, also in black and white. In its formal

269

high focus, she looked nothing like the attractively tentative girl in the snap. Buried beneath the past, her youth was reined in by oppressively moulded waves and dark lipstick, her unplucked eyebrows and fierce, pale-eyed, off-camera stare suggestive of rebellion or bluestocking integrity. She looked much more definite than she had next to Tony Frome.

'This was taken a few years earlier, perhaps when Prunella came out.'

Seeing Harmony's confusion, Lara added that she'd been coming out as a debutante. 'As in, into society?'

Still largely unenlightened, Harmony asked if she had had any children. Well, said Lara. That was a whole can of worms.

'She's pregnant, in the photo,' said Mel. Had this really passed Harmony by?

Lara nodded, pulling a face, as though pregnancy was the least of what she had to say on the matter. 'The baby was born here. A girl. That was kind of a big deal, in those days, given her situation.'

Mel could imagine. Her own mother used to tell a story about her engagement, in the early 1950s. She and Mel's father had spent their spare evenings wallpapering the room they had found to rent after their marriage, while they waited to proceed up the council list for a house. After Mrs Ansholm's return on one of these evenings, upon the discovery of a smear of wallpaper paste on the skirt of her coat by her mother, she had been thrashed. As she told the story to Mel, her own mother's hysteria and rage had been all the more terrible because she couldn't explain it in any way, and Mrs Ansholm had been too innocent to understand until after she was married. Mel's grandmother had assumed the stain to be ejaculate.

London bohemians might have been given more leeway, but Evensand was Evensand. From the look of her, Prunella Webster lacked the hardness, or worldliness, or even wealth, that might have eased her passage in the difficult life she had apparently chosen for herself.

And when had Prunella Webster died, Harmony wanted to know? Well, this was a good question, Lara said. It was difficult to find out what had happened to her after the war. She'd broken off her engagement, despite or perhaps because of the child. She hadn't got married to Tony Frome, who had stayed with his forbearing wife until much later. It was possible that she'd gotten married to someone else, and the unknown change of name meant it had been impossible to track her down so far.

'We don't even know if she kept the baby. There are adoption records to go through . . . '

She hadn't given up, Lara reassured them. She'd gotten very interested in Prunella in the course of her research into Tony . . . in some ways, she was the more interesting character.

Mel realised she should have been paying more attention to what Lara had been saying at the beginning of the tour.

'Sorry. What is it they did, exactly?'

OK, said Lara, taking Mel's ignorance in her mellifluous stride, so they didn't know this? Tony and Prunella had written a book together. A really important book? It just had Tony's name on it, but Prunella had contributed a lot of the research, easily half, and had done the joe jobs, as Lara called them, of collating the interviews and typing them up and typing the book itself and organising the footnotes and editing. And possibly, she concluded, Prunella had done quite a bit of the writing, as Tony in later life seemed to have a big problem with finishing a book to completion. Though there might have been other reasons ... Lara side-eyed the drinks. Apart from a dirty, dried-blood rime in the bottom of the vermouth bottle, they were empty.

'I thought he was a politician,' said Mel.

Lara said that came later. Mel's impatience leapt at her niece. What did any of it have to do with Storm? Harmony, matching her impatience, snapped that this was what she'd come to find out. She took a piece of paper from her pocket, the same piece of paper Aurora had brandished at Mel – Mel saw her sketches for the rainbow banner pencilled across the fold as Harmony smoothed the sheet out and handed it to Lara.

'It's Storm. You know, the missing girl. The girl they found. My auntie found her, actually.'

This with a note of pride. Lara glanced at Mel in surprised acknowledgement, then at the paper.

'She wrote it when I went to visit her. She's at this clinic. They've taken her there to see why she can't remember anything.'

Lara nodded. 'OK ... right. OK.'

'Prunella Webster.'

'So I see.'

The young woman continued to nod, white top teeth pushed hard into the plush red of her lower lip as she considered the piece of paper. Her quickened breathing hoisted the darted bodice of the retro print. All her irony had evaporated, and some of her warmth, diverted into the suddenly troubled business of just being herself.

'OK ... Holy shit.'

The game, whatever it was, was up.

Someone might have thought to inform Dan, before he trekked out to the clinic, that Storm had been moved. If not Lottie, which might have been asking too much, Melanie Bale at least, with her hectoring, tidy way of doing things. But Mason knew that, along with everyone else, Mrs Bale imagined a process in which, as a member of the police force, he had updates delivered to his desk by inhuman agents of efficiency. Dan really wished it was like that. Instead, it was left to one of the nurses to tell him Storm was gone. Young, with bloodhound circles under her eyes. She seemed pissed off when he flourished his folder of mugshots at her, wanting to gain access.

'She's gone.' She was already walking away as she said it, stamping out the spark of his surprise with the declaration that he'd have to talk to Lennox if he wanted to know any more about what was happening.

At least it was one of the days Lennox was in the building, although he made Dan wait. Sitting outside a consultation room – this is what the sign on the door told him – Dan wondered what piece of medical wisdom had processed the girl further into the system. From the girl, his thoughts wandered to what he'd taken to CID the previous day. Although his knackers went watery every time, returning to it was irresistible.

He'd gone into the station early, having taken the trouble to find out that DS Compton would be at the end of his shift. Compton was the most approachable of the Evensand detectives, without the side of his younger colleagues, who all fancied themselves in the job a bit too much from what Dan had observed, making them unlikely to listen to a uniform uncompetitively. He needed to lay it out, plainly: Storm, the vans, Nicu, trafficking. And from there, to raise the possibility that Soccolo had no desire to see the truth come out, and to explore the reasons why. Since Dan had understood his partner's dodginess, it had tainted him like some unpurged toxin. Even Soccolo had noticed, out in the car. What was wrong, he asked, was Dan in love or summat?

Without Soccolo to talk to, he was alone in the world. Despite assiduous attempts to get hold of Lottie, she had remained elusive beyond that one missed call that had coincided with him putting the pieces together about Soccolo, out in the patrol car. Missing her call was clearly a test he'd failed. Truth was, she may have wanted him to fail it. Which was a shame, given how low his own expectations had been of any relationship they might manage to have. Yet he liked her so much.

When Mason intercepted Compton, the older man had suggested they go downstairs to the bay just outside the emergency door which was the station's unofficial smoking area. A career smoker, he bolstered himself with patches and vaping but escaped the building whenever possible to top up his real levels. Dan could hardly say no, though telling his tale alongside Claire and the admin gang (why did so many of those girls smoke?), plus a couple of additional PCs who couldn't get through a shift without tabs, was far from ideal. It was even worse when the snarkiest DC in the department, a bearded wazzock from Sunderland called Hubbard, headed down the stairwell after them, intent on making one of his poncey little rollies. Hubbard caught up with Compton and chatted about a case with no entry point for Mason, who had already decided that he would have to find another opportunity to get Compton on his own. When, though? He could hardly ask him out for a drink. It'd be easier to shag him.

But as Compton pushed at the bar of the emergency door, he nodded to Hubbard, amputating their conversation. With Dan following, he strode through the scree of trampled fag butts in the bay and set out in a diagonal across the car park. They stopped at the end corner outside the holding cells, nice and private. This is what you got in CID, thought Mason, a bit of nous, a bit of actual proaction.

'Now then, what can I do you for?'

Stopping and starting, Dan got it all out, bar the revelation about Soccolo. Along the way, Compton, inhaling committedly, asked questions that showed he was listening. Their blunt acuity made Dan uncomfortable. There were more questions at the end, doubling back and testing connections. Dan was reminded of emerging with some toiled-over creation at primary school, seeing, even as he announced that the haphazardly painted yogurt pots and taped Frosties boxes were the *Titanic*, the flat fact of his delusion. But while Compton didn't enthuse, nor did he deride. Could Dan put it all down in an email, with dates and names? Dan was encouraged. If not the *Titanic*, not a yogurt pot, either. Now was the time.

'One thing I've been wondering about … Dave Soccolo. He's not been too keen on me looking into any of this.'

Compton was on to his second cigarette, lit from his first.

'Dave's a lazy bastard.'

'Yeah, no. Not just that, though.'

Compton's grey face desiccated the remains of its smile at Soccolo's indolence. 'What are you saying?'

'Just … he's not keen. He's prevented me investigating further. I'm wondering why, Sarge.'

When they'd attended on the dead twoccer, after they'd been to the mum's house and Soccolo had delivered the news, Dan had seen his partner cry. They were back in the car, Soccolo insisting on driving as per, and as he put the key in the ignition, the day had surged out of him in a series of full, sobbing heaves. He'd wiped the tears from his eyes and, calling himself a soft bastard, started the car. Dan thought of this as he dobbed him in to Compton. He thought of it now, waiting for Lennox, the immediate relentlessness with which Soccolo had launched into quizzing him about his preferences in nipples. Pink, brown, big, small? Jelly babies or peanuts? Had he ever had a Thai lass? What about black lasses? On and on it had gone, all the way back to the station, bludgeoning away the softness Dan had witnessed.

Today, this morning, he'd only glimpsed Soccolo during the ruck of their briefing meeting. Nothing unusual about that. After that, he'd disappeared. It was Claire who told Mason he'd had a call out to Andjati. Hedge Wars. Dan had had to cadge a lift to the clinic from Lisa and Jade. What if Compton had already said something? Had the wheels of disciplinary machinery been set in motion? His knackers dissolved all over again. Mrs Soccolo, who he'd never met, had baked Dan a Christmas cake. Even though he couldn't stand fruit cake, Dan was touched that she even knew he existed, the conversations about him implied by her offering, surmounted by its plastic robin.

Lennox's door opened, releasing a large-framed Asian man with Lennox close behind him. The man was weeping abjectly, as unselfconscious as a child. Lennox placed a steadying hand on the man's shoulder before he was taken away by a nurse. Mason saw that Lennox might not be that bad. This was an unhelpful thought.

For no reason Dan could see beyond the desire to get rid of the hour he'd just spent, Lennox told him that the departing patient had been hit by a car as he walked his son back from school in Birmingham. The boy had been killed outright, the father left with head injuries that consigned him to a waking present of five minutes. He woke into each loop knowing something was terribly wrong, but unaware that the boy was dead. None of the doctors or nurses ever told him, even though he would forget the news within five minutes. Lennox's account of this was completely devoid of his usual jargon. Like a lass leaving her make-up off for the first time now that they knew each other better, it wasn't entirely welcome. It didn't suit Dan to think of Lennox as a human being. He cut to the chase.

'I hear she's been moved. Storm. The nurse downstairs said.'

Lennox expressed surprise Dan hadn't been told properly. By who, exactly? Everyone believed in this person who didn't exist. Those old ladies in Easingwold, even now, had faith that someone, God himself probably, was trying to find the garden furniture that had been flogged at some pub months ago. In the case of Storm, wasn't Lennox supposed to be God? Or was it Mason himself? He was trying. He'd tried.

Lennox leaned back against the wall. Dan had forgotten this propensity to lean, and the irritating way it seemed to claim ownership, rather than announce weakness. Storm had just walked out, Lennox said. A friend had come for her, her girlfriend, partner, Lennox thought. A woman called Lara. Lennox's foot slid down the smooth plaster behind him. Now he thought of it, Mason was just the man to talk to, given the massive waste of time and resources. Shouldn't the girl be prosecuted? Mason got him to back up.

'So she's got her memory back? She's *talking*?'

Hands in pockets, Lennox looked down at the scuffed tops of his shoes. The hinges of his jaw worked.

'It was all a wind-up.'

But the girl had almost died; had been as good as dead, the rain and sea driving down on her that night. Dan, unlike the shrink, had been there, seen and touched her bloodless body. She'd been so close to death the paramedics wouldn't call it.

'Sorry, not a wind-up.' Lennox glared up from his shoes. 'Art. She's some kind of, I don't know. Artist. Art student.'

Dan was off before he remembered Soccolo had the car. Art? Lennox said he'd be glad if Dan could make some sense of the situation, not that it would make any medical difference, and trying to get a prosecution would probably be setting even more good money chasing after bad. But for the satisfaction. Art. Here, at last, the two of them found common ground. Lennox almost verged on matey. But with Storm out of the picture, Dan wasn't inclined to hang around.

He needed the car, needed Soccolo, to go and sort all this out. It was a brisk trot from the clinic up to Andjati's. If Mason was lucky, he might catch him. The girl – he couldn't think of her as Storm any more, though Lennox didn't know her real name – had staged it all, for some sort of project or performance. Or that seemed to be the claim. How could she give a performance to the open sky? Put her life at risk? He'd give her fucking *art*.

The neatly similar residential roads that led to the Andjati house may as well have been the background in a computer game. The minutes Dan walked their grid gave him time to consider the real cost of the art student's shenanigans, to borrow one of Soccolo's words. Dan had already sent the email to Compton, concerning Nicu and the vans. If CID had spent any time on it at all, Dan would be arsehole of the year. Even if they hadn't, and Hubbard had got a whiff of it, he'd still suffer. This was bad enough to set Dan thinking about putting in for a transfer, let alone the matter of his own judgement and trust – yes, trust – in human nature. He'd wanted to help the lass, above everything, soft bastard that he was; had hated the thought of her being so lost and what might have been done to her. But worse than all this, a great steaming, stinking pile of shit that Dan felt descending on him, which was only right and proper ... Soccolo. He'd grassed up Soccolo for being involved in trafficking girls, for Christ's sake. What was he, the fucking Gestapo?

The fucking joke Gestapo, at that. King of yogurt pots. Soccolo was right. These streets with their Everest windows and decked back gardens, this was it: domestics, burglary, vandalism, some drunk and disorderly, bit of dealing, assault. This was life, right here. Dan picked up his pace to a run. By the time he caught sight of the yellow-green mass of the leylandii, he was going at a sprint, chasing himself. For a crucial second, as he slowed to a stop outside the house, the scene before him lacked meaning. Standing, gasping, his brain processed the tableau into sense: shouting and motion, men, a woman, the living wall of the hedge. Nathan Latimer had hold of an electric hedge trimmer – reason told Dan it probably belonged to Laurence Andjati – and was swinging it by its orange flex like a medieval weapon, as Soccolo imposed himself between Latimer and Andjati, who was screaming abuse at his neighbour while making reckless sorties to grab the trimmer from him. The trimmer was switched on. Mrs Andjati stood at the open front door, filming on her phone, ignoring Soccolo's shouted commands for her to switch off the power in favour of her husband's orders to keep filming.

As Latimer looped the cable faster and faster over his head in a berserking orbit, the trimmer roared, catching the hedge behind him. Amid a spray of severed pine needles, Latimer staggered slightly, readjusted his balance and advanced. Dan saw Soccolo's dilemma: if he abandoned Andjati to go and cut off the power supply, Latimer would kill Andjati. If he didn't cut off the power supply, Latimer would kill them both. The insane momentum of the flex had a looping rhythm. Like jumping in in a game of skipping, Dan saw there was an optimum moment. He hadn't been the lasses' playground pet for nothing. On the next revolution, as the blades glanced the hedge, he launched himself at Latimer's legs. The two of them crunched to the ground. There was an electrical squeal as the trimmer too hit the ground, mingled with human screaming. Dan forced his eyes open as he gained purchase around Latimer's thighs and grappled up his body to straddle him in some kind of restraint. Peripherally, as Dan flailed for the cuffs hanging from his belt, he saw the confusion of movement as Andjati lurched for the trimmer and Soccolo got there before him. While Mason was ratcheting the metal pincers around

Latimer's meaty wrists, every atom of training in the muscle memory of snap and lock, the noise of the trimmer stopped, either through malfunction on impact or Mrs Andjati finally cutting the power. Andjati, all enraged, skinny tenacity, continued to struggle with Soccolo. As Dan heaved Nathan to his feet, he saw the serrated edge of the kitchen knife in Andjati's hand, his lunge at the bare mass of the neighbour's white torso where his t-shirt had rucked. Before Dan could wrench Latimer away, Soccolo had broadsided Andjati with his own uniformed body to block him and Dan saw the blade slide, impossibly, into the top of Soccolo's leg.

It was Soccolo's animal scream, rather than his own action, that finally shocked Andjati into stillness.

'Fucking hell.' This was Latimer, who had also ceased to struggle.

The blade had gone all the way in. Only the black plastic handle stood proud of Soccolo's haunch. Soccolo automatically reached for the knife and Dan shouted a warning not to touch it. One-handed, he was grabbing his radio, calling for backup and an ambulance.

When it came, Soccolo was stretchered into the back, the knife intact for the hospital to deal with. He'd passed out from the shock. Dan had no difficulty in arresting Andjati and Latimer, ensuring they were taken away in separate cars. He almost had to make a third arrest on Mrs Andjati, who turned on him as her husband was taken away, baying obscenities at Mason's unfairness, since Latimer had started it.

At the hospital, they laboured for hours. Andjati's bread knife had torn Soccolo's artery, and while the emergency team and then the surgeon tried to seal off the damage, the blood pumped out of him faster than they could pump bag after bag of blood back in. When Dan went in to see him, drained plasma bags still littered the floor next to the trolley, the lino glossed with saffron and red swathes of barely mopped blood. Someone should pick those up, he heard himself say, from deep down a well of shock.

Soccolo didn't look asleep, like people said. He definitely looked dead, the life violently mugged out of him. On the top shelf of a trolley Dan saw the bread knife. It sat in a kidney dish, ready for the next loaf.

What had Soccolo said to him, his last words? On the Andjatis' lawn, nothing: just shouting and chaos; shouting at Andjati to calm down, to Mrs Andjati to turn the power off. Had there been a *careful* in there, as Dan had tackled Latimer? The *chuffing hell*, as Soccolo sank heavily on the grass, staring at the knife handle akimbo from his leg, had been a general address. A squeeze of the hand, as Dan had helped the paramedic get him up to roll on to the stretcher, might just have been a transfer of weight. Everything else, the words they'd exchanged the previous day, had been routine. No acknowledgement, at least, of Dan's betrayal. No accusation.

By the time Mrs Soccolo arrived, his partner had been arranged into peace, bare legs covered with a blanket, black socks still on. Dan was startled to see that she was a woman so beautiful not even her shock and grief could make her ugly. Dazed, he let her cry into his neck. She'd made Soccolo a cooked breakfast every day and worried about his blood pressure. She had, Dan knew, the kind of nipples Soccolo liked best, large and pink. She'd baked Dan a Christmas cake, and had no idea her husband fucked around. She loved him to bits, she wept, on and on. To bits. Just to bits. She loved him to bits.

Storm, whose name wasn't even Storm, didn't care if she was in trouble. Lara had said things like that didn't mean much to her, when Mel raised the possibility on the way to the clinic. From her tone, Harmony thought Lara might not mind some police intervention. In the car to Whitby she didn't say much about what her girlfriend had been doing, despite Mel's barrage of interrogation, but her anger had been clear, if complicated, from the moment Harmony showed her the Prunella Webster note. Perhaps this made it easier for Mel to offer her help. Why would the stupid girl put her life at risk, Mel asked? What was the point? And how, forgive her ignorance, was giving so many people the runaround meant to be 'art'?

Lara said these were all good questions. She'd been thankful for the lift. The Berlingo they'd seen on the way to the Frome house was hers, but there was a problem with the transmission. Harmony knew that Mel driving Lara to the clinic was less a gesture of kindness than Mel's need to see Storm and get all the gories. Harmony was eager to witness them herself, although she already dreaded what Mel might have to say.

At the Frome house, after Harmony had shown Lara the note and Lara had admitted – no, declared – that she knew exactly who Storm was, they had followed her into the other ground-floor room to get her bag and phone. Tony Frome's study was as painstakingly arranged as the living room, its piles of books with maroon and brown bindings and stacks of foolscap even duller. Set diagonally across the room's far corner was a dun-coloured canvas screen, which Lara moved to reveal a thrillingly chaotic, triangular backstage space used for her own life. As well as a sprawled motley of admin forms and computer-printed sheets, Harmony spotted on the small desk a pot of bright blue Essie nail varnish, a drum of evening primrose oil capsules from Holland & Barrett, two crumpled Club biscuit wrappers, a fanned copy of a book called *Citizen*, tweezers and a dirty mug with Marge Simpson on it. Next to the mug, the yellow, radiating moisture from a used herbal teabag, its string dangling from the desk's edge, had bled into the print on a Specsavers flyer.

'It'd be much better if the rest of the house was like this,' Harmony told Lara as she pulled her bag – an outsize tote – free from a pink sweater entangled in its handles. Lara stopped to look at the desk, unable to see what Harmony saw.

'Are you crazy?'

There was a doorway into a small kitchen, where Lara found her keys. It wasn't even trying to be Tony Frome's kitchen, but retained the unluxurious fixtures of whoever had lived in the cottage after him and into the 1990s. Mel wondered how Lara managed. Lara said she did, somehow.

If they raised more money, the kitchen would be a priority for the next curator.

At the clinic, the knackered nurse had answered their buzzer as incuriously as on Harmony's previous visit. When they reached the third floor, Harmony and Mel hung back a little so Lara could see Storm first, but not so far that they didn't have a good view. Storm was sitting on her bed, cross-legged. She faced the window, staring through the view with the same absorbed, unsettling vacancy Harmony had already witnessed. This time, Harmony wondered if it was meditation, or yoga. When Lara said hey, taming her big voice to the silence, Storm turned her head and Harmony saw her eyes widen as though something had been thrown at her. The rest of her body didn't stir for the seconds it took Lara to reach the bed, then she untangled her legs and threw off her vacancy as suddenly and comprehensively as a blanket. The two women held each other, Lara so much taller and bigger-boned that Storm disappeared.

'Nice outfit,' Lara said when she stepped back.

'Thanks.'

And so, Storm spoke. The word stuck, and she had to clear her throat to expel it, but Harmony recognised the someone she had seen printing PRUNELLA WEBSTER on the piece of paper: as pointed as the pen nib. Dee, Lara had called her in the car.

'You're a fucking lunatic, you know that?'

Dee's smile was a light switched on, then off. Lara said she meant it, and Harmony saw again that her anger was the real thing. Mel asked if she should go and get a nurse, or one of the doctors.

'I can do it,' said Dee. 'It should be me.' Harmony was amazed by the girl's lack of both apology and embarrassment in suddenly talking; and to Mel, of all people. As she crossed to the door, she stopped and faced the older woman.

'I've got a lot to thank you for.'

Mel was the one who had to look away, embarrassed for both of them, and as angry in her way as Lara. In this sentence, Harmony heard that the girl was, like Lara, American. Except she wasn't. Lara filled them in while Storm – Dee – was out of the room, discharging herself. Both women were Canadian. There was a connection between Tony Frome and their graduate school, money he'd left to endow the scholarship which had brought Lara to Evensand. Dee was on a different scholarship, for fine arts. While they'd been in Evensand, she'd gotten very interested in the erased history of Prunella Webster.

'Well, more kind of obsessed. I mean ... ' Lara, giving a hard stare at a point beyond the smudged paintwork of the opposite wall, flinched, as though Dee's obsession had scuttled up there in front of her.

In answer to Mel's question, she said yes, of course she'd known what Dee was doing, fetching up on the beach. Sort of. She'd even driven her as far as The Walk, where Dee had insisted on leaving some of her clothes.

'Kind of as a clue, I guess?' She shrugged. 'Like that worked.'

Lara had taken away the rest, on the beach. They'd had a fight. Sort of about her piece, but sort of about everything. Dee had made her promise not to wreck it, whatever happened, and Lara had, in the end, promised. So when she saw Dee on the news, it was genuinely hard to tell how much was the piece and how much was her just acting out, because of their fight. When Lara said this, 'acting out', she pinched the 'ou' towards an 'oo'.

'Which was kind of the point, I guess ... or not.'

Harmony didn't understand. But she could already tell that confusion was something Dee relished.

'OK, we can go.'

Dee leaned in from the corridor, nonchalant. Her voice had cleared from the talking she'd been doing downstairs, but it was still light and a little frail, as insubstantial as she herself suddenly wasn't. She avoided looking at Lara.

'Hey.' She was talking to Harmony. 'Harmony, right?'

She walked right up to the window where Harmony was standing and held the top of her arm, looked her in the eye. They were almost exactly the same height.

'I hope you know it couldn't just be anyone.'

What the hell did that mean? Harmony didn't feel she could ask. Although Storm didn't exist any more, the girl – woman, she probably preferred woman – still pulled questions out of you. Days later, Harmony was still asking them. There had been stuff on the news. Dee, amazingly, was D for Debra. Debra Moscavido, always known simply as D. From the living room of the Frome house she spoke to news cameras in her sketch of a voice, telling them that 'Storm' would be the name of the performance piece she would be mounting as a site-specific work on Evensand beach, in tribute to 'forgotten pioneer' Prunella Webster. It asked a lot of questions, she told the baffled, jocund *Look North* reporter. Not the young woman with the scraped-back hair, but the large-eared, 25-year-old man with the bass delivery of a 50-year-old.

'About othering in our society.' D pinched 'about' towards 'aboot', in the same way Lara had her 'out'. Before the reporter could speak, she continued. The spare assertion of her speech made you hear the completion of her sentences, rendering them hard to interrupt.

'About feelings towards refugees.'

'Feelings towards immigrants.'

Once more, the reporter started a question.

'Misogyny.' D hammered each lightly spoken word, her full stops the seated nails.

'The narratives of femininity cherished by our culture.'

'Wow,' said the reporter, having left a silence, just in case. 'That's a lot of questions! Talking of questions' – Harmony could hear how pleased he was with his segue – 'a lot of people are asking about the resources you've relied on since February, at a time when maybe they're thinking, the NHS, the police force – these are precious resources, particularly at the moment.'

For sure, said D, beadily. In her own clothes, although all that was visible in shot was a khaki band t-shirt with the sleeves rolled up to her thin shoulders, she looked older than she had as Storm. She said she had nothing but praise for the NHS. She also namechecked Mel, for saving her life. The reporter seized on this: had she actually been trying to kill herself?

'It's an interesting thought.'

To this reply, after she'd allowed it full resonance as a sentence, D added a final question: would this have enhanced the value of her piece?

There followed the customary shots of Brazen beach, as the reporter stood to camera alone, shouting over the wind. Questions had indeed been raised, he intoned, and would continue to be asked. East Yorkshire Police may not know much about art, but they knew what they didn't like ... the screen cut to sexy PC Mason, frowning heavily outside the police station, where he said what D had done was wasting police time, pure and simple.

REPORTER: So you were unaware at any point that this wasn't a missing persons investigation, but a 'work of art'?

MASON: We knew nothing about that, as I say. We took the case very seriously.

REPORTER: Can you put a price on that?

MASON: Well, we'll be looking at the man-hours, definitely. All I can say is, I lost my partner on Friday, more or less as a direct result of me not being there to provide backup because I was looking into what was going on with this young lady.

REPORTER: That's a high price to pay.

MASON: Aye, it is. I hope she's proud of herself.

This interchange spooled into the deep-voiced reporter declaiming about a neighbour dispute, as a grainy insert was flashed up of the 'dead officer'. Harmony was surprised to recognise the fat copper who had caught her out as a liar at the police station. It sounded to her as though D didn't deserve to be in trouble for him having got in the way of someone going mental with a bread knife. Though she suspected D would not only not mind getting into more trouble, but would quite enjoy the experience of being arrested.

She wondered if D and Lara might split up if that happened. Lara had told them, just before Harmony and Mel headed into the clinic with her, that D was an extraordinary human being, she really was, but she was so committed to being extraordinary that sometimes she was just full of shit. Yet Harmony had noted the careful way Lara had reapplied her excellent red lipstick in the car, checking herself in the rear-view mirror as well as in her compact. And if she'd been so pissed off with what Storm – D – was doing, couldn't she have grassed her up at any time? Now Harmony regretted not having asked Lara more about why she hadn't. What if D had died? What if Harmony herself had done nothing about the note with PRUNELLA WEBSTER on it? It was hard to imagine even someone as determined as D following her own rules and staying in the clinic for ever, pretending to be no one. Perhaps she had been working to some self-imposed time scheme all along, and one day would have just walked out.

In the car, Lara had added, after kissing her own lips to set their velvety colour, that D was no fool. The faculty had been indifferent to the degree project she'd first proposed, with D straightforwardly assuming the identity of Prunella Webster.

'They called it historical re-enactment – she was so pissed off!'

She capped the lipstick and replaced it in her bag, suddenly crestfallen.

'I guess that's more my line.'

Later on that memorable day, when they had dropped the two women back at the cottage, Mel said that D reminded her of Aurora at that age. Harmony pointed out that D looked nothing like her mum, which was obvious. Mel said she wasn't talking about looks, but an attitude. Surprisingly, Mel's tone implied as much admiration as its opposite.

'What happened, then?'

Like D, and Lara, Mel said this was a good question.

'It's easy to be young,' she said, finally.

'No it isn't!'

Harmony's violence surprised them both. All right, said Mel, steady on.

Mum, with her new downstairs ways, had watched quite a lot of the news coverage about D. She seemed to find it interesting, but not so much that it got through what Harmony thought of as her hand cream barrier. She'd moved the pot next to the sewing machine on the living room table, breaking off from sewing the strips for Mel's rainbow banner to smarm it over her busy hands, keeping them raised after each anointing like an ungloved surgeon so that they could dry off enough not to mark the parachute silk as she worked. Occasionally she went as far as making herself a slice of toast or a cup of tea. On her first attempt with the tea she had forgotten to switch the kettle on. Once this would have amused her, a joke called out to Harmony about how she was losing it, but Harmony saw tears glaze Aurora's eyes as she realised her mistake, fruitlessly squeezing the bag up against the wall of the mug with her teaspoon and failing to transform the pallid mixture of milk and cold water. Before this, Harmony had assumed Aurora was making progress back to where she'd been. But now she saw that once someone had broken, they mended differently. To make her feel better, she claimed she often forgot to switch the kettle on herself.

A stroke of luck. What was that meant to be? A stroke like stroking a cat? Or firmer, a cricketer stepping forward with a bat, like one of those boys at St Ben's? Harmony didn't feel the luck now bestowed on her was as fleeting as an action of any kind. It was a thing she'd been given, as substantial as a present under the Christmas tree. D had given it to her. *It couldn't just be anyone*, she'd said. She wasn't. She wouldn't be. She would make herself count, finally.

At first she couldn't see how, but the gift was delivered exactly when it was needed. It was Thursday, the day of the last Declan lesson. Stu had left at bumcrack for a classic car rally down in Kent, and wouldn't be back until the early hours of the morning. Mum had been spending more and more time downstairs, sewing, and Harmony had resigned herself to going over to Mel's for the lesson, as arranged. Nothing would happen. She was squeezing an irresistibly yielding, yellowish whitehead that had bloomed overnight in the fold between the cheek of her nostril and her actual cheek, when Aurora came into the bathroom and wondered how long Harmony would be. She had to get ready to go out, she announced. Mel was picking her up, so that Aurora could take the finished rainbow banner to the civic centre and install it herself before Mel's dress rehearsal, which she would watch, in case of logistical problems in attaching the different-coloured strips. Harmony busied herself applying a flannel to the dot of blood at the side of her nose. How long would that take? Most of the day, Aurora imagined. Possibly into the evening. Harmony weighed her luck, solidly wrapped. The house, free, and Auntie Mel out of action as the bow on top.

'What do you think looks better?'

Aurora held up two different shirts, switching them across her torso for Harmony to judge. The red, said Harmony.

'Really?'

Aurora looked down at her small body and said that she preferred the pink.

'Well, wear that then.'

'With my black jeans?'

Fired by her desire to see Mum leave the house as soon as possible, Harmony manufactured some enthusiasm. Yeah, black jeans were a great idea.

There was a slight delay when Mel arrived and told Mum to bring a jacket as it was always freezing in the civic centre auditorium and Aurora, rattled, ended up changing entirely. When she reappeared, re-clad, Harmony insisted on helping to shepherd the banner out to the car. Even complete, it weighed nothing, but had become almost too voluminous to be contained in Aurora's arms. Under the guise of ensuring no ends trailed and dirtied on the ground, Harmony shepherded Mum out of the house and into the car before she had the chance to change her mind and not just her outfit. The back of Mel's people carrier was stuffed with costumes and props, so Aurora had to sit with the rainbow crammed in her lap. When the two of them finally drove off, they looked like a couple of harassed children's entertainers.

Upstairs, Harmony couldn't resist posting on MySecretHeart: *The coast is clear! Only need the guts to do it* ☺ *wish me luck*

Next, she texted Declan.

Hi Declan, v soz but have hurt ankle and can't get to Mel's. Don't want to miss last lesson do u mind coming to our house instead? Thanks. See you at 3. Harmony

At the back of the bathroom cupboard, she found an elastic bandage from when Aurora had sprained her wrist falling off a stepladder when they first moved in and she was decorating. While she was doing this, Trujet79 had responded on MySecretHeart:

I think you should really consider what you're doing in your parents home, this is really disrespectful to them imo. Also your love is a feeling that may not ever bear the brutal light of reality SandyChick1, trust me I know something about that the world is a harsh and brutal place you have to protect your heart believe me, its a precious organ you only get one & no one will look out for it in fact some people get there kicks from hurting other people. Sad but true ☺

'I have spread my dreams beneath your feet. Tread softly for you tread on my dreams.'

Harmony asked her to pick her fucking dreams up if she didn't want them trodden on. She hadn't asked her to spread them all over the floor, had she?

In preparation for Declan, she had a bath, washed her hair and shaved her legs and underarms with Stu's blunt razor, which resulted in cuts. Never mind. Mum, when she was lecturing Harmony about not removing her body hair, had said that porn was like the McDonald's of sex. Human appetite was infinitely various, Aurora declared, but all you could get from McDonald's was a hamburger and chips. Harmony knew, because since Aurora's withdrawal she and Stu had taken to nipping into a McDonald's from time to time, that you could get anything there these days: wraps, smoothies, pretty much whatever you liked. But she understood what Mum meant. She just didn't agree.

Harmony didn't have many memories from Bristol, but one of the clearest was just before their return to Evensand. She only knew it was the refuge because that was the story Mum had told her. Her own memory of the place was restricted to a flecked, pale green tabletop, branded near the edge with a trio of perfectly circular cigarette burns, dark brown at the centre, lightening to tan, then a ring of dirty yellow. It was pleasing to explore these tiny craters with her fingertips as she waited for food, the ridges they formed in the otherwise untroubled Formica. With one finger settled in the dip of the nearest burn, Harmony had been distressed to bite into a slice of cheese on toast, at the time her favourite food in the world, and find it tasted totally unlike itself. The alarm of finding that there wasn't a universal slice of cheese on toast had been much worse than leaving their flat in the middle of the night and running through the streets until Mum found a taxi, Mum with blood down her coat from a broken nose. There in the refuge, for the first time Harmony encountered the slimy, white-bread fact that home was smaller than the world. Well, that was a lesson she'd continued to learn. So McDonald's had a point, as far as she was concerned. There was a comfort in consistency.

By two, a thin rain was peppering the windows. Harmony had felt too excited even to eat all day, which was unprecedented. She posted again on MySecretHeart: *OMG an hour & counting wish me luck!!!* Perhaps because of international time differences, no one did. She assumed she had offended Trujet79.

Harmony had bought condoms, although the various scenarios she'd spent so long concocting faded out at the kissing stage, time-lapsing into penetration, one very specific touch of Declan's six-pack, and then the two of them in bed, afterwards. Carefully, she removed the plastic film from the condom box, so there would be no gauche scrabbling. Would it be too much to open one of the individual envelopes, or was there a question of evaporation, as with a moist towelette, which might affect its contraceptive power? She decided it might. She slipped the packaged condom under her pillow, exactly in the centre.

Doing anything for the first time was shit. On the afternoon Harmony had spent with Aidan and Finn on The Walk, she had waved away the offered spliff because she didn't know how to inhale. She left the boys to it, the two of them giggling ever more obscurely and exclusively, as the whites of Aidan's eyes reddened as though he'd been swimming lengths in an over-chlorinated pool and Finn, no longer aloof, pissed himself trying to remember knock-knock jokes to tell her.

D had said she was chosen. She couldn't be just anyone. She would do this frightening thing and speak her heart to Declan, before offering her body.

He was on time, naturally. Harmony counted to ten before answering the door, to add credibility to her bandaged ankle, which she kept hoisted a few centimetres above the hall rug as though it wouldn't bear her weight.

'What happened?'

She hopped up the hall, explaining that she'd just gone over on it, which satisfied him, since he was really only being polite. She thanked him for the change of plan and he said it was no problem. Only belatedly, as Declan settled himself amid the sewing detritus at the table and wondered if her bad foot should be resting on a chair, did it occur to Harmony that the fake injury might be counter-seductive. In spite of her bath, her bare toes were already grubby from the floor. Harmony wasn't sure the sight of them sticking out of the end of a greying bandage would be very alluring. She was fine, she told him. It really wasn't that bad.

Now that the moment was here, she didn't feel up to it. She knew her blushing must be obvious. Nothing Declan hadn't seen before. Trying to calm herself, she breathed his shower-gel-outdoor atmosphere, lightly and deliciously cut with fresh sweat. The grey North Face sat on the back of the chair, despite the weather. The possibility twitched that Declan, if you knew him properly, might be slightly boring.

'So. The last lesson. What would you like to do, Harmony?'

Her name pierced her. He was the only one ever to use it like that. What would she like to do? To tell him, to give him the outpourings of her heart, to feed him marshmallows, to run her fingers through his tortured, beautiful hair, bite his bottom lip, be understood.

He was waiting. Action, not words. A stroke is as good as a gift. Blindly, she lurched her hand out for his. At the brief searing of skin on skin Declan recoiled backwards so forcefully his chair tipped and he had to grip the table edge to rescue himself.

'No. That's not—' He righted his chair. 'No. Come on.'

It was the way he said 'come on'; so kind, so reasonable, that exterminated all hope.

She started to cry.

'Oh Harmony.'

She couldn't help it. She cried like a six-year-old, with snotty, gasping entirety. When Declan stood and left the room, she thought he was leaving altogether, but he came back with a glass of water and placed it carefully by her maths papers. She could feel him standing by her shoulder as she wept, her eyes squeezed hotly against the sight of him. He said that he was sorry; not sorry for her, she knew, just sorry about the lesson. He thought he'd better go. She nodded. She wasn't going to open her eyes until he was gone. The tears came in great panting wails now, torn from her heart.

'Hey.' He sounded alarmed. Good.

The feelings soared out of her with a terrible, limitless exhilaration. She was a seagull, fighting the storm. Whatever this had to do with him had turned into Mum and Stu and Severn Oak and the glass at St Benedict's and the impervious girls and jeering boys, Flakes and biscuits, her peeling bedroom wall, all the days since and the days still to come. Maybe this was what going mad was like. On and on she went, honking and wailing, until a cold shock of water hit her face and shoulders.

He'd thrown the glass of water at her.

'Fucking hell.'

It was a full glass. It may as well have been a bucket, she was so drenched.

'You need to calm down.'

The wetness stilled her long enough for his voice to lasso her in.

'Harmony.'

She heard herself saying she was sorry. She was. When she looked through her spread fingers, Declan was standing with his arms braced away from his side, oddly formal. Suddenly, he turned and left the room. She thought again he might be leaving altogether but she heard him in the kitchen. He came back quickly, holding out a wad of kitchen paper he'd wet under the tap. Apparently he set quite a lot of store by water, as though she was a fire that needed to be put out. The offering was for her to wipe her face, which was already wet enough. He seemed to think it would be soothing. She got up herself to get a towel.

'Don't tell anyone,' she said.

'I'll have to.'

'Please.'

'I have to. I'm sorry.'

It was the only proper look he flicked at her before he left. The very last thing he said was good luck for the exam.

On her phone, ten minutes later, another poster was wondering what had happened to Beetlebutt.

The light was an assault when Mel and Aurora left the civic centre. After hours in the dark auditorium, Mel wouldn't have been surprised to emerge from the rehearsal to find that an unwitnessed apocalypse had devastated the car park into ash, the cars scorched to black skeletons. But life went on, in watery sunshine. Her Fiat stood intact, beneath the pale, ailing branches of a tethered municipal sapling. It was barely six o'clock. No one really cared about the Spectacular, except Aurora, in just the wrong way. Not enough for Aurora that the rainbow banner, bar the odd trip over its hem, and accounting for Kitty Sue and Lola learning the ways of the Velcro strips, had done what it was supposed to.

'Not sure about those girls.'

Mel was too tired to respond. Her voice was raw from shouting instructions, her knees two grinding points of pain. Levering herself into the driving seat, she wondered if she'd have the energy ever to get out. Ian would have to wave an open bottle of Pinot Grigio under the window to lure her to their front door.

'Mrs Beagles would cream herself over those two.' Aurora paused as she loaded herself into the car to mimic the rictus of Kitty Sue's stage smile.

When Aurora, as Dawn, had been one of Mrs Beagles' girls, Mrs Beagles was forever wrenching her by the shoulders to correct her line, mocking her sickled feet. The teacher's constant, carping attention was really a perverse recognition of Dawn's ability. She had been a naturally gifted dancer, flexibly light and expressive. But she hated, always, being told what to do. One day, during a ballet lesson in which Mrs Beagles had repeatedly batted at her stretched leg to straighten it, she'd simply walked out. The teacher, who had returned to the front of the studio, didn't notice her drop out of the line near the back of the barre, leaving a gap. Mel, one girl behind her, thought Dawn had just gone to the loo. But she didn't come back. The full magnificence of the gesture was revealed by the end of the hour, when Mrs Beagles had been forced to cover for Dawn's ongoing absence with the token hope that she hadn't been taken ill. Despite an imminent exam, and a Spectacular in which Dawn was meant to play a prominent part, she never returned, or even, as far as Mel knew, communicated to Mrs Beagles that she would no longer be coming to classes.

If Dawn had stayed, Mel, much more ungainly and averse to performance, might have been the one to leave Mrs Beagles. If Dawn had stayed, maybe Mel wouldn't be facing the ordeal of her eleventh Spectacular. Dawn would be the one clapping time for rhythm-deaf kids and trying to find enough junior-size sombreros to kit out a Mexican number. She'd have the music collection of a 12-year-old, and be forced to master the street dance syllabus. Aurora's feet, her tired, tired feet, would be the ones that perpetually smelled like supermarket Parmesan.

Although Mel wouldn't have had it any other way, it would have been nice to have the choice. How strange to sit next to this wraith of her oldest friend, whose greatest achievement might be the garish billows of parachute silk that were currently threatening to submerge her, and feel that Aurora had squandered, not just her own choices, but Mel's as well. It wasn't fair.

'If you want fair, get yoursen' down to't racecourse next bank holiday.'

Aurora delivered this in her 'happen, Alderman' voice they'd both nicked from *Billy Liar*. It was so long since she'd either done the voice or her mind-reading act that Mel's throat clogged. Aurora wasn't looking at her, but out of the window. Her comment, Mel saw, may have been connected to her own train of thought, and quite coincidental.

A beam of low, late sun sliced the windscreen, incising a mesh of lines around Aurora's eyes. At this commonality, Mel softened. What did it matter, at their age? Perhaps you were stuffed, either way. You let circumstances, other people, make the choices for you and lived a life that felt rented, or you took what you thought you wanted, like Aurora, and it bankrupted you.

'It looked good, anyway. Your banner thing, whatever we're calling it.'

She could see Aurora's cynicism suspiciously filtering this uncharacteristic kindness. But it was true, so she may as well say it. Rejecting the offering, Aurora drily acknowledged the 'Summer Spectacular' poster as they turned on to the main road.

'You've missed a trick, haven't you? "Over the Rainbow"? Surprised you could resist.'

'I'd already had it printed.'

Aurora cocked a look, a phantom of former ironies. 'Mrs Beagles will be spinning in her grave.'

Teenage Dawn, reading about the Moonies, had once likened Mrs Beagles to a cult leader. This was shortly before she walked out of that final ballet class. She'd laid it all out for Mel according to the article: suspicion and denigration of other religions – in Mrs Beagles' case, the other dancing schools they competed with (*'You can always tell one of Maureen's girls – arms like pigeon wings!'*) – check. Demand for absolute loyalty – check. Cult of personality – Dawn invoked the gallery of shots from Mrs Beagles' Bluebell Girl heyday that adorned the changing room, the assiduously polished trophies kept on the studio piano, the framed certificates – check. Brainwashing – what else was ballet, with its mindless repetition and physically perverse demands but that? – check. Also, Dawn pointed out as she showed Mel the photo of Sun Myung Moon, cult leaders and dictators always had a strong look. Like Hitler: it wasn't as though everyone in the 1930s had the smarmed-down hair and the moustache. With Mrs Beagles it was the beetle-green eyeshadow and sequins.

'And the moustache.'

Laughing, Mel had felt the relief of sharing the lonely knowledge she had hung on to since she was four, when she first set foot in the studio, clutching her mum's hand: Mrs Beagles was as ridiculous as she was terrifying. There was another girl in their ballet class called, unfortunately, Regina. During a lesson Mrs Beagles had inevitably started to address her as 'V—', leading to explosions of laughter all along the barre, as well as Regina's blushing mortification, though God knew she must have been used to it. Rather than joining in, which would have been unthinkable, or mocking herself for her mistake, which was entirely beyond her, Mrs Beagles botched together a frosty mitigation. In her bizarrely enunciated delivery, a cut-price version of Mrs Thatcher's, the teacher pronounced that Regina's name was of course reminiscent of Victoria Regina, 'as the Queen Victoria was known'. She had been, she explained, on the verge of mistakenly saying the first word.

'Not fanny, then.'

Dawn was sent out, even though Mrs Beagles hadn't heard her properly. Afterwards, Dawn polished this jewel in her diadem of ridicule.

'The Queen Victoria,' said Mel now, earning a diluted smile. For a time it had been their favourite phrase: 'the footballer, Kevin Keegan', 'the vegetable, cauliflower', 'the sanitary towel, Bodyform'. No one, Mel knew now from her own years of teaching, laughed as much as 14-year-old girls.

She and Aurora were on the same side. Weren't they still? Did Aurora remember that day, she asked, the day she walked out? Of course, Aurora said. It had been then, that day of the ridiculous speech about poor Vagina. She couldn't bear it any more.

The two exits were distinct in Mel's mind: one, a punishment; the other, a stylish act of defiance. Surely. But no – according to Aurora, Mrs Beagles had sent her out and that was that. She had sat on a bench in the changing room, still giggling at the thought of Mrs Beagles saying, or having, a fanny. On the wall in front of her had been the biggest photo of Mrs Beagles in full Bluebell Girl regalia – she didn't know if Mel remembered it – fishnets and ostrich feathers and Mrs S with a smile set like concrete, as though enduring the impossible height of her heels. All in black and white. Mel did remember, as Aurora conjured it. The cult of personality.

'Yeah.'

In the car, Aurora smoothed the bunched parachute silk across her lap, coaxing her own memory. It was like – she raised her small hands and waved them around her head – an out-of-body experience. Not really. But a sort of . . . Mel waited for the word.

'An overview.'

What of? That laughing at Mrs Beagles wasn't enough to make her bearable, said Aurora. That laughing at her made them feel better but it didn't change anything. Her being a cow, hitting their legs, her godawful Spectaculars. She had no idea she was ridiculous, which was how she got away with it. And them laughing at her allowed her to get away with it, because it made all of them feel *they* had power over *her*. But they didn't. She still controlled them. They were Mrs Beagles' girls. Realising this – Aurora didn't know if she was explaining it properly – had been overwhelming. The one thing she could always rely on was taking the piss out of anything. Like at home, with her parents and Malcolm: Mel remembered the routine she'd worked up about that?

Mel did. In all the time she and Dawn were at school together, she'd never had an invitation back to the Whites'. As a family, they existed for her entirely in Dawn's remorseless off-the-peg sitcom rendition: her dad a tyrant, her mum a doormat, her brother a mong. By conjuring Malcolm as the playground stereotype invoked for most forms of disability – in Dawn's anecdotes, he was represented mainly as a tongue padding out the bottom lip and a Neanderthalic grunt – Dawn pre-empted curiosity about her brother's condition for all of the years when it might have been used as a weapon against her. By the time they had reached a more civilised age, it had also made a genuine conversation about Dawn's family situation impossible.

So, seeing the way she and all the rest of them were trapped by Mrs Beagles, persisted Aurora, seeing how she got away with her cruelty . . .

'Cruelty?'

'Yeah.'

'That's a bit strong, isn't it?' objected Mel. The late sun dazzled her as they turned west out of town.

Come off it, said Aurora, more Dawn than she'd been for years. What about the little fat kids? Or the only black girl in their modern class, who Mrs Beagles had singled out over the pretext of her hair, practically scalping her every week with that needle-toothed tail comb she kept on the piano? And surely Mel hadn't forgotten the way she sucked up to the richer parents, giving their offspring the choicest parts and shoving the council house girls to the back rows in every show?

Mel couldn't disagree, although all these memories were bizarrely pleasurable, simply in evoking a time no one else had shared. Also, she realised now, smelling the sour hairspray on that vicious comb, when Mrs Beagles had concentrated her angry energies on a scapegoat, it had brought the addictive relief of herself escaping potential persecution. It had put her on Mrs Beagles' side.

So, said Aurora, the day with poor old Regina-the-Vag, the way all of them excused Mrs Beagles' behaviour as absurdity had suddenly seemed not just totally inadequate, but wrong. And it made her see that even if the way she herself laughed at Malcolm was different from the arseholes who followed him home pulling faces and calling him spaz, the difference didn't excuse it. It didn't help, was the point. The laughter was aimed at something unshiftable, as pointless and lonely as throwing a ball at a wall and catching it on the rebound.

'It was like, I don't know. Losing. Losing a superpower or something. If I couldn't laugh at any of it any more . . . '

Aurora ran her fingers softly across her lips. 'I think that's when I knew I'd have to get away.'

They were out of the centre now, filtering into the top of the beach road where it joined the route down from Brazen Point. Aurora turned to watch the beach as the last of it ribboned past them in parallel, the sun flaring back in mirrored lozenges from the windows of the houses high on Whitecliff Road. Mel had no idea how long it had been since Aurora had visited her dad, or Malcolm. She had, at least, attended her mother's funeral. Mel only knew this because she herself had gone, paying her respects, as though she had respects to pay. She and Aurora had never spoken about what it had been like, for all that time. *Beechdale.* The one thing Aurora had said as they left the crematorium was that it was the first time her mother had left the house in about thirty years.

Aurora's fingers clenched back on her lap, as though ordered to leave her mouth alone. 'I used to think I might be able to turn into someone else completely.'

Oh God. They were on the same side, weren't they? Mel had to ask it.

'You don't think – I'm not turning into Mrs Beagles, am I?'

Aurora's 'no' was reassuringly swift. But this was not,

Mel then saw, a brisk dismissal of an impossibility, but a distraction.

'Is that Harmony?'

'Where?'

By the time it was safe for Mel to take her eyes off the road, they were already metres along from the turning back to the Point. Aurora twisted back in her seat, still clutching the colours of the rainbow.

'What's she doing?'

Mel had no idea. Going for a walk? It didn't sound much like Harmony. Wasn't she supposed to be at their house around now? Brazen Point was in the opposite direction to theirs. Mel hoped Harmony hadn't forgotten her lesson, or Declan would have been twiddling his thumbs. They'd mucked him about enough recently. Aurora suggested they pick Harmony up. Having never learned to drive, she remained cavalier about the realities governing the road. Mel pointed out the difficulty of turning the car round with traffic behind her. Her first opportunity would come at the golf club entrance, a few hundred yards along. She was indicating to pull off into the discreetly signed turning circle when two police cars barrelled towards them at speed, snaking in and out of lane, sirens screaming. Mel thought she caught a flash of PC Mason's puppy dog profile, intent at the wheel of the first car. By the time she had turned out of the golf club in the opposite direction, the blue lights were flashing halfway up to the Point. Then, as the car reached the base of the same road, she had to shift on to the hard shoulder to allow a hurtling fire engine to pass.

'Must be the vans.'

Aurora craned to find Harmony, who had disappeared from view as she continued to climb the cliff path. They would soon catch her up. It was a stiff slope up to the top, walking. Mel privately thought it was a shame to be picking her up. The exercise was bound to do her good.

'I think Stu and I are over, by the way.'

Aurora said this as though the fire engine had reminded her. Talking of emergencies . . .

Mel relaxed her hands on the steering wheel, in case Aurora inferred something from the way her knuckles had whitened.

'Oh.'

Had he told her about Australia? Better to feign ignorance.

'It's fine, and everything. It'll be fine. Better all round.'

'I'm sorry.'

'Yeah. Fuck off, Mel.'

It was weary, gentle even. *You never thought we should be together in the first place*, is what she meant. Then, suddenly, she was grabbing at the handle to open the car door, thwarted by the child locks. Mel warned her to wait, even though she had slowed the car to a crawl, this close to the top of the Point. She herself could see Harmony's foreshortened legs stretched out on the grass at the cliff edge, the rest of her dipped out of view. She hadn't quite braked before Aurora was fighting the spilling parachute silk to clamber out. Mel followed. The grass up here was the lurid green of a dream or a tourist ad, strewn with roundels of black shit pellets from the rabbits that nibbled the ground close and mined it with their holes.

'Careful!'

Their holes threatened your ankles if you weren't looking and stepped into one. Mel was confused by the smell of smoke attacking her throat, before she realised it was blowing from the vans, behind her; hence the fire engine and police. Ahead, Aurora was shouting at Harmony to get away from the cliff edge. Harmony rolled over on to one shoulder with a normalising lack of urgency. Her face, though, was raw with distress. This intensified when she saw her mother.

'Leave me alone!'

What had happened? Harmony shimmied forward on her stomach, her instinct to escape. Aurora, with a swiftness Mel thought she had lost for ever, lunged to snatch the hem of her jumper and pull her back. This provoked Harmony into a struggle. What the hell was she doing, she yelled at her mother? Mel, calling at them both to calm down, was striding over when she buckled, felled by a rabbit hole. Her knees hit plush grass. Preoccupied by their skirmish, neither Aurora nor Harmony noticed. Ignoring her own agony, Mel stood and limped towards them. Getting closer, she saw that they were further back from the drop than it appeared on the approach, a safe couple of metres.

Then she saw something else. Spread far below was the north end of the beach, where she had found Storm. D. Now, at strong high tide, the shingle was half-covered by slate waves that broke and foamed into grubby lace. A figure, a boy, ran towards the water then backed away, calling to a dark speck that bobbed in and out of sight with the swell. Mel shuffled right up to the unreliable edge of the cliff. The sea wasn't safe: the red flags were clear to see. She watched as the boy ran in up to his waist, frantic, lost his balance and stumbled down into the water. After some false starts, he managed to right himself and stagger heavy-legged to shore, turned all the time back to the vanishing speck, which must be a head. His wail tore itself away from the ragged complaints of the gulls. It was a high, thin voice, in distress.

It was Eddy.

Before Mel could move, Harmony was already up and starting to run down the cliff path to the beach. Mel's phone was in the car. Limping back to it, coughing in the pall of smoke blowing from the vans, Mel had some thought of calling the coast guard, but she didn't know the number. She tried ringing 999 as she screamed after Aurora, who had taken off down the cliff in tardy pursuit of Harmony, but the call wouldn't connect. No coverage up here. The hurtling path Harmony had taken down to the beach was more direct than the road, but she would easily catch up in the car. Driving took her briefly out of view of the water. All the time she prayed that Eddy hadn't launched himself back in, making desperate bargains about saving him: take Harmony, Aurora, Ian, Joe, Aidan. Take me. As she rounded the bottom end of the cliff road and ploughed the car into the shingle, she thanked God to catch sight of him again, alive, parrying the breaking waves and shouting.

'Eddy!'

He turned and saw not her, but Harmony, floundering down from the cliff path into the tussocked sand close to him. He was frantic, his face bone white.

'Toothpaste!'

He wasn't allowed to bring the bloody dog on to the beach, for this very reason. Aidan was supposed to be doing the walk. She'd kill him, the idle little sod. And Joe, probably still in bed, pining. As Mel cleared the shingle, her ankle uncertain from the fall, Eddy saw her. Mel commanded him not to go back in the water, but her voice had stopped working. Eddy continued to shout, desperate for anyone to make it unhappen.

'Toothpaste!'

Once more, Eddy staggered dangerously close to the

waterline. But Harmony was there, hoicking him back by the soaked waist of his jeans so that he arced round her, losing his balance, bringing both of them to the ground. Mel limped on, thanking God, the gods, promising she'd be a better person and expect nothing for the rest of her life, buy nothing, want nothing, treasure every dull, taxing, precious, unwanted hour as Harmony crouched to speak to Eddy, hands cupped round his face. Mel had lost sight of Toothpaste's head, cresting and dipping. Eddy was nodding. Harmony handed him something from her pocket – her phone – and pointed him to the cliff path, where Aurora accelerated down the last steep metres, shrieking her daughter's name. If Harmony heard, she gave no sign. The girl struck out, no longer stumbling, and as her mother continued to call, propelled herself against the tide, lifted and dropped, out and out to the horizon, buoyant, on and impossibly on, towards the dog not one of them could see.

A secret isn't the same as a lie. A lie is what a secret gives birth to, when it mates with speech. Its father's child, as well as its mother's.

Sometimes we call it a story. Little bastard.

Handwritten fragment, ink on paper, single sheet. Anthony Frome collection.

Evensand, 1945–6